THE ELEMENTAL
DETECTIVE

A MIDLIFE MAGIC MYSTERY
KIRSTEN WEISS

misterio press

ABOUT THE BOOK

MERMAIDS, MIDDLE AGE, AND murder.

Metaphysical detective Riga Hayworth just wants to relax with her new husband on their Hawaiian honeymoon. But the bodies of a murdered man and a seal found on a Kauai beach pull them into an investigation and send the supernatural world into an uproar.

When Riga detects traces of magic at the murder scene, she knows she can't ignore the call. There's necromancy afoot, and she must prepare for the battle to come. But can Riga fight the elemental forces of nature? Or will they destroy her and everyone she loves?

Book four in the Riga Hayworth series of urban fantasy and paranormal mystery novels, *The Elemental Detective* is fun, fast-paced paranormal women's fiction. If you're looking for a page-turner with a complicated, 40-something heroine, scroll up and buy *The Elemental Detective* today!

COPYRIGHT

Misterio Press / print edition December 2022

Cover image by Dar Albert

Interior images licensed by DepositPhotos.com

ISBN: 978-1-9447670-8-2

Visit the author website: https://kirstenweiss.com

CONTENTS

CHAPTER 1

THE PALMS RATTLED LIKE bones, awakening Riga. A warm salt breeze slipped through the open door and shivered across her bare skin. Beside her, the mattress sagged, the bed frame creaking an accompaniment to her own, steady breathing.

One breath, rising and falling. Her breath.

Muddled by sleep, she stilled, her heart leaping with a jolt of adrenaline. It wasn't her husband beside her, weighting the bed.

Riga kept her breathing steady and extended her other senses, probing. She opened her eyes, peering through her lashes. Through the open glass door, the moon illuminated a winged figure, hunched beside her on the hotel's bed.

"Brigitte." Riga sat up, torn between annoyance and the panic rising in her throat. She clutched the sheet to her chest. "What are you doing here? Where's Donovan?"

The gargoyle shrugged, the sound of rocks grating together, and the bed shifted. "Monsieur Mosse left an hour ago," she graveled, a French-accented Lauren Bacall. "And his whereabouts are the least of your worries."

Riga lurched left and reached for the bedside lamp. Instead, her fingers found emptiness, fumbled in the dark, then touched a wooden leg, upright, seemingly supporting nothing.

Where the hell had the tabletop gone? Her fingers brushed a rounded stump, and something fell with a crash. Where had the *lamp* gone?

She swung her feet out of bed, took two steps, and bashed her shin into something hard. Riga felt along the wall. She smacked the light switch.

Uncomprehending, she stared. Everything but the bed had been turned upside down. Cushioned wicker chairs. Wooden table. Television...

She grabbed her silk robe, draped over an upside-down ottoman, and slipped it on, walked to the entertainment center. That was still upright, but the TV inside had been inverted.

Wonder leaked past her anxiety. She sniffed. A trace of magic lingered, wild like a forest glade and elemental. *Fae?* She regarded the creative destruction she'd slept through and amended that thought. *Stealth fae. Dammit.* She fumbled the belt of her robe.

"What happened to Donovan? Where is he?" Riga's voice sounded shrill even to her ears.

"Your husband left of his own accord."

"Alone?" Riga motioned toward the mess. No, it couldn't be happening again. Not another run-in with the faery world. Not *here. Not now.* "Did you see who—"

Brigitte's stone-feathered head reared backwards. "I do not spy!"

"But you saw Donovan leave."

"And then I waited by ze rocks until you woke up."

"*You* woke me up."

The gargoyle picked at her feathers. "I grew bored, and the sun will rise soon, and we have much to discuss."

The diamond on Riga's finger glinted. She rubbed the back of her wedding rings with her thumb.

She and Donovan hadn't yet adjusted to island time, and both were rising well before daybreak. Donovan had probably woken up while she was sleeping and grown restless, hadn't wanted to wake her.

Of course he was safe. It couldn't be happening again. That would be stretching the bounds of... She worked the knot on her robe. He was safe.

She swallowed, despising the remnants of fear that made her muscles twitch, and flipped her emotions to anger. Anger was simpler.

"For Pete's sake. We're on our honeymoon. Whatever the problem is, it can wait." Only two weeks ago, she and Donovan had had an undead crisis at their wedding. She'd recently learned her niece may be a necromancer.

She'd just learned that she, herself, was a necromancer, albeit an unusual one, and connected in horrifying ways to dark magic. And Donovan was... God only knew what he was.

Brigitte tossed her head. "You and your niece *are* necromancers, even if you happen to be a terrible disappointment at the art. And I am here because I sensed dark magic, black necromancy, and not your own."

"Well, of course not mine. I would hardly—"

"Black magic, Riga. Big magic. You cannot ignore this."

"Faery tricks? Oh yes, I can ignore them." She allowed herself to hope. After all, these were just silly pranks. It wasn't as if someone had died.

"Not ze furniture. Something else, something terrible. This is serious."

"No," Riga snarled. "It's *always* serious. And there's always something terrible coming. Let someone else deal with it this time."

Riga righted the bedside table and replaced the clock and lamp. "It's four AM, and I'm on my honeymoon. Go away."

Well-traveled and just north of forty, Riga was experienced enough to know she had a lifetime ahead of her with the man she loved. This honeymoon was only an interlude. But their first week in Hawaii had been blissfully supernatural-free, and she'd hoped...

The gargoyle flapped her wings. "Ze honeymoon is over. Put your big-girl pants on and stop ze dark magic."

"Put your big girl... Did you get that from my niece? And you're supposed to be watching her, training her."

"Pen is fine. You, however, are headed for big trouble."

Riga righted a chair. Her stomach tingled unpleasantly. "This is Hawaii. I'm sure they've got their own shamans and kahunas. They don't need my help."

The gargoyle shook her head. "But this magic is—"

The lock on the bungalow door clicked.

"Get out," Riga hissed.

"But—"

"Out!"

The gargoyle's stone muscles tensed beneath her stony feathers. She leaped, her wings angling to soar through the open glass doors.

Donovan edged inside carrying a wooden tray laden with fruit and juices, and relief flooded her senses. Rumpled raven-black hair, broad shoulders, chiseled features, emerald eyes that crinkled around the edges.

He stopped and took in the disarray, his expression shifting to surprise. "Redecorating?"

"Please." She snorted. "You know how I feel about morning exercise."

His eyes glinted. "Not all morning exercise."

Riga's heart beat faster, warmth spreading through her veins. She contemplated her new husband – her first. She was his first, too, which had struck her as miraculous given his age (also mid-forties) and astonishing good looks.

Donovan owned a chain of casinos, and the patina of money and power made him even easier on the eyes to many women. While she couldn't claim immunity to those charms, Donovan was so much more. He was someone to grow old with, an idea she'd once found trite but no longer.

As for herself, Riga knew why she'd stayed on the shelf. Ever since her college years, she'd been a magical freak and a powerful one. Last year, her life had changed, and that power had flickered, turned erratic. And life had grown dangerous.

"What happened?" he asked.

"I'm not sure. Menehunes, maybe." She grimaced. "This has the smell of the fae."

He nudged the door shut with his bare foot. The tray wobbled, threatening to stain his loose, white linen shirt with orange juice. Catlike, he regained control. "What are menehunes?"

"The Hawaiian little people."

He eyed the overturned bureau. "How little?"

Smiling, Riga righted a chair. "I've never actually met one."

"And they turned our bungalow upside down because...?"

"They're known as tricksters."

"Annoyances is more like it." He handed her the tray and ran his hands down her arms to settle on her hips.

"Or they might just want to let us know they know we're here."

"That's one of the many things I love about being with you. You introduce me to the most unusual... people."

Her heart turned over. And that was one of the many things she loved about him. He didn't just accept the magic, he embraced it as another adventure. But he was new to the magical world, and the fae weren't the cutesy faeries of Victorian greeting cards. They could be capricious and deadly. "The fae aren't people. And I'd rather they stay out of our honeymoon."

"Hold that thought." He flipped the table, took the tray from her, and placed it on top. "You were saying?"

"They might have been trying to send us a message. Brigitte—"

"Forget the faeries." His mouth claimed hers, and her blood hummed. His lips drifted to the arch of her neck, and his attention drifted lower.

She gasped. "But..." There was something she had to tell him. Something...

He smelled of ancient forests, wild and primal, and heat rose inside her. She found the buttons of his shirt. "Later," she said, her voice husky.

Their lovemaking was slow and sweet. And when they lay curled in a drowsy knot, he bent over her and brushed her lips, and heat flared between them again.

Afterward, he pulled her into the wide shower. Then they settled down for breakfast on their balcony and watched the stars dim. The sky over the Pacific lightened to gray, and the curve of Hanalei Bay took on definition, mountains rising in the background.

She sighed. "Is this heaven?"

Donovan's broad hand covered her own. "It ought to be."

"Only one week left in paradise." Riga brushed a fleck of croissant off her short-sleeved blouse, and it fell to the lap of her white skort.

"I couldn't take more time away," he said.

"You were a marvel to manage two weeks." Donovan's casino in South Lake Tahoe was still in rocky condition. And he owned other casinos as well in Las Vegas and Macau. But she hadn't seen him check his e-mail once, or more than glance at his phone.

"And we can always come back." His thumb traced a pattern in her palm, leaving it tingling.

"Mm..."

He rose. "Shall we?"

She let him pull her from the chair. Donovan unlatched the patio gate, and they stepped into soft sand. They were staying in one of the hotel's private bungalows, tucked amidst kukui trees behind a small private beach.

They walked past a tangled banyan tree and clambered onto a pile of smooth rock, slick with sea spray. Donovan froze, the grip on her hand tightening. "Do you hear that?"

She strained to listen and caught a woman's soft sobbing.

Slowly, they picked their way over the pile of large rocks. At the top, a woman's outline, semi-transparent, blurred. The Christmas lights on a kukui tree shimmered through her bathing suit, through her slim arms and legs, glittering off the water droplets in her hair.

"Hello," Donovan said. "Can we help?"

She ignored them, and Donovan gave Riga an apologetic look. It wasn't the first ghost they'd seen on the islands. None had been aware of their presence.

"I had to try," he said. "There's nothing worse than hearing a woman crying."

The ghost turned and walked through him.

He winced. "I take it back. That's worse." But he watched the woman disappear into the trees, his expression regretful.

Riga watched too, her scalp prickling. She touched his hand. They both knew the ghost would become aware when she was ready. "We'll be here another week. Who knows? Maybe she'll notice us."

He nodded and led her onto a long stretch of beach, curving around the bay. Gentle waves lapped the sand, covering their feet and ankles, and Riga felt that strange disorientation of the earth being sucked from beneath her. She stooped to pick up a cowry shell.

A sweet miasma choked her throat. The world slipped sideways, and she stumbled as her other senses recoiled from the scent of dark magic, rotting, sulfurous. And then it was gone, as if carried off by the wind.

Donovan caught her arm. "Careful."

Not now. "Thanks." The fae were one thing, but dark magic was quite another.

They walked on, skirting rocks and bits of driftwood. Palm trees still wrapped in Christmas lights twinkled along the shore.

"What do you think of our hotel?" Donovan asked.

"I love it, of course," she said, looking at him curiously. Donovan had chosen the hotel, and it wasn't in his nature to seek approval or validation.

"But what do you think about it?"

"Spectacular location, recently renovated interior with a modern, eco-chic feel, a bar and restaurant that makes me want to stay in... What's not to like? Why? Has it given you ideas for your casinos?"

The sky above the mountains pinked, shot through with ribbons of gold. But a chill rippled through her. The sense of dark magic had returned, crawling along the edge of her awareness, making her want to run. She stopped, tightening her grip on his hand, probing with her senses.

"It's *our* casino, now," he corrected. "And no. Those are two different worlds. I'm thinking of..." He stopped, frowning.

She followed his gaze. Something lay still on the beach. No, she realized, two somethings. But one was bloated, misshapen. Its image flickered, as if a television channel had been switched. "Oh, my God."

Donovan was running across the sand.

Too late.

Riga already knew – the somethings were dead.

CHAPTER 2

BARE FEET DRAGGING IN the damp sand, Riga trudged toward Donovan and the two motionless figures. Donovan knelt beside the smaller lump.

She neared, her chest tightening, the full horror revealing itself. Orange tape flapped loosely, tied to two pegs in the ground before a man and a... She blinked. A seal? Blood stained the sand, and her stomach rolled.

A shutter dropped over her mind, and she tried to view the scene dispassionately. Bullet wounds to both heads. A good bit of damage, so a larger caliber.

Dark magic tugged at her senses, a sickly-sweet cocktail that both repelled and attracted Riga. She clapped her hand over her mouth, acid rising in her throat, and focused on the torsos.

The man was well-dressed, in expensive boating shoes and creased khakis. He wore a blue windbreaker with the logo from their hotel. A guest? An employee? "That's a hotel jacket," she said.

Donovan looked up. "It's Dennis Glasgow, the owner."

She nodded. Of *course* they'd chosen a hotel where the owner would be murdered. On the other hand, *they* hadn't picked the hotel, Donovan had. Which meant... She rubbed a spot above her left eyebrow. What *did* it mean?

The morning light had turned pale gray. If there were footprints in the sand, Riga couldn't interpret them, so she looked for other signs. And they were there, a circle drawn around the bodies as if with a stick.

She squinted. The slanting pre-dawn light illuminated magical sigils carved in the loose sand. A sour taste rose in the back of her mouth. The magical symbols could only mean one thing.

"This tape..." She motioned toward the pegs and the plastic, orange ribbon.

"It looks like the beginning of one of those barriers people put up around the seals, to warn others away," Donovan said.

She relaxed her gaze and turned to the seal. Its image flickered again, something with a long tail, scales, and then it was just a poor, dead seal. Opening herself, she probed deeper and let her boundaries fall away.

Terror. Rage. A dark wave washed over her, nauseating. She gagged, stumbled toward the ocean, and fell to her hands and knees, retching.

Behind her, Donovan's footsteps pounded in the sand. He touched her shoulders. "Are you okay?"

She nodded and wiped her mouth with the back of one hand. Cold sand pressed into her palms and knees. "Magic," her voice trembled. "A sacrifice. Black necromancy."

He rubbed his broad hand along her back, and a soothing warmth spread where he touched. "I'll call the police." His voice was tight. Donovan drew his phone from his pocket and called 9-1-1.

She sat in the sand, her legs crossed. Half listening to the conversation, she stared at the roll and swell of the ocean. The wind picked up, tossing her auburn hair.

Magic was involved. Which meant she was involved. She was a metaphysical detective, with a PI's license. Walking away from this type of murder would be like an off-duty paramedic walking away from a choking victim – legally correct, but soul destroying and morally wrong.

But now, on her honeymoon? She scrubbed a hand over her face, torn between frustration and guilt over her desire to walk away.

Donovan ended the call. "I need to make sure no one disturbs the body."

She nodded and began to rise. He laid a hand on her shoulder. "You can stay here, catch your breath," he said.

"Thanks," she said, grateful. "It's hard to tell in this light, but I think someone drew a magic circle and sigils around the bodies. Be careful where you step."

She watched him trudge back to the bodies. Dark magic they could handle. Donovan had known what he was in for when they married, and he brought magic of his own to the partnership. But she'd hoped they'd catch a break on the islands, that mayhem wouldn't prick their bubble of happiness.

She wasn't used to being responsible for the happiness of another, though Donovan would consider his happiness his sole responsibility. And she wanted to make him happy.

A wave washed her stomach contents into the bay. At least she'd made some fishes happy.

She looked over her shoulder. Donovan stood relaxed, the wind pressing his loose linen shirt and trousers against his muscular frame. And now her new husband was guarding two corpses.

The police arrived quickly. First a white squad car. Then an ambulance. Then another squad car. A man in uniform drew Donovan aside and took notes in a small pad. Donovan rubbed the back of his neck. He pointed down the beach, toward their hotel.

Riga stood, brushing the sand from the back of her skort. Her mouth tasted of bile. Until she could get back to the hotel and her toothbrush, she'd need to keep downwind of Donovan and the detective. A tingle of energy tickled the edge of her awareness.

"Have a peppermint," a male voice said, close by.

She turned, bewildered, and saw only beach and the far-off policemen and Donovan.

A laugh, rich and rolling. "Here."

Riga looked down. Beside her stood an elderly man, his chubby arm upraised, offering a candy wrapped in pink foil. He was waist-high to Riga, and his red and white Hawaiian shirt fluttered in the strengthening breeze.

She assumed there were pants or shorts beneath the shirt, but from her high angle, his beach-ball stomach hid whatever came below. His fisherman's hat threatened to blow away. He clutched it to his shock of white hair, hair that accentuated the deep bronze of his skin.

"Thank you." She took the candy and unwrapped it slowly, popped it in her mouth. It was a buttery peppermint, recalling the candy bowl her father had kept at his office when she was a child.

They watched the remnants of waves edge toward their feet. She drew in her energetic center then blew it outward with her breath, extending her psychic senses.

A ripple feathered across the edge of her perception, and her skin twitched in response. The man was magic, or he had magic, but it was like nothing she'd ever encountered.

When it was clear he wouldn't say anything more, Riga spoke. "Did you see what happened here?"

"I didn't need to see it happen. I can see what has happened. And it's clear what *will* happen."

"Oh?"

"Sacrifice has returned to Kauai."

"Returned?"

"It came to this island long ago. The old kings used it to increase their power, their mana."

"And did it work?" she asked.

He nodded. "For a time, but there was a terrible price. It's bad magic. Your kind of magic, sorceress."

"I don't kill people," she said sharply. "Or animals." At least, not intentionally. And not for magic.

"But the creature who did this is one of your kind. Which, I believe, makes you responsible."

She drew breath to argue, but he was right. She'd known she was responsible – not because whoever had done this was her kind, but because she could stop him. "Who are you?"

"Just a humble kupua."

"What's that?"

"You would call me a shaman. You would be wrong, but shaman is close enough."

"What do you know about this?" She motioned toward the bodies on the beach.

He clucked his tongue. "Big trouble is coming. Big trouble for your kind. Big trouble for mine."

She pressed her lips together. *Why, why, why did magicians insist on being cryptic?* She suspected it was because it made them seem wise and mysterious. Across the bay, the sun broke the mountaintops, sent shadows slanting across the dry sand.

"I don't suppose you can be more specific?" she asked.

He didn't reply, and she looked down. The little man had vanished.

"Damn, he's good."

A uniformed policeman labored through the white sand toward her. He flipped through the pages of a leather-bound notepad. "Mrs. Mosse?"

She didn't bother asking if he'd seen the kupua. "Technically, my last name is still Hayworth. Riga Hayworth."

"I know who you are." Impassive, he scrawled notes in his pad. He was too young to recognize the closeness to the name of the silver screen goddess, Rita Hayworth. And he'd been born too late to acknowledge the strange resemblance between the two women.

Riga answered his questions. He dismissed her, just an unlucky tourist who'd stumbled on a body.

She rejoined Donovan. They walked slowly toward their hotel.

He cleared his throat. "There's something I need to tell you. I wanted it to be a surprise, partly because I wasn't sure if he was going to go through with it."

"Tell me you're not a suspect."

He arched a brow. "No. Why would you think that?"

She didn't respond, and he smiled. "Fair enough. But one of the reasons we came here was because the hotel might be for sale. I was thinking of buying it."

She tugged at his hand to stop. "Buying it? But it's not a casino."

"I've decided to diversify, but I want to stick to an industry I know. And I know resorts. And if we owned this place—"

"We'd have more excuses to return," she finished for him. "So that's why you wanted to know what I thought of the hotel. But that doesn't make you a suspect, does it? Dennis Glasgow's death doesn't benefit you."

One corner of his mouth tugged upward. "No. I'm not a suspect. Dennis and his brother both own the hotel, and both were interested in selling, though the younger brother is more eager. Dennis's death doesn't change anything for me."

"Which was killed?"

"The older brother."

The one less enthusiastic about selling. Riga furrowed her brows. So to an investigator, it might look like Donovan had a motive, that he'd cleared a path to buying the hotel.

He chuckled. "Don't look so worried. I'm not a suspect. But I don't like the timing."

"There's something I need to tell you," she said. "I was right – there was magic involved in the murder. While you were talking to the police, I was approached by a local kupua, a sort of shaman. He told me the murder had been committed by one of my kind."

"And I assume by 'your kind' he didn't mean mainlander."

"I don't know what's more disturbing – that magical people can see what I am so easily, or that we've only been in the islands a week before finding a body."

"This wasn't your fault," he said.

She bit her lip. "No, but it's my responsibility. This is magic. The police may not be able to take care of this."

Unwelcome, a memory rose in Riga's mind. Tangled white hair and wild eyes. A woman she'd met who had the same powers. And like Riga, she'd attracted violent deaths, magical deaths. But she had ignored the calls of the dead and gone mad.

"What are you thinking?" he asked.

Her jaw tightened. Why did this have to happen to them now? So much had come between them before the wedding, and she'd hoped... "I don't think I can ignore this. Not a magical death, not necromancy."

"The police have the crime scene and will interview the people at the hotel who knew Dennis, as well as anyone on the beach who might've seen something. We can't do anything for now."

"We?" Suddenly, she felt lighter. Donovan was with her. He understood.

"If Dennis was killed by someone for magical reasons, it's unlikely the police'll be able to manage." He squeezed her hand. "Besides, I have a stake in this too."

"The hotel." She gnawed her lower lip. The hotel purchase would both ease and complicate things. "But we're more likely to hear truths when people are off balance. We should talk to the victim's wife and brother as soon as possible."

"And if they're innocent, we'll be harassing them for no reason."

And making it harder for him to buy the hotel, she thought cynically. "Donovan—"

"If I was your client, would you do things my way?"

"No."

He barked a laugh.

"Okay," she relented, "for you and only you, yes. But you're not my client. Besides, how would you pay me?"

"I think I can afford your rates."

"You said when we got married that what's yours is mine and what's mine is yours – it would be like paying myself."

He cocked his head, his dark brows drawing together. "What if I told you I hadn't actually meant that?"

Despite the situation, she almost laughed. "No take-backs."

He rubbed his chin. "Well, I do believe a wedding present is traditional, and you still haven't gotten me one."

"Oh." She'd wanted to get him something, but it had been one of those man-who-has-everything conundrums. "I suppose that would work."

"Then I suggest we go on with our plans for the day, and use your celebrity status to gossip with the locals."

"What celebrity status? You're the one in the business pages. I'm an afterthought."

"That's what you think. Did you see the tabloid pictures of our wedding?"

"Wait a minute." Her eyes narrowed. "If you're trying to buy the hotel... Is our honeymoon a tax deduction?"

"No." He darted a glance at her. "Not all of it."

Lightly, she pinched his arm. "You rat."

"Not our time on the last island and only part of our stay here. You did say it was a lovely hotel. You're not really angry, are you?"

"No. But don't think you're off the hook just because I'm madly in love with you."

"Madly?"

Riga's mouth twitched. "Maybe."

CHAPTER 3

THE CATAMARAN POWERED ATOP the crystalline waters and bounced against the waves. Riga sat on Donovan's lap beside the captain in swivel chairs beneath a blue awning. The warm wind streamed through her hair, and she knotted it at the nape of her neck. Strands flew out, striking her skin.

Glad she'd taken the motion sickness pills, Riga's hand drifted to her stomach. Maybe she should take them every day to ward off these random bouts of dark-magic nausea.

She itched to be back on land investigating the murder. But Donovan had been right. For now, the police were in charge, and there was nothing to be done. And she was on an island paradise, and Donovan was beside her and God, oh God she loved him.

But a trickle of unease leaked past. How long could this last? Necromancy had nearly taken Donovan from her once, and she was now a necromancer, whether she liked it or not.

While she wanted to believe she could make necromantic magic her own, create a system for herself she could use for good, that sort of thing was years in the making. She had a feeling she'd need magical help a whole lot sooner. For her, there was no vacation from the supernatural.

Donovan's arm tightened around her waist. She leaned into his muscular form.

"There it is." The captain, bronzed and bare-chested, shouted over the roar of the motor. "Na Pali."

Fingers of mountain, red earth and green, cascaded into turquoise water that grew dark as it edged from the island. They rounded the bend, and a deep cleft appeared in the dagger-like cliffs, a call to Shangri-La.

Donovan's grip tightened. A dozen inadequate platitudes about the beauty of the place poised on Riga's lips. She said nothing and laid her hand on his bare knee.

"Those are called 'Pali.'" The captain scratched his beard. "The cliffs are carved by waterfalls at the top and shaped by the sea at the bottom. According to legend, Pele, the volcano goddess, came to Na Pali coast searching for a home. But her angry sister, the goddess of the sea, Namakaokaha'i, drove her away. The elements are still battling here. Fire, earth, air and water are still shaping these islands. The volcanoes grow the islands, and the water chips them away. We'll visit a lava tube later."

"Are there any other legends about Kauai?" Donovan asked.

"Lots. Ever heard of the menehunes? They're our little people. According to legend, they built the sacred sites, the heiau, overnight. There's also a cave near the Na Pali coast trailhead that's believed to be menehune."

Riga made a face. *Menehunes.* That would be one cave she'd be steering clear of. Donovan glanced at her, his emerald eyes dancing. Grudging, she broke into a smile.

"And now this trip is research," Donovan said.

"Research?" The captain asked. "What are you researching?"

"She's a writer," Donovan lied. "She's interested in local magic and legends. Especially about – what did you call them? Menehunes?"

"Well in that case..." The captain droned on about gods and ghosts as they traveled up the coast. He turned the boat in a wide arc, and pointed. "Spinners." Suddenly they were racing a pod of dolphins, flashing mercury in the waves.

Riga gasped with delight and hurried to the side. Donovan followed, steadying her against the rail.

The dolphins slipped in and out of the water in an effortless display of grace and muscle. One leapt from the water, twisting its body and exposing the white patch on its belly, then splashing onto its side. Riga could almost feel the water streaming across her skin, the freedom of skimming through the waves.

"They're magnificent." Donovan's voice was a low rumble. He turned to the captain. "How fast are we going?"

"Fifteen knots. That's roughly seventeen miles per hour."

Donovan braced one hand on the rail and studied the dolphins as if to learn their secrets.

"We're coming up on our snorkel spot," the captain said. "Looks like we may be in luck."

He navigated into a crescent-shaped bay and to more shallow waters. They shimmered cerulean, the water clear enough to see wavery patterns in the white sand below.

The captain cut the engine and Riga's ears rang in the abrupt quiet, broken only by the lap of water against the boat. The captain dropped anchor. Riga and Donovan went down below and changed – Donovan into a pair of black trunks and Riga into a white two-piece.

Sunlight shimmered invitingly off the water. Riga ran to the back of the boat and dove. The water was a cool shock to her skin, and she broke the surface with a yelp.

Donovan stood on the platform at the rear of the boat. "Cold?"

But Riga was already growing used to the temperature. "Not anymore."

He twisted behind him and picked up a mask, tossed it to her. It plopped into the water. "You forgot this."

She reached for it and a shadow slipped beneath Riga. A dolphin popped up beside her, and she gasped, startled, then laughed. "Well, hello."

The dolphin chattered, bobbing its head, and swam in a circle around her. She watched, entranced.

The captain appeared beside Donovan. "I think it likes you," the captain shouted.

"The feeling's mutual," she said.

The dolphin brushed her leg, its skin soft and slick.

"He might even let you go for a ride," the captain said. "See if he'll let you touch him."

Slowly, she swept her hand across the animal's silky back. It continued to circle.

"Take his fin," the captain said. "Gently."

Carefully, she took hold. The dolphin moved forward slowly, then with increasing speed, pulling Riga in its wake. For a moment she was flying, free, powerful. Then she let go, uncertain if the dolphin was trying to escape. But it circled toward her with two more members of its pod.

The captain leaned close to Donovan and said something. Donovan looked startled then grinned, shaking his head.

More dolphins appeared. Some chattered at her urgently. Others circled.

Donovan dove, his body arcing through the air. He swam toward them, his strokes smooth and powerful. A dolphin blocked him, chirping, and he stopped, treading water.

"It looks like they're protecting you," he said.

She arched a brow. "They can sense your intent. Do I need protecting from you?"

He swam more slowly toward her, but another dolphin cut in front of him. Donovan's lips turned down.

And Riga was suddenly aware of how large the dolphins were. She looked toward the boat. The captain had vanished.

Riga shook her head. She was being ridiculous. The dolphins were playing, and there was nothing wrong.

The air pressure changed, pressing on her. She shivered in the rapidly cooling water. The dolphins darted around her, silvery blurs, their circle closing. Suddenly, she wanted out.

"Swim toward me, Riga." Donovan's voice was rough, commanding.

She had the sense of doors sliding open, of reality shifting. Blood drained from her face. Magic. Cold, menacing. They needed to get out of the water. "Dono—"

Something jerked him beneath the waves.

Riga stared for a moment, stunned, waiting for him to reappear. He didn't. "Donovan!" She took a deep breath, and dove. The dolphins flashed around her then parted before her. Salt stung her eyes.

Coils of deep pink bloomed in the water. Her chest tightened. Her stomach turned to stone. No, no, God, no. Not Donovan. She swam through a rose-colored tide. Blood everywhere, and where was he, where was he?

She swam toward the surface, thinking she might see him from there, and touched sand. Her heart thundered against her ribs. Disoriented, Riga pushed off the bottom, her vision obscured by the coiling pink clouds.

Fire burned her lungs. Blindly, she reached out for Donovan. But she couldn't find him, couldn't find the surface. *Air*, she needed air.

And then her fingers brushed the sandy bottom again. Her senses lurched, twisted.

Riga stood on a beach, alone. She staggered, confused by the sudden shift in reality. A wave, as tall as a lighthouse, raced toward her. Fear clubbed her, a leaden weight from above weakening her knees.

Someone grasped her wrist and she turned, gasped. She was choking, blinded.

"Riga!"

Donovan. She grabbed for him, tears welling behind her eyelids. His arms went around her, and he towed her roughly toward the boat. She coughed, spitting water, and twisted, determined to see, to know how he'd been hurt.

But he gripped her firmly. "Don't struggle. You're safe."

She coughed and kicked out. "I'm okay. Are you hurt?"

He relaxed his hold and turned her in his arms. His green eyes darkened with worry. "Something—"

"Hey, you two." The captain leaned over the side of the boat. "What's going on out there?"

"Riga got a cramp," Donovan said loudly. "We're coming in."

Riga pushed the hair from her eyes. The dolphins had vanished. The water was clear and still. And on the beach stood a diminutive, pot-bellied figure in a Hawaiian shirt. He beckoned to her.

She turned to Donovan. "On the beach, do you see him?" She looked back. The figure was gone.

"See who?"

"I thought I saw someone. From a distance, he looked like the shaman I met near Dennis's body."

On the hill above the beach, something twinkled. Magic tugged her gaze upward toward a cut in the hillside, a trail. She extended her senses and felt that odd prickling of magic. Riga probed deeper, but all she could sense that magic was there, but not its cause.

She ground her teeth. There had been a time when she could have sent her senses flying and seen, known, acted. But now her magic limped, and she was back at beginner's level. Sensing without understanding. Relying on the crutches of candles and cards, sigils and stones to cast her spells.

"There's no one there now," Donovan said.

"But there was. And there's something up further on that trail. I think we need to find it."

She let Donovan pull her to the boat and hoist her up to the captain, who helped her climb the ladder. A breeze brushed her skin, and her flesh pebbled. The captain dropped a towel around her shoulders.

Donovan climbed the ladder. Only when he was completely out of the water, his dark hair plastered to his muscular legs and chest, did she relax.

"Lunch?" the captain asked brightly.

Donovan nodded. The captain went below deck.

"Someone grabbed my ankle, pulled me under," Donovan said in a low voice. But his eyes glittered.

She stared in disbelief. He was actually enjoying this. And then reason reasserted itself. Of course he'd enjoy it. It was something to battle, a problem to solve.

But she hadn't enjoyed it. Riga looked away. The beach, white and shining, seemed to bob with the rhythm of the boat.

Magic was her first love. She'd never grow bored with its mysteries. But Riga didn't like when its forces played with her, dragged her into terrors, shoved visions into her head. It made her feel small, weak, insignificant. She liked it even less when the people she loved got hauled along for the ride.

She ran her fingers over Donovan's arms, assuring herself he was unhurt. A band of angry red circled one of his ankles. "Someone pulled you under? Or something?"

"Someone." He lifted his ankle, tilting his head to examine it. "Teeth would have left more of a mark, though whoever it was moved inhumanly fast. I was under the boat before I knew what was happening. And then there was a sort of surge of energy, and whoever grabbed me, let go. I saw you floating underwater unconscious." He grasped her hand, his expression darkening. "Your turn."

"I saw you go under." She put her head in her hands, felt the towel slip from her shoulders. "It was like a scene from Jaws, all that blood in the water."

"Blood?"

She bent and picked up her towel from the wooden deck. Still shaken, Riga was having a hard time meeting his gaze. "It must have been part of the vision. It seemed real until I found myself on a beach with a tidal wave headed in my direction."

A band squeezed her chest. Her struggle to find the surface had been no trick, no vision. It had been real. She didn't know if she'd come close to drowning, but it had felt like it.

He didn't respond. She straightened. Looking thoughtful, he toweled off his arms.

"What?" she asked.

"The two events – your vision and my attack – came so close together I thought they were related. Now I'm not so sure." He ambled to a white-cushioned bench and sat, one leg extended, the other drawn up, his hand dangling off his knee.

She sat beside him and curled her legs beneath her. "You said you felt a sort of shock, and then the hand released you?" That implied magical aid – aid she hadn't delivered – and competing forces at work. Unless Donovan himself had somehow done it.

He rubbed the faint cross-shaped scar on his jaw. "In dreams, water represents the emotions, and a tidal wave could mean you feel swamped by an emotional upheaval. Our marriage could account for that."

"But not the blood I saw in the water. Or the dolphins behaving so strangely."

He tilted his head back to study the awning above them, and his lips parted. Then he snapped his jaw shut.

Donovan's phone lay on the table, and she picked it up. "I'm calling Pen," she said.

Her niece was probably awake by now and without Brigitte as protection. Were her other loved ones under attack? Pen only had the meager protective spells she'd been taught – spells Riga suspected the teenager wasn't practicing.

But there was no service, no signal, no luck. She put the phone down, frustrated.

"Pen's fine," Donovan said.

She pressed her lips together. Now was the time to tell him about Brigitte's appearance here on the island. "Donovan—"

"Can we agree the attack underwater is related to the bodies we found?" he asked. "Which Pen has nothing to do with?"

"Bodies?" The captain clambered onto the deck, a wicker basket in one hand and a metal bucket filled with ice, juice, and hard liquors in the other. He stopped in front of them. "You found bodies?"

"On the beach this morning," Donovan said, "between Princeton and Hanalei. A man and a seal, both shot."

The captain whistled. "They killed a man? Now they've gone too far."

"They?" Riga asked sharply.

"I don't know if it's a 'they' – might just be a 'he.' Or a 'she.' Someone's been killing the seals." He put a finger to his temple. "Shot through the head." He raised the bucket. "Drink?"

"No thanks," Riga said, leaning in. "But why?" Something like this had happened before?

Sketching a bow, he opened the basket on the table before them and whipped a red and white checked cloth over the table, followed by plates, sandwiches, and plastic containers filled with food. "The popular theory is that it's a local pissed off at the haole seal-lovers. You know, the ones who block off the beach around the seals. The Hawaiians have been walking those beaches their entire lives. Now whenever a seal shows up, they can't. It makes people angry. You know who got shot?"

"Dennis Glasgow," Donovan said. "He owns the Aloha Princeton Resort."

The captain nodded. "That explains it. He's part of that group that protects the seals. Probably got in the way of the killer. Sure you don't want anything to drink?"

"Just juice," Riga said absently. It was too hot for alcohol.

The captain's theory was neat, clean, logical.

And she knew in her bones it was wrong.

CHAPTER 4

IN UNSPOKEN AGREEMENT, RIGA and Donovan headed straight to the hotel bar. It was sleek, modern, and neutral-colored with pale slate tiles and windows facing the bay. The bar's only concession to island style was hibiscus flowers in tabletop vases.

Mid-afternoon, the bar's single customer was a man in rumpled khakis. He slouched on a leather couch, half a dozen empty glasses on his low table.

Donovan steered her to a table by the windows beneath a slowly turning fan. A waitress hurried to them, her blond hair held in a bun by chopsticks. She placed two glasses of water, rattling with ice, on the round table. "Would you like menus?"

"No, I'll have a brandy," Donovan said. He looked to Riga.

"Can you do a lychee martini?" Riga asked.

Donovan's expression flickered.

"Sure," the waitress said. "Anything else?"

"No thanks."

The woman walked away. Riga reached for the ice water.

"I guess this means you're not pregnant," Donovan said.

Riga choked. Donovan's eyes crinkled, his smile lopsided.

She slapped her palm against her chest, coughing. "Pregnant? What made you think that?"

"The captain told me that dolphins were attracted to pregnant women. And then you turned down the alcohol on the boat."

Was it *that* unusual for her to turn down a drink? And was this where things would fall apart? She looked away, toward the ocean. Donovan knew how old she was. He knew the odds were low.

The waitress returned with their glasses, setting them atop square napkins. Riga took a sip.

Yes, she thought, it *was* unusual. And she wasn't going to dwell on her age. Not when she had a martini this delicious. "A pregnancy would put a spoke in my plan to drink every type of tropical martini ever invented on our honeymoon."

"Was that your plan? How greedy."

"Don't sneer." A lychee fruit, speared by a toothpick, lay against the inside of her glass. With two fingers, she extracted the toothpick, and pointed it at him. "At least martinis don't come with umbrellas." She put the fruit in her mouth and slid it off the toothpick with her teeth.

"Then I'll chalk up the dolphin behavior to your animal magnetism."

Head lowered, she pressed the point of the toothpick into her napkin, bending the tip. "Donovan... You know at my age the odds are—"

He lay a hand over hers. "I know. Don't read anything into it."

They'd talked about the possibility of children before getting married. Before she'd become involved with Donovan, she hadn't considered a family. But now she wondered, dullness fogging her chest. If they'd met earlier in life, if she was only five years younger. *If, if, if.*

He wanted a family. But he'd been raised in foster homes and had told her the idea of adopting delighted him.

"Hey!" Two meaty hands slammed on their table.

Riga's drink tipped, spilling. Donovan was out of his chair before she could react, a broad hand on the man's chest, pushing him backward. The man stumbled and sat hard on the tiled floor.

"Can I help you?" Donovan's voice was cold iron.

Eyes wide, the waitress scurried to Riga's side. She blotted up the drink with a towel, her eyes darting to the men.

The man scratched his grizzled jowls like a confused bear. His legs bowed, his stomach pressed hard against the buttons of his pale blue shirt. He looked up. "I heard you found my friend."

"Your friend?" Riga prompted.

"My friend is dead."

The tension in Donovan's shoulders relaxed. He looked at Riga, questioning.

The upside of interrogating those who'd over-imbibed: they said more than they should. The downside: slobber. Disgust warred with curiosity. She hated drunks. Was his even a true expression of grief? Or was grief an excuse to overindulge?

Curiosity won out. "I think we should buy this man a drink," she said.

Donovan hauled the man to his feet and grabbed a chair from a nearby table, plunking it in front of their own. "One of the same for the gentleman," Donovan said. "And another martini for the lady."

The waitress laughed shakily. She hurried away without comment. Wary, silent, Donovan watched the man. The waitress returned with his drink – something a mellow golden brown, no ice.

When the waitress had gone, Riga said, "You knew Dennis Glasgow?"

The man belched, his expression mournful. "Friend of mine. Now he's dead. Too young, the good die young."

"I'm Riga Hayworth. What's your name?"

"Garfield. Grover Garfield. I'm the lighthouse keeper, up on the point."

Riga raised a brow. Heaven help the shipping industry if he was on duty today.

"Off duty," Grover said. "Came to meet my buddy. But he's dead. Heard you found him." Oblivious to Donovan's growl, Grover put a hand on her wrist, lying across the table, and her muscles tensed. "I just wanted to know – was it quick? I don't want to think about him being in pain."

Donovan lifted his hand off hers. Dropped it. "It was quick."

The lighthouse keeper slumped in his chair. "That's a relief."

"How did you two know each other?" Riga asked.

His eyes widened. "I'm the lighthouse keeper. Course we know each other." He shook his head. "Good man."

Riga pressed her lips together. Grover had passed the optimal intoxication point and was unable to talk sensibly. "Who do you think killed him?"

"Who killed him? Who killed him?" He lurched to his feet, swaying. His voice rose to a roar. "Who would want to kill him? He was a good man."

Another man wearing a blue-denim shirt with the hotel logo entered the bar and looked around. A brick-red birthmark splashed across his tanned face. He shoved his sunglasses to the top of his head, ruffling his brown hair. Expression grim, he beelined for their table.

Gently, he took Grover's elbow. "Come along, Grover. You don't want to bother these people."

The lighthouse keeper pointed a wavering finger at Riga and Donovan. "They started it."

The man shot Donovan an apologetic look. "He's had a rough day."

Donovan rose. "So have you." He extended a hand. "I'm sorry about your brother."

Riga looked at the newcomer with interest. So this was the murder victim's younger brother and the co-owner of the hotel.

She relaxed her vision. His aura was the bruised purple of mourning flecked with black. Feeling like a voyeur, she looked away.

The black specks of hatred made her uneasy. But his brother had just been killed, so they were understandable. And she'd never found aura reading terribly reliable. They could be as confused as people's emotions, changeable, tangled.

She glanced at Grover, looking intently at a spot on the wall. She had no desire to look at the lighthouse keeper's aura.

Donovan and the newcomer clasped hands. "I don't believe you've met my wife," Donovan said. "Riga, this is Paul Glasgow."

Lightly, Paul took her hand. He turned to Donovan and swallowed. "I understand you found my brother."

"That got around quickly," Donovan said, his voice deceptively light, "and we haven't told anyone."

"No, no, of course not. But it's a small island. You can't keep secrets for long. The police told me he'd been shot, but—"

"He was too young." Grover clutched Paul's shoulder, leaning into it, and Paul took a step back to brace himself. "Too. Young." He used his finger to accent each word with a poke to Paul's chest.

"Yeah. Let's get you home, Grover." The hotel owner began to pull him away, then stopped, released Grover and turned.

Grover studied his open palms, his expression perplexed.

"I still want to sell," Paul said. "I don't want to run this place without my brother. It's not..." Abruptly, he departed with the lighthouse keeper.

Donovan lowered himself into the chair opposite her. "Well, that was—"

"Useless," Riga finished.

"Let's hope this really is Grover's day off, or there'll be ships running aground. And Grover Garfield? Could he be named after the presidents?"

Riga laughed. "I didn't want to ask."

He took a sip of his drink. "What would you have asked?"

"If Grover had been more sober? I'd try to get him talking about the murder victim, his habits, his friends, his enemies. And I'd find out where Grover was when Dennis was killed. We should talk to him again, later."

"And to Dennis Glasgow's brother." Donovan rubbed his jaw.

"The captain mentioned Dennis belonged to a group protecting the seals. They may know more about who's attacking them. It's still unclear who was the primary target – Dennis, or the seal."

"Dennis was married."

"Oh." She enjoyed interviewing grieving widows about as much as she'd enjoy talking to a grieving brother, but both had to be done. *Soon*. When people were emotional, ugly truths were more likely to slip.

"And if you had a Hawaiian PI's license, who else would you talk to?" he asked.

"Other colleagues, people near the murder site who might have seen something. The police have likely already begun that. They won't be happy if they think we're interfering."

Donovan closed his eyes. "There was a house overlooking the site. Its owners are wealthy."

"Are you channeling this information?" she joked.

He opened his eyes. "It overlooks the ocean and was a very nice house. I'm surprised you didn't notice it."

"I was distracted."

"I'll find out who they are and get an introduction."

"That easy?"

"People with money run in the same circles," he said.

"And you know they run in your circles because..."

"It's the sort of house I might buy. Some day."

She placed her hand on his. "Donovan. Thanks for this." It wasn't the honeymoon he'd planned, but he'd shifted gears effortlessly, without complaint.

"The sooner we figure this out, the sooner you're free of it and we're back to our honeymoon."

"This will still take time." Riga conjured mental lists of suspects, timetables. "If we split up, we can cover more territory."

"I'm not letting you out of my sight. My first priority is for my bride to survive the honeymoon."

"What's your second?"

"To see she enjoys it."

She arched a brow. "How do you propose to accomplish that?"

His eyes darkened. "Is that a challenge?" His voice grew husky.

Awareness of his masculinity tingled through her, and Riga's lists evaporated in a curl of smoke. Romance, she thought—not for the first time—was not the detective's friend.

CHAPTER 5

A WARM BREEZE BRUSHED Riga's cheek, waking her, and she reached for Donovan. His side of the bed was deserted. She flipped on the table lamp.

She sighed. At least the furniture this morning was upright. But a trail of child-sized footprints led from the bedroom and out the open patio doors.

Menehunes. Again.

Riga dressed in white-pleated shorts, a cotton tank top, and sneakers, and walked outside, following the trail of muddy feet across the tile patio, past their private swimming pool. The trail stopped at a banyan tree near the beach. In the darkness, the tree's aerial roots felt alien, threatening.

The hell with the menehunes. Following the sound of waves, she turned from the tree.

Riga clambered atop the pile of rocks that isolated "their" strip of beach and watched the stars fade. Unaware of Riga's presence, the dripping ghost beside her sobbed, raking hands through her glistening hair. Something fluttered to the rocks and scrabbled toward them.

Riga didn't turn her head toward the gargoyle. They sat, listening to the ebb and crush of the waves. The sound blended with the ghost's whimpers. Finally, Riga said, "Thanks for not saying 'I told you so.'"

Brigitte overbalanced and flapped her stony wings, scraping Riga's left arm. "I *did* tell you so." The gargoyle nipped at an unruly stone feather on her chest. "What happened?"

Rubbing her arm, Riga told the gargoyle about the body they'd found and the underwater attack when they'd gone sailing. "It all feels connected. But I didn't sense dark magic when I was in the water. It was something else." The attack had confused her, but the magic hadn't left her with that sick feeling.

"What?"

"I don't know."

"And your next step?"

Riga rose and brushed the back of her shorts with her hand. "I don't know that either."

"Marriage has made you lose your focus."

"Most likely." Riga followed the ghost toward the hotel. The spirit vanished behind the same banyan as the menehune footprints. Was there something special about the tree, something that related to the ghost? Or were the menehunes just being annoying?

Riga circled the wide tree but sensed nothing to indicate murder or magic. And why had she thought murder? The ghost was certainly a mystery – but she could have died a natural death. Yet something told her that wasn't the case.

Her jaw tightened. She returned through the rear balcony door just as Donovan was entering through the front, breakfast tray in hand.

"You don't need to collect our breakfast every morning," she said. "But I love it that you do."

"I was awake. Thought I'd make good use of my time." He slid the tray onto the circular table and drew her into his arms. "Though I can think of better uses," he rumbled.

❧❧❧❧❧ ❦❦❦❦❦

Lips burning from the morning's lovemaking, Riga strolled through the hotel lobby with Donovan at her side. The sleeves of his loose white linen shirt rippled in the balmy island air that drifted through the open hotel doors.

Nearby, a uniformed employee unwound Christmas lights from a potted palm. Donovan walked to the valet podium and slipped the man behind it a folded bill.

The valet nodded and darted down the circular driveway. A red Ferrari with the top off purred up the drive, halted in front of them.

Riga pushed aside her jealousy – she'd love to drive a Magnum PI car – and checked her watch, impatient for their rental Mercedes. The Aquatic Protection Society, where the murdered hotel owner had volunteered, would open soon. She wanted to be there when it did, counting on the twin elements of surprise and nuisance.

The valet exited the car and handed Donovan the keys.

He hopped over the driver's door and into the front seat, grinning. "You coming?"

Her eyes widened. "That's not our car. Is it?"

He ran his hands over the wheel. "I wanted this one from the beginning, but the only red Ferrari on the island was unavailable until today."

"You sneaky devil." She sank into the low seat, her bare legs sliding across the buttery leather, and tried not to look impressed. It even smelled like new car, though it was a 1980s model. Was there an air freshener with that smell? If so, she wanted it. "You warned me marrying you had its benefits. I thought you meant in bed."

"I did." He revved the engine, and they sped out of the lot onto the winding road draped with greenery.

His eyes held a proprietary gleam. "Er, you didn't want to drive, did you?"

She just gave him a look. The wind whipped Riga's hair. She knotted it loosely at the base of her neck, pulled a silk scarf from her leather satchel and tied it under her chin.

"You're one of the few women I know who can pull off that look without looking like a babushka," Donovan said.

"Compliments will get you everywhere."

"What else is in that bag of yours?"

"Sunscreen. Bug spray. Tarot cards. Emergency magic kit. Latex gloves—"

"You brought latex gloves on our honeymoon? Kinky."

"I'd forgotten they were in the bag." She never knew when she'd stumble across a crime scene. Or create one. She was especially proud of her emergency magic kit – a candle, spell paper, herbs, magical oil, and a piece of quartz – which she'd crammed inside an old mint tin.

"That reminds me," she continued, "I want to pick up some of that red Hawaiian salt." When it came to magical protection, salt was salt, but she had a secret passion for the more exotic flavors. Volcanic black salt, Dead Sea salt, the pink stuff laced with iron from the Himalayas...

"Not a problem," he said. "According to the desk clerk, the Aquatic Protection Society is in a shopping center."

But it was the wrong kind of shopping center, a green-painted two-story wooden complex inhabited by tourist traps, their windows filled with shells and cheap pearl jewelry. Colorful sarongs fluttered from clothing racks lining the sidewalks.

Donovan parked in front of an ice cream parlor. A small, blond boy stood outside it in Batman swim trunks and nothing else, earnestly trying to catch the drips curling down the sides of his cone. The kid wiped his hand on his bare chest, leaving a streak of strawberry. Riga's chest pinched.

Donovan chuckled. "His parents will have their hands full." He nodded toward a staircase on the left. "Up that way."

The wooden stairs echoed hollowly beneath their feet. Down an open corridor, past more souvenir shops, and then a small office with posters plastered on the windows. A vintage *Save the Whales. Happy Earth Day. Be Kind to Animals.*

"My keen, animal instincts tell me this might be the place," Donovan said.

Riga laughed. "I'll make a detective of you yet."

The door stood open, exposing an empty room. They strolled inside. A ceiling fan wheeled slowly, making little progress stirring the warm air.

Riga walked to a bookcase and frowned at an ugly glass and bronze sculpture of a dolphin riding a wave. She tapped the plaque beneath it: *The Hannah James Memorial.* "I wonder what Hannah did to deserve this?"

A twenty-something with a wisp of a beard hurried out of a back room and adjusted his glasses. His shorts and t-shirt were slouchy, wrinkled. "Can I help you?"

She smiled at him. "We're interested in learning more about the seal killings and your work protecting the animals."

"Are you press?"

"Interested parties," Donovan said.

He crossed his arms, his nose wrinkling with disdain. The nail on his index finger was unnaturally long. He was a guitar player, Riga guessed, but the nail repelled her, a touch of the vampiric. "And you just got interested when you heard about the murder," he said.

"Exactly. I'm a private investigator." She dug in her bag and flipped open her wallet. It was a California PI license, worthless in Hawaii. She picked up a brochure lying on a steel desk. "Surely the Society's work is public information?"

"Sorry." He rested against the desk, bracing his hands behind him. "I thought you were just a couple of morbid tourists."

"Only one of us," Donovan said. He grasped the man's hand. "Donovan Mosse. The private investigator's husband."

He frowned. "Wait a minute. I've heard of you two."

"Then you have us at a disadvantage." Riga stiffened. Donovan was a public figure, though mainly on the business pages. And not all of the publicity surrounding him lately had been fair.

"Oh. Sorry. I'm Jay Sylvan. Assistant to the director."

"We're sorry for your loss," Riga said. "Dennis's murder must be hard on your organization."

"No one's ever been killed before – no one human, that is," Jay said, his voice bitter.

Donovan walked to a bulletin board and studied the flyers there. His head tilted.

Sweat trickled down Riga's back. "Do you always have a volunteer standing guard over the seals?"

"No," Jay said. "We don't have enough people. But when our responders can get out to keep a seal from being disturbed, they do."

"How was Dennis connected to the Society?" she asked.

"He is – was – one of our founding members. He was president of the board."

"Any idea who's attacking the seals?" Donovan asked.

Jay plucked at the strands of hair dotting his chin. "I really couldn't say."

Donovan turned from the bulletin board. "You must have some idea."

"Look. I get where people are coming from. The locals have been walking those beaches for a long time. Now we come in and rope them off, all so a handful of monk seals – which they don't see as even being native to the islands – can get some sleep. They don't believe they're worth protecting. But the monk seals are endangered, and they were here before the Polynesians arrived. The early Polynesians killed most of them off, and now they've returned to the islands. The species as a whole is headed for extinction. And when they arrive on the beaches, they need to rest undisturbed."

"It sounds like being president of your organization could be controversial," Riga said. "Did Dennis have any run-ins?"

"I couldn't say."

"Oh, I think you could if you wanted to." She winked. "How well did you know Dennis?"

"Me?" Jay's eyes widened. "I only saw him once a month. I work with the Executive Director, not the board."

"The seal killer," Donovan said. "Or killers. You must have put some thought into who's responsible." He tapped a wanted poster on the bulletin board with the back of one finger. Forty-thousand-dollar reward for information leading to the arrest of the monk seal killer.

"We've had conflicts with certain individuals," Jay said.

"With whom, exactly?" Riga forced a smile.

Jay made an exasperated motion with his hands. "Look, the cops were here yesterday. They've got reports of all our incidents, but I can't release that information to you. If I could help you, I would, but my hands are tied. Killing an endangered species here is a state and federal offense."

Riga gave a minute shake of her head. "And killing a human?"

Breathing noisily, Jay straightened off the desk. "It's the job of the police to protect people. It's my job to protect the seals. If you find that offensive—"

A throat cleared behind them, and they wheeled toward the doorway. An egg-shaped man stood there, his face red. A droplet of sweat hung from one tip of his curled, white moustache. He pulled a handkerchief from the pocket of his crisply tailored khakis and wiped his head. "Good morning, Jay. What's so offensive?" He glanced at Donovan and gave a start of recognition. "You're not Donovan Mosse, are you?"

One corner of Donovan's mouth curved upward. "I am. And you are?"

The man strode toward Donovan, hand outstretched. "I'd heard you were in the islands and recognized you from the papers. My name is Townsend, Townsend Murray. I'm the executive director." He clasped Donovan's hand, pumping vigorously. "What brings you to our offices? Considering a donation, I hope?"

"I'm always looking for worthy charities," Donovan said. "This is my wife, Riga Hayworth."

The little man wrung her hand. Then he turned his back on her. Grateful, she wiped her palm dry on her shorts.

Townsend bounced on the toes of his boating shoes. They were leather, spotless, and expensive looking. Did the Aquatic Protection Society paid well or did his money came from another source?

"How can I help you?" he asked Donovan.

Riga suppressed a twinge of annoyance and smiled harder. She was used to being both lead and sole detective in her investigations. But if Townsend related better to Donovan, she'd be a fool not to leverage that.

"Perhaps we can help each other," Donovan said. "I'm considering an investment on the island and would like to learn more about potential environmental issues and about your organization, since it appears we'll be neighbors." Donovan frowned. "I apologize for dropping in on you like this, but we only became aware of your organization this morning, when we learned Dennis Glasgow had been a member. My wife and I found his body on the beach yesterday, alongside the seal."

Townsend shook his head. "Terrible, terrible. Man truly is the planet's most destructive animal. Yes, of course you have questions. Would you like to come into my office?" He motioned toward a door at the back of the room.

Riga took a micro step forward. She wasn't sure if Townsend was a suspect yet or just an information source, but he was willing to talk.

Donovan checked his watch. "My wife and I have another appointment, but maybe we can take you to lunch later today or tomorrow and discuss this further?"

Riga sagged.

"I'm free today. There's an excellent Mediterranean restaurant on the beach not far from here. Shall we say noon?"

"Perfect," Donovan said.

They did another round of handshaking and Riga and Donovan left. "Interesting technique," she said, following him down the stairs.

"You would have handled things differently?"

"We-ll." Yes, she *would* have. He stopped at the base of the stairs and turned to her.

"I would have interrogated him before he had a chance to prepare. But in this case," she admitted, "your methods may well be an improvement on mine. The delay gives Townsend time to fantasize about that fat donation you dangled."

Donovan arched a brow. "Did I?"

She laughed, her annoyance evaporating, and wrapped an arm around his waist. "We've got over an hour until lunch. Shall we wander?"

Hanalei rested between misty green mountains and a bay. As they walked past turquoise-painted wooden buildings with corrugated tin roofs, and picnic tables with palm umbrellas, their gaze kept drifting to the conical hills. When they grew bored with the art galleries, they turned to the beach, removing their sandals and letting the cool waves wash over their feet.

"What did you think of them?" Donovan asked.

"The men at the Protection Society?" She shrugged. "Jay is young, earnest, and afraid of saying the wrong thing. Though I got the feeling he was more upset by the murder of the seal than of Dennis. Townsend is awfully well-dressed for the director of a small non-profit. If he has his own wealth, I'm surprised he didn't take a cushy board position rather than a director's job, which requires actual work. Either he's a true believer, or something's up."

He kissed her forehead. "I do love your suspicious mind."

"So that's why you married me, for my mind?"

"There might have been some other factors." His hand caressed her back.

"What did you pick up from the interview?" Riga asked.

"Mr. Townsend Murray is one of the few men I've met who's more interested in me than in you."

"More interested in your money, another good reason for you to take point on the questions."

"I noticed you were unusually quiet back there."

"Why should I do the work when I've got a big strong man to do it for me?"

"For that, you're going in the water." He threw her over his shoulder and charged into the waves.

"Stop!" She shrieked, laughing. "We're meeting a suspect!"

Gently, he put her down, knee-deep in the surf. He traced the line of her lip with his thumb. "Thanks for marrying me."

"I couldn't stand to watch you beg." She stood on her tiptoes and brushed his lips with hers. Their kiss deepened, and a familiar, hot longing surged through her. They broke apart, their breathing quick and fast.

"We're meeting a suspect in ten minutes," Riga said.

Groaning, Donovan strode deeper into the ocean, unbuttoning his shirt. He tossed it over his shoulder and dove, slicing cleanly through the low waves. She caught the shirt, scooping it to her chest.

He surfaced, wiping his face with both hands. Donovan walked to her, water cascading from his bronzed chest. Her lips parted, her body aching.

"I needed to cool off," he said.

She dug a small towel out of her satchel and handed it to him, along with his shirt. "Now, so do I."

CHAPTER 6

THE DIRECTOR OF THE Aquatic Protection Society relaxed at a round table on a deck overlooking the beach. He glanced curiously at Donovan's water-darkened shorts but didn't comment.

"Hello, Townsend." Riga sat in the wooden chair beside him and smiled. For a suspect – or for a man about to solicit money – he seemed utterly tranquil. His fingers dangled over the arms of the chair like tiny sausages, a plain gold band biting into his ring finger.

"Is an outdoor table all right?" he asked. "Or would you prefer to sit inside?"

"Outside is fine." Donovan signaled for the waitress, and they ordered drinks.

"How long have you lived here?" Riga asked after the waitress had departed. Yes, yes. She'd told herself she'd let Donovan take lead. But she wasn't about to sit there like a bump on a log.

Townsend shifted in his chair. "Just over three years now. I learned about the plight of the monk seals not long after I arrived and found others as outraged as I was. So I took over as executive director of the Society."

The waitress arrived with their drinks– a tropical martini for Riga, brandy for Donovan. When she had left, Donovan asked, "So who's killing the seals?"

Townsend choked on his beer and placed the bottle down carefully. "You get straight to the point, don't you?"

"Why waste each other's time?" he asked.

"If I knew who our seal killer was," Townsend said, "he'd be in jail."

Riga stirred her sunset-colored drink with a wedge of pineapple. "You must have some suspicions."

"Suspicions, yes." Townsend smiled complacently. "But that's not enough for an arrest."

Patronizing. Riga's teeth hurt, and she realized her smile had become a rictus grin. She loosened her jaw, took a sip of her drink.

"Who do you suspect, then?" Donovan asked.

"The most aggressive gang is led by a fellow named Kimo Kalani."

Riga arched a brow. "Gang?"

Townsend tilted his head. It gleamed in the sunlight. "Technically, not a gang. More like a band of merry men. Some of their encounters with our responders have been... threatening."

"How threatening?" Riga said. "Verbally? Physically?"

"Both. But they're clever, use double meanings, use their size and body language to intimidate rather than their fists. It's never enough to file charges, not that the police would do much anyway." Townsend's expression grew pinched.

"The police aren't sympathetic?" Donovan asked.

"Oh, they are, just not to the plight of the seals. The seals are being assassinated – there's no other word for it. And they're federally protected."

"Where can we find Kimo?" Riga asked.

Townsend blotted his head with the napkin. "Somewhere in the Koloa area, though I don't know why you'd want to bother. He's got a restaurant and fishing boat."

A boat sped past, and the crush of the waves grew louder. "Any other suspects?" Riga asked.

He laughed politely. "You sound like a detective."

"I am." She watched for his reaction.

He merely shrugged. "It could be anyone. Kimo and his buddies are just at the top of the list. The seals have many enemies on the island. But why are you two so interested?"

"I'm considering buying Dennis's hotel," Donovan said. "Finding his body on the beach beside the seal highlighted another angle I need to consider. Are there any other environmental issues I should be aware of?"

Townsend mopped his head with a cocktail napkin. "Dennis did a good job creating a sustainable resort, but really, there shouldn't be a hotel there at all. The more hotel rooms, the more people, the more pressure on the local environment – and not just to the seals. If I had my way, I'd turn back the clock. But I can't, so all I can do is advocate for sustainable development, so we don't ruin the very thing people come so far to enjoy. I suppose I stand with the local hippy colony on that one."

Riga sipped her drink. "Hippy colony?"

"They live out along the Na Pali coast," Townsend said. "They're quite remarkable, actually, living off the land and only bringing in the supplies they can carry on their backs."

Donovan glanced at Riga. "We're heading out to the trail after lunch."

"I hope you're not going to try to hike the entire trail. It's at least a two-day march in, and the trail becomes treacherous quickly, especially now during the rainy season. There's another, shorter trail to a waterfall I'd recommend for day hikers. There's also a cave near the trailhead, which is supposed to be haunted by menehunes, our local little people, if you're interested in that sort of thing. But if you'd like to learn more about the ecology..." Townsend launched into a dissertation on the sad state of the environment, the Aquatic Protection Society, and its desperate need for funding.

Riga's gaze drifted to the beach. Something glinted at the edge of her awareness. She turned her head sharply but saw only waves, sand, beachgoers in swimsuits and floppy hats. Riga relaxed her gaze and probed outward with her other senses. A psychic door slammed shut, cold and hard, and she winced.

A familiar-looking Hawaiian shirt fluttered across the beach, caught like a kite in the breeze. *The kupua. Dammit.* He'd blocked her probing. She swallowed her pride, vowing to ask him how he'd done it next time they met.

Townsend leaned across the table. "Are you all right?"

"I just realized my glass was empty," Riga said.

"A crisis easily averted." Donovan motioned to the waitress then returned his attention to Townsend. "You were saying about the sea turtles?"

❦ ❦

The parking lot at the Kalalau trailhead was full, but Donovan maneuvered the Ferrari between two Jeeps on the street, across from a shallow, wide-mouthed cave. He extracted a backpack from the trunk and slung it over his shoulders.

"Last chance to back out," he said. "This is one of the most dangerous trails in the United States."

"Are you suggesting I'm unfit for duty?" She'd heard enough warnings about this trail along the Na Pali coast and had no intention of cutting short her honeymoon with a slide down a rock cliff. On the other hand, she hadn't been regularly working out for over a month. Riga tucked some bottles of water in her satchel and slung it diagonally across her chest.

"I'm suggesting we probably got a better view of the coast from the boat. And this trail sounds like a lot of work, especially during the rainy season. It's going to be a muddy mess."

"You're not afraid of a little exercise, are you?"

He grinned. "I can think of better workouts for our honeymoon. And there are other leads we can follow. This seems a bit thin."

"Exactly." This is what it meant to be a metaphysical detective – following coincidences, hunches, the unusual. "I just have a feeling that shaman wants us here, and it's somehow connected to this case."

She also suspected they might owe the tiny man. There had been magic yesterday along that coast. Something had attacked them, and something had defended. The diminutive shaman had been there.

And there'd been something else, higher up where the trail should have been. She badly wanted to know more about that magic.

Riga glanced at the cave. Two tourists in shorts and t-shirts stood inside, pointing at the ceiling. One snapped a photo, illuminating the slick, black rock with his flash.

Donovan nudged her. "The menehune cave, you think?"

"If it is, I'm not getting any vibes off it." Just an odd sense of resignation. Probably sick of the parade of visitors, she thought wryly.

They trekked along the road and past a kiosk to the red-dirt trail. When she stepped on the path a wave of energy flowed through her feet, a current that raced to the roots of her hair.

"Did you feel that?" Donovan asked.

Now *this* was magic, the magic of the earth, the magic of a place. Her heart leapt. "Donovan..."

A muscular Polynesian in a loincloth materialized ahead of them, his form translucent. A hiker brushed past her and walked through the ghost. Oblivious, the hiker shrugged the backpack on his shoulders, hurried forward, and staggered sideways in the mud.

"You were right," Donovan said. "There is magic here. Big magic."

Around the bend in the trail they saw more ghosts marching. Suddenly, she felt like an intruder.

"We should ask permission," she said in a low voice.

"Nonsense. We belong here. Can't you feel it?" He grasped her hand, and they moved forward.

But she couldn't feel what Donovan did. And that disturbed her.

The uneven trail was slick and climbed quickly through lush foliage. Riga slipped and clung to Donovan for support, sending a silent request for safe passage to whoever might be listening. Mud spattered Riga's legs, and as she struggled up the hill, she found it difficult to admire the exotic climbing vines winding around thick tree trunks.

She'd seen plenty of ghosts in her day, but the ghostly marchers unnerved her with their sheer, noiseless numbers. Some of the spirits wore skirts and capes of Ti leaves, but many were naked. All were barefooted.

Water dripped from a wide leaf and splashed onto Riga's cheek. The humidity which had been bearable at the beach clogged her lungs, and her shirt soon stuck unpleasantly to her skin.

Several of the hikers who passed them in the opposite direction were covered in mud. Wearily, Riga predicted a mud bath was in her near future. The hikers going their way thinned out, defeated by the slick trail. But the ghosts tramped on by their sides, mute, determined.

Donovan, surefooted, kept an easy pace. But Riga was gasping when they crested the first ridge and glimpsed a slice of turbulent ocean in varying shades of blue. View followed upon view – the beach they'd left behind, the scalloped red-green cliffs and ocean, ocean, ocean.

The trail leveled out after the first mile, and they paused beside a pandanus tree's teepee of exposed roots. Riga dug the water bottles out of her bag and tossed one to Donovan.

"This place is incredible," she said, panting. She wiped the back of her hand across her forehead. It was a useless gesture; both hand and head were covered in sweat. She wrenched the cap off and drank deeply. The bag had begun biting into her shoulder, and she'd rather drink the water than carry it.

"It does have a certain feeling to it, doesn't it?" he asked.

Riga examined her legs. Her socks were coated with mud, and she was sure some of it had oozed into her shoes. But they had farther to go, and she couldn't spare water to clean up, even though the sweat and muck left her itching like crazy. She replaced the bottle in her bag.

Donovan took a sip and stared into the tangle of leaves and vines. He wasn't even sweating, she thought crossly, and there was only a thin crust of mud near the soles of his boots. How did he *do* that?

He pointed. "There's a heiau in there, one of the Hawaiian sacred places."

She peered into the dense brush but saw nothing but green. "Where?"

"Just past the ginger flowers. See the stones?"

A line of ankle-high stones, jagged and uneven, disappeared beneath the greenery. It was nearly invisible. "How did you spot them?"

He shrugged. "Good eye, I guess."

Rejoining the spirits of the dead, they continued on. They passed wild orchids and a battered, tsunami-warning sign, and then the trail descended. Donovan took her hand, steadying her when she slipped on a rock.

He grinned. "Having fun yet?"

"The views alone are worth it," she said, sucking in air, hoping she sounded convincing. Donovan had been right. They were closeted in a jungle, and the views from the boat had been more spectacular. But the trail had been her idea, and she'd be damned if she'd complain.

A roar of water drifted up to them. They neared the bottom of the slope. The sound of rushing water grew louder.

He frowned. "There's supposed to be a beach around here somewhere."

They rounded a bend. The path ended in a fast-moving river.

Riga balanced on a rock, hands on her hips, and caught her breath, relieved by the unscheduled break. They'd been hiking nearly two hours. Her knees ached from the strain of the downhill climb.

Donovan crouched on a rock and placed his hand in the noisy torrent. He snatched it away. "If this is the stream I think it is," he shouted over the roaring water, "we're at the end of the line. It's moving too fast."

"What a shame," she lied. "But it was lovely while it lasted."

Footsteps pounded behind her. "Look out," a man snarled, knocking her sideways.

She twisted, bracing herself, but the rocks slipped beneath her, and she fell. Donovan shouted.

Icy water clutched her legs, ripped her into the current. She bashed against a rock. Her knee exploded with pain. She grasped for something, anything, but the water moved too fast, and she was a helpless piece of driftwood caught in its flow.

As she contemplated her fate (doomed), her mind had a moment of marvelous clarity. Then one set of hands grasped her wrist. Another gripped beneath her shoulders, and she was dragged onto a rock beneath a broad-leafed banana tree.

She untangled herself from her bag, strapped cross-ways over her shoulder and now near wrapped around her neck. Two men peered down at her: Donovan, white-faced and grim, and a shirtless twenty-something with a tangle of beard and a peeling tan.

Panting, the stranger sprawled on the rock beside her. His feet were bare and muddy, broad and hairy. "Dude. That was, like, totally uncool."

Donovan ran his hands over her arms and legs. Her knee was swollen, seeping blood, her palms raw. She trembled from the chill and damp.

A muscle pulsed in Donovan's jaw. "How badly are you hurt?"

Cautiously, she flexed her knee. "Nothing's broken."

"You were lucky," the stranger said. "That guy was like, totally out of control." He shifted forward into a squat and pointed to the other side of the creek, where a man with an expensive-looking pack and hiking gear clambered over rocks.

Riga's muscles tensed. Anger flared in her chest. The hiker must have known he'd knocked her into the raging river. But he'd plowed onward, indifferent.

Her fingers twitched, and dark energy flowed through her. A rockslide would be easy work, tear him from the cliff, drive him into the river. And then...

She blinked, shame flooding her face. *God.* What was she thinking? She'd never used her magic for revenge.

Donovan's eyes narrowed, watching the man climbing the opposite slope. His lips peeled back in a snarl, and he started for the river.

"Donovan," Riga said.

"He ain't worth it man," the stranger said. "If she was my lady, I'd be pissed too. But I've been hanging here for two days now waiting for the water to recede. That guy's lucky he made it across. A woman drowned out here last month. Swept right out to sea." He made a whooshing noise.

"You know who he is?" Donovan's voice was controlled, but Riga felt his fury, flowing from him in a black wave.

"Nah, man. Just some tourist." The stranger scratched at a mosquito bite on his shoulder. "But take my advice and chill. He's got a bad attitude, and bad attitude's got no place out here on the trail. The trail will eat you, man. With karma like that, he's his own worst enemy."

She grasped Donovan's hand. He looked down at her and blinked. Shaking his head, he knelt beside her. "I don't suppose you've got a first aid kit in that bag of yours?"

"You know my motto: semper paratus."

Donovan smiled. "I think "always ready" is the Coast Guard's motto."

"They can share."

Her bag was soaked. She dug past sodden towels and extracted a plastic container with a red cross on the lid. Thanks to the dunking, at least she was clean.

Donovan took the tin from her hand. He paused and reached across Riga, his hand extended toward the stranger. "Thank you. The name's Donovan."

The other man gripped Donovan's hand, let go. "Aw, it's just life along the trail. I'm Trader."

"And this is my wife, Riga."

Trader tipped an imaginary hat. "Howdy."

Donovan pawed through the tin, found a tube of lotion, and handed it to the man. "Here. Your need is greater."

Trader squinted at the label. "Itch be-gone? All riiiight. Told you – it's all about the karma." He unscrewed the top and rubbed it on the red bumps dotting his arms.

Donovan smiled crookedly. He splashed antiseptic on Riga's knee.

She flinched. "Mother... Mary that stings."

"Baby," Donovan chided, his eyes glinting with humor.

"Trader," she said through gritted teeth, "how long have you been in Kauai?"

His forehead wrinkled. "Just over a year, now. I live out at the other end of the trail." He nodded to a duffle bag beneath a banana tree. "I'm bringing back supplies."

"Then you must have heard about the seal attacks," she said.

He nodded. "Too many people think it's man against nature. But it's just in their heads. Everything's in your head, man. But your head is like, ginormous." He knit his stained fingers together. "See, we don't have to fight nature. We can, like, live in harmony. Killing seals ain't right. They're just seals, just swimming, just eating, just sleeping. The seals get it. And then... WHAM." He slammed his open palm on the rock. "They're dead. I'm just saying, it ain't right."

Donovan taped gauze to Riga's knee. "Is there any talk about who's behind the killings?"

He shrugged. "Probably. But I don't hear it. I keep myself to myself. I don't like to listen to negativity. It gets in your head, and you can't get it out."

"You say you've been waiting here for two days," Donovan said. "How's your food supply?"

"There's plenty of food out here. You just need to know where to look."

Donovan unzipped his pack, and drew out a baguette, a round of cheese, and a bottle of wine, setting each on the rock. "We won't be needing these. They're yours if you want them."

Trader licked his lips, his eyes fixed on the cheese. "Oh, hey man, I couldn't take your food."

"Consider it karma." Donovan shrugged and tossed him the backpack. "May as well take this too."

"Thanks, Karma." Trader jammed the food into the pack and vanished into the brush.

"I hope you don't mind giving away our picnic," he said in a low voice. "It seemed the least I could do after..." He rubbed his ear. "He got to you before I did."

"You sound jealous," she joked.

"I am. It's my job to rescue you."

"I can't wait to see how you'll make up for this lapse."

Donovan examined her hands and swabbed them with more antiseptic. "Do you think you can stand?"

She reached for him, and he helped her up. Gingerly, she put weight on her damaged leg. It throbbed dully. "I can walk out of here."

"Maybe. But it's a steep trail, and you might make the injury worse. I'll carry you."

"How? I am not letting you use a fireman-carry to get me out of here. That's just uncomfortable. For me." Donovan had been spry as a goat on the trail, but it was slick and messy. He was strong, but she couldn't see how he'd manage carrying her all that way.

"Piggyback. I've had lots of practice with my nieces and nephews."

"I outweigh your nieces and nephews by... never mind by how much."

"I enjoy a challenge." He turned around and bent at the knees. "Hop up."

She hesitated.

"You're not going to make me look silly squatting here, are you?" he asked.

She slung her bag over her back and pressed against him, her arms loose around his neck and chest. He grabbed her around the thighs and hefted her up. Donovan strode easily up the muddy hill, Riga's legs clamped around his waist.

She held her breath, waiting for a stumble, a slip. But his movements were smooth and sure. At the top of the hill, he wasn't even breathing hard.

He was quiet for a time, then, "We got lucky. If Trader hadn't grabbed you..." His muscles tensed beneath his shirt. "You have the oddest guardian angels."

"I count you as one," she said in his ear.

He chuckled. "How are you doing back there?"

"I've got the easy job. You?"

"I'm great."

A hiker passed them. He slipped and cursed beneath his oversized backpack.

Donovan's chest rose and fell easily beneath her locked wrists, his breath unhurried. He was in good shape, but this was a rough trail even under dry conditions. Wet, it was a nightmare. Her eyes narrowed. "Donovan, how are you doing this?"

"Doing what?"

"Walking the trail."

"I'm just walking."

"Hm." She relaxed her gaze, extended her senses.

The jungle breathed around them. Multi-colored auras shimmered off the trees and rocks and earth, bending toward them as they passed.

Donovan's aura glowed bright gold, shot with green and pale purple. The aura of a kukui tree, green tinted with gold, reached for him, mingled with Donovan's energy body. Where they touched, both flared brightly.

"Wow." Her eyes widened.

"What?"

She squeezed him more tightly. "Your aura is... interacting with the auras of the trees, and even with the mud path. It's like an aurora borealis of energy fields."

"And that's not normal?"

She thought about it. "I've never been that good at aura reading," she said slowly. "And I haven't seen auras surrounding plants and stones before. It makes sense that the spirit of a place would affect a person's aura, just like it would affect their mood. But this is amazing." She laughed, giddy.

"What does my aura look like?"

"Mardi Gras," she said promptly.

"Mm. The Big Easy. We should go to New Orleans. I know a bar in the French Quarter that makes the best hurricane."

She kissed him beneath his ear. "Promise me beignets, and I'll follow you anywhere."

Without Riga slowing them down, the return trip took half the time. Soon they were passing the trailhead, tramping down the road lined with cars. Donovan deposited her at the Ferrari.

He examined his shoes critically. A thin layer of mud crusted the soles. "I'm going to wash these off before getting in the car. Wait here. I'll get some water, so we can both clean up." He grabbed the empty water bottles and headed for the picnic area near the beach.

Riga looked at her shoes. Since she'd been Donovan's passenger, they looked fairly clean after their soaking in the river.

On the opposite side of the street, the cave waited, empty. Straightening off the car, she hobbled across the road.

Riga hesitated in the cave's mouth. It was wide enough that the afternoon sun easily lit the expanse. It was empty, safe.

Still, Riga made no move to go inside. She had no idea why the shaman had wanted her on the trail. To see the auras? The ghosts? Or was it the cave that held the secret?

Menehunes – the Hawaiian fae. She shuddered. More faeries. Did she *really* want to know why they'd been invading their bungalow? But it was magic, and despite her misgivings, she couldn't resist.

Riga forced herself to relax and focused on her breathing, extending her senses into the cave. Her skin tingled, as if brushed by soft fur. Something was inside. A friendly.

The cave had a soft, sandy floor dotted by occasional smooth rocks. Its high ceiling of dark, uneven stone glistened with damp. Wary of another twist that would send her knee past the point of no return, she bowed her head, watching every step.

Rocks grated against each other, and she looked up. The rock breathed, swelling. Riga froze.

Stone shifted, a piece separating from the main. Brigitte's head twisted toward her, owl-like.

"I knew you would find me," the gargoyle said.

Riga exhaled, embarrassed to have thought the cave wall had been... "I wasn't looking. What are you doing here?"

"Camouflage. This lovely stone perfectly matches ze color of my wings. And ze magic of the place..." Brigitte's feathers rippled. "It is delightful. But what are you doing here, if not seeking me out?"

Riga jerked her thumb toward the cave entrance. "Donovan and I were hiking the trail."

"Hiking? Hiking! You are supposed to be investigating. You have a duty to ze dead."

"I have a duty to my husband too. We *are* on our honeymoon. And—"

"And he knows ze consequences if you reject your calling."

"My calling is death, Brigitte. And it goes on whether I'm there or not."

"Faugh! You can be such a teenage girl. Not even your niece, ze brave Pen, wallows in drama as much as you do. In ze first place, any fool can see your husband craves excitement. Nothing would make him happier than to assist me on a case."

"Assist *you*?"

"And," the gargoyle continued loudly, "your calling is not death. It is to avenge wrongful death. Ze dead are here, and they deserve peace."

"Magic is here, too, a magic that's very different from my own. I felt something call me to the trail. That's why we were exploring."

"And did you find anything?"

"No," Riga admitted. "Though someone did nearly kill me."

"Well, that at least is promising."

"Besides, subtract the tourists, and this is a small community. Every local I talk to is a potential information source."

Brigitte sniffed. "There are not many locals on this trail."

"Not live ones," Riga muttered.

"What?"

"So this is the menehune cave," Riga said. Voices drifted to her, and she turned quickly. Three silhouettes of hikers jogged past the mouth of the cave.

"Ah, ze Hawaiian little people?" Brigitte shrugged. "Perhaps. I heard that it is the cave of an evil mermaid who lures handsome men to their deaths."

"Where did you hear that?"

"Ze tourists. They have been coming and going all day. One even took a photo of me. She thought I was an intriguing rock formation. Which is, of course, true."

"Seen any mermaids?"

"No." Brigitte sighed. "I would like to see a mermaid. There is something about the magic of these islands. Ze elements, they are closer, do you not feel it?"

Brigitte was right. The water, the trade winds, the volcanoes spewing fire and earth, here they all seemed more raw, more powerful.

"When Donovan was attacked yesterday, when we were swimming," Riga said, "he was pulled under. And then he felt magic and was released. But none of it seemed dark. Just wild, like the elements. But the bodies we found on the beach... The magic I sensed there was clearly black necromancy."

"Mermaids? Menehunes? Hawaiian magic? I cannot help you with these things. But we know how to deal with ze black necromancy. My advice is to play to your strengths."

Riga gnawed her lower lip. "There's a flaw in that plan."

"Oh?"

"The local magic. It's somehow involved too. I can't ignore it. And Donovan..."

"What about Monsieur Mosse?"

"Nothing," she said quickly. She didn't want to tell Brigitte about his experience on the trail, how he'd thrived on that magic. That was Donovan's secret to tell. But he'd always had a special connection to nature. It was a part of him, and perhaps she was worrying for nothing.

A breeze scented with malice lifted Riga's hair. She turned sharply, senses straining. Magic buzzed through her, unpleasant, cloying.

Then it was gone. She rubbed the back of her neck. "Brigitte, did you sense magic just now?"

"I always sense magic. It is everywhere, especially here." Brigitte shifted on the rock face. "And that is what you must remember. Magic is magic. Ze principles are always ze same. It is like that alchemist, Newton's, laws – you cannot escape gravity."

"But that's not true. Newtonian physics – his laws of gravity – don't work on Mercury. That's why quantum physics was developed." A smile played at the corners of her mouth. Of course things had gone haywire on Mercury. He was the trickster god.

Brigitte sniffed. "We stand on ze planet Earth, not Mercury. Do not talk nonsense. You know how to protect yourself."

Riga twisted the rings on her finger. But could she protect the one she loved?

CHAPTER 7

"Riga?" Donovan's figure was a broad-shouldered silhouette at the cave mouth.

The gargoyle ducked her head and vanished into the rock ceiling. Limping, Riga hurried to him.

"We have to go," he said. "Now."

"What's wrong?"

He placed a hand beneath her elbow and steered her across the street. "Melee on the beach. And it's growing."

She stopped beside the Ferrari, astonished. "A melee? An actual brawl?"

He opened the car door for her. "And if we get involved, it'll just get worse. I've called the police. They're on their way. We need to go."

She nodded and slid into the car, her leg twisting. Pain sparked in her knee, and she winced.

Donovan closed the door and leaned in, his eyes darkening with concern. He handed her a water bottle. "It's cold. If you hold it against your knee, it might help with the swelling until we can get you to an icepack."

"Thank you." She pressed the bottle to her knee. It rolled awkwardly over her leg, but the cool was a blessed relief, and muscles she didn't realize were clenched, relaxed.

The wind carried sounds of the fight from the beach. Shouts. A woman's angry scream.

Striding to the driver's side of the convertible, Donovan vaulted the door and maneuvered them out of the tight parking spot. They flashed past ramshackle homes and taro fields and stopped beneath a tunnel of trees at a one-lane bridge, waiting for the cars coming in the opposite direction to pass.

"What's going on?" she said. "First some jerk knocks me into a river and now a brawl on the beach? This is Kauai. How can you be angry in paradise?" Riga thought of what she'd wanted to do to that man on the trail and flushed.

Dumb question. She knew how to be angry anywhere. Oh, how she knew. Propping her elbow on the car door, she blew out her breath.

"I didn't see the fight start," he said, "but it built quickly. That sort of thing always does. You should see the security footage of the knockdown, drag-outs at the casinos."

"Yeah, people can be jerks. But this..." She pressed the bottle to her forehead. A dull ache had sprouted behind her eyes. "A necromancer killed Dennis. The magic I sensed, the sigils drawn around his body all point to it. But there's something else going on. It pulled you underwater and sent me a vision. I'd like to talk to a local shaman or magician. I just don't know where to look for one."

"I might be able to get you a lead. I wanted it to be a surprise, but I've arranged for a lomi lomi massage. We're headed there now. I thought it would be a treat after our hike."

She put the bottle down and gazed at him in admiration. "You're a sexy genius."

"Agreed. But maybe we should find you a doctor first. I don't like the look of that knee."

"No, no, no. Don't dangle magic Hawaiian massages in front of me and then yank them away. That's just cruel. My knee will be fine. And a lomi lomi masseuse might know some local magical practitioners."

He grinned. "Good, because we're almost there." His cell phone rang. He touched a button on the steering wheel. "Mosse here."

"Mr. Mosse." A woman's voice emerged from the speakers near their heads. "I've arranged for cocktails on the beach at seven o'clock tonight with Mr. and Mrs. Rogin, the owners of the home on the beach where Mr. Glasgow was found."

"Excellent. Thank you." He hung up.

The voice had sounded vaguely familiar to Riga. Someone from the hotel? "It must be nice to have minions."

"It is."

He slowed, consulted a map folded on the seat between them, and turned down a narrow red-dirt road lined with palms and blossoming red and yellow hibiscus. They bumped to a stop at the end of a drive, before a complex of small tin-roofed homes with wide verandas.

Donovan jumped from the car. He opened Riga's door, helping her out.

"Seriously, my knee's not that bad," she said, laughing.

"Any excuse," he rumbled, putting his arms around her.

"Oi!" A large Hawaiian woman emerged onto one of the verandas. Her mumu swayed in the breeze of an overhead fan. "None of 'dat here." But she was grinning.

They broke apart, sheepish, and Donovan walked to stand at the base of the wooden steps. "Hello. I'm Donovan Mosse, and this is Riga. We have an appointment with Aunty 'Akamu."

Her black hair, streaked with gray, was knotted in a bun. She smoothed it, tucking the plumeria blossom over her ear in more firmly. "Aloha. I'm Aunty. And I know who you are. Come in, come in." She stood aside from the front door, and her wide brow creased when she saw Riga's knee. "You've been on da Kalalau trail, haven't you?"

Riga grimaced. "Is it that obvious?"

"You're not da first tourist who thought it would be a good idea to hike that trail and then get a massage. You won't be the last." She ushered them into a simple room with a rag rug and cushioned, bamboo-frame chairs and couches.

Riga and Donovan sat beside each other on a couch.

Using a table for leverage, Aunty got on one knee and examined Riga's leg, tsking. She grunted, hauling herself to her feet. "Manuku!"

A young man with a thick shock of dark hair entered the room from a side door, wiping his hands on a rough towel. "Yes, Aunty?"

"You take Mr. Mosse to da pavilion. I will work with Mrs. Mosse."

He nodded to Donovan. "Aloha. This way, sir."

Aunty 'Akamu watched them leave and sighed. "If I was thirty years younger... You have a handsome husband, Mrs. Mosse."

"I agree. And please call me Riga."

She laughed. "Like da city in Latvia? I thought you were going to tell me your name was Rita, like that actress. You look just like her you know, Rita Hayworth. Though maybe you don't know. She was a pin-up girl a long time ago."

Riga's smile was brief. "She was more than a pin-up."

"Yes. She led an eventful and sad life, like so many beauties of her day and ours. Come with me." Aunty 'Akamu turned and lumbered into a narrow hallway and then out a rear door into a grassy yard.

The afternoon sun made long shadows on the lawn. Riga walked behind the woman to a corner sectioned off by tall white screens. Water trickled somewhere – low, steady, soothing.

"This way." The older woman vanished behind one of the screens.

Riga followed. The screens had been arranged to form a square out-door room, with a massage table covered by a white sheet in the center. In one corner, a bamboo fountain trickled water into a stone bowl. In another, stood two Adirondack chairs.

Aunty 'Akamu lowered herself into one. "Sit."

Riga sat.

The Hawaiian woman leaned forward, hands on her knees. "So, before we get started, let's talk about lomi lomi. Lomi lomi is a massage based on huna. Huna means secret. And da secret is that everything and everyone wants harmony and love, and that harmony and love is all energy. Lomi lomi will help your body unblock the energies so you can relax, feel better in body, feel better in your mind. And it helps if you set an intention for this healing. What would you like?"

To find a killer and get on with my honeymoon. "Unblocking energies would be great."

"Okey dokey." She rose. "Plenty of privacy here. Take off your clothing and hang it there." She pointed to a metal hanger hooked over the edge of one of the screens. "Wash up there." She pointed to a metal bucket filled with water and a towel folded neatly on a small table in a corner. "Then dry off and get under da sheet. I'll be back in a few minutes."

Riga undressed, grateful to be free of her sweat-soaked clothing, then sponged herself off with the cool water from the bucket. On the table, the light sheet skimmed across her skin, and she tried to relax.

The running water, the warm breeze scented with salt and steaming vegetation, were all ingredients for Nirvana. But her rage at the hiker, the horror of Dennis's death, nagged. She needed to let it go.

Aunty 'Akamu coughed. "Are you ready?"

"Mm hm..."

There was a shuffling sound, and Riga looked up. The woman folded one of the screens inward, revealing the conical mountains carpeted in emerald. "Plenty of privacy," she repeated. "But we want to enjoy the view, too, eh?"

"It's lovely," Riga said. "What an amazing place to live."

"Yes," she said, non-committal, "but even paradise had a serpent."

Aunty 'Akamu stood beside Riga and closed her eyes, resting her hand lightly on Riga's back. She stood this way for several minutes, and warmth spread through Riga.

The massage began. With fluid, wavelike motions, Aunty 'Akamu used her forearms and hands.

Riga's muscles dissolved. She didn't want to fall asleep and tried to focus on what the woman was doing. Beneath the hole in the table for her head, Aunty had placed a bowl of water where a hibiscus blossom floated. Riga watched it drift, gently scraping the bowl's sides.

The woman shuffled around the table, her hips swaying. Was this hula or huna or something else? And then Riga was drifting, rocking as if on a surfboard rolling gently up and down.

Riga lurched hard to the side, and her eyes flew open. The ground trembled. She clutched the table bucking beneath her, the earthquake growing in strength. A red gash opened on a mountain, widened. With horror, she realized she was watching a mudslide.

"Be aware now. It's over." Aunty 'Akamu's voice broke the spell, and Riga jerked, gasped, her heart pounding.

She wrapped the sheet around her and sat up. "Sorry. I must have fallen asleep."

"Don't lie to Aunty. I felt your energy. That was no dream. You had a vision."

The woman lowered herself into the Adirondack chair. It squeaked beneath her bulk. "You have magic. Big magic. But your energies are chaotic. You've been repressing them, until recently. Now they're all over da place. Some have turned dark. So I worked on smoothing them out. Things should be better for you now. But you must be careful."

"Thanks," she said, unsure if her gratitude stemmed from the massage or just from having someone else to talk to openly about the supernatural. "I've been feeling magic everywhere. Some I recognize, some I don't, and some scares the hell out of me."

The woman shook her head. "Lots of negativity around. I can't figure out why. A man even got murdered on da beach yesterday. Darkness infected da killer. Holding hate and grudges makes him sick. It will make you sick too."

"Him?" Riga asked sharply.

She shrugged, her flesh rippling. "Him? Maybe her? I don't know. All I know is there is much hihia and hukihuki about."

"What can you tell me about Hawaiian magic?"

"Nothing. I'm no kupua. But if you like, I can introduce you to a friend of mine. He's da local kupua."

"*The* kupua? Is he the only one?" Riga asked, thinking of the little man she'd met on the beach.

"Only one I know. And I know everyone. So what's your story?"

"I'm a metaphysical detective. Donovan and I found the murder victim on the beach, alongside the dead seal. There was magic there."

"You don't think da kupua did this?" Aunty 'Akamu asked sharply.

"No," Riga said. "The sense I got was that the magic was... from the mainland." *Necromancy.* Riga's kind of magic.

The masseuse made a wry face. "Not all our visitors are welcome. But they come anyway." She heaved herself up. "I'll call my friend. You take your time, get dressed. Then come back to da house."

Charcoal-colored clouds massed behind the steep mountains and threatened rain. Riga dressed slowly, hating to put on her muddy clothing. Eyeing the darkening sky, she hoped the masseuse was right about the privacy. She was in no mood to give any random hikers a show.

Once dressed, she returned to the house and found Donovan stretched out on one of the couches. "Nice massage?" she asked.

He didn't open his eyes. "Let's just say it was enlightening. You?"

"Apparently, my energy is blocked."

He opened one startling green eye. "I may be able to help you with that."

Aunty 'Akamu swept into the room and handed Riga a slip of paper. "He says he would be happy to meet with you. Just call this number."

Donovan swung his feet off the couch and stood, stretched.

"Thank you," Riga said. "And thank you for the massage."

Donovan handed the woman an envelope. "It was everything promised. Enjoy your evening."

He walked Riga to the car. "You're not limping."

Surprised, she looked down. The swelling was gone. All that remained was a faint pink mark on her knee.

"Well, so much for milking that injury," she said. "And I had such plans for taking advantage of you."

He helped her into the Ferrari, and they drove slowly down the bumpy road. "I take it you found your kupua," he said.

She folded the paper into her wallet. "According to Aunty 'Akamu, there's only one in this area. Now, explain what was so enlightening about your massage."

"I got the lomi lomi lecture. Though in fairness, I asked for it."

"Anything useful? Useful to our little problem, I mean."

"Nothing I didn't already know. Love is happiness, that sort of thing. But according to my masseur, the locals had something of a love-hate relationship with Dennis."

"Wasn't Dennis a local?"

"Yes, he was. Dennis employed a lot of people in his hotel. But they resented an outsider dictating how they should protect their island."

The car glided to a stop at a one-way bridge, and a pickup truck rumbled past. Donovan shifted the Ferrari into gear, and they purred forward.

"And apparently there's been some sabotage at the hotel," he continued.

"What kind of sabotage?"

"Stopping up the plumbing, a fire in one of the kitchens, bogus online reviews. Petty stuff, but it adds up. What did you learn?"

"Aside from the kupua's phone number? I fell asleep and had a vision."

"Bad?"

"An earthquake, a landslide. I honestly don't know what to make of it. I've had visions before. I've seen people who've given me messages, or astral traveled, but these seem... pushed. Like someone's forcing them on me." A layer of her newfound relaxation evaporated. She didn't like being toyed with.

He risked a glance at her. "Who?"

"That's the question. Maybe Mark will have an idea."

"Mark?"

She held up the strip of paper Aunty 'Akamu had given her. "The kupua."

Riga called him, and they arranged a meeting for early the next day. She hung up, frowning.

"What's wrong?" Donovan asked.

"He wasn't the kupua I met on the beach."

"Kauai must have more than one."

"Aunty 'Akamu said she knew all the locals, but I'll ask Mark when we meet him tomorrow." She checked her watch. It was well after lunch in San Francisco. Surely her niece would be awake. But when she rang Pen's cell phone, it went to voicemail. Riga left a message and dropped the phone into her bag.

"I'm sure Pen's fine," Donovan said. "If there was a problem, your sister would call you. And she's got Brigitte."

"Donovan, about Br—" A Volkswagen Bug barreled around a curve on their side of the road.

Donovan slammed on the brakes and pulled up tight against the mountainside. Riga's jaw clenched. She gripped the door handle, one foot stomping an invisible brake.

The woman in the VW brandished her fist at them. Shrieking, the woman leaned her head out the window.

"You okay?" Donovan asked.

Riga's heart banged against her chest. "Fine. But my post-massage Zen is officially gone." More honking sounded up the hillside.

He grinned at her and pulled back onto the road. "I think I know a way to get it back."

CHAPTER 8

NIGHT HAD FALLEN WHEN they returned to the hotel to shower, and the air outside had cooled. There was a gust of wind, and a sound like pebbles striking the walk.

Riga looked out the window, unsure if she was hearing rain or the rattling of palm fronds. But in the light of the tiki torch, she saw no tell-tale droplets on the patio outside.

She changed into her mainland uniform, wide-legged khakis and a crisp white cotton blouse. Riga fumbled with the clasp of a thick shell choker she'd bought from a street vendor on the island of Hawaii.

"Here." Donovan brushed her hair to the side and hooked the necklace.

His arms came around her waist, and she watched him in the mirror. He'd returned to his comfort clothing as well – a black shirt and jacket, black pants. Experimentally, she rubbed her bare foot against his and touched the smooth leather of cowboy boots.

"Are you flirting with me?" he asked.

"Yes."

He nuzzled her neck.

"What time did you say we were meeting the Rogins for cocktails?" she asked.

"Let's be fashionably late."

They pulled into the beach house driveway, the Ferrari's tires crunching across the gravel. Spotlights artistically lit the palm trees lining the drive, their fronds waving five-fingered shadows.

The house was an elegant sprawl, an updated mid-century modern that she wouldn't mind living in, and Riga had to remind herself that a death had occurred on its beach. That on the other side of that house, Dennis had died.

Donovan checked his watch. "Right on time."

"Mm." She leaned across the seat and kissed him. "Good thing you mixed up the schedule."

"Who said I mixed it up?"

"So how did you arrange this? What's our connection?"

He grinned. "Mr. Dirk Rogin loves Vegas."

"But how did you learn that?"

"Like you said. Minions." He hopped from the Ferrari.

"I really need to get some of those," Riga muttered. A gargoyle was great when it came to magic, but she wouldn't mind assistance with the everyday stuff.

They walked past birds of paradise and spiky purple and yellow pineapple bushes. A gong hung beside the wooden door.

Donovan quirked a brow. "Do you want to do the honors?"

"Absolutely." Riga took the padded hammer and struck the gong, which rang a high, golden note.

There was the sound of laughter, and the door was opened by a fit-looking sixty-something, her graying hair done up in a bun. She smoothed the front of her sarong-style dress with one hand. Smiling, she extended the other to Riga.

"You must be Riga and Donovan. I'm Dirk's wife, Jane." She kissed them on both cheeks. "It's lovely to meet you both. Come in, come in."

It was, as Donovan had observed, a very nice house, with high ceilings and burnished natural wood and cork floors.

"We send the staff home at night," Jane said. "So you're stuck with Dirk's bartending. Though I love having someone else doing the cleaning, I do like the privacy."

Riga smiled. "I've always found the concept of live-in staff awkward." And she suspected it was equally odd for the staff not to have a place fully their own to go home to.

"Exactly." Beaming, Jane led them to a semi-enclosed tile patio that ended in a swathe of green lawn. A firepit in the center of the tiles warmed the outdoor room. Donovan gravitated toward the bar and regarded the row of bottles on the wall behind it.

Riga eyed the surf boards hung on one wall. "Do you surf?"

Jane laughed. "Not anymore. Lately I've gotten into stand-up paddleboarding. It's a fantastic core workout."

A silver-haired man in shorts and a crisp, white shirt entered the patio. "Aloha! Looks like I'm just in time to mix you a drink. I'm Dirk." He laughed, and they shook hands. "Fun with Dirk and Jane, eh?" he said. "What are you drinking?"

"How are your skills in the way of tropical martinis?" Riga asked, grinning.

He winked. "I make a mean coconut martini, with real slices of fresh coconut. It will send you to Tahiti and back."

Dirk whipped up drinks. Soon they were settled in wooden chairs around the firepit, Riga with a coconut martini that lived up to his promise.

Dirk gripped his bare knee and leaned forward. His drink sloshed onto the tile patio. "Well, I have to say I was tickled when I heard you were here and wanted to meet up. Though with all the cash I've dropped in that casino of yours, you should be buying *me* drinks."

"Then next time you're in Vegas, stay at our casino as our guest," Donovan said. "I'll even comp the drinks."

"With pleasure." Dirk leaned back comfortably in his chair. "And for the record, I never believed that stuff they said about you in the papers."

Riga's smile turned brittle.

"But I've got to say," Dirk continued, "this is some customer outreach."

His wife gave a little shake of her head. "And on your honeymoon."

"Actually," Riga said, "what brought us here was my business. Donovan was kind enough to use the casino as an introduction."

"And what sort of business are you in?" Jane asked.

"I'm a metaphysical detective, a private detective."

"No kidding?" Dirk said. "What's a metaphysical detective?"

"The study of metaphysics is the study of first causes," she said. "So in a sense, most detectives are metaphysical. But on a day-to-day basis, I deal with a lot of haunted houses and things that have gone missing. My PI license is handy for the latter."

Jane laughed. "You mean the ooga-boogas aren't always responsible when Aunt Milly's pearl necklace disappears?"

"Usually the culprit is a very much alive cousin Jeff," Riga said wryly. "But I do occasionally get a murder case. We found Dennis Glasgow's body on the beach outside your home and were wondering if you'd noticed anything."

"The police asked us that, too," Dirk said. "But we didn't see or hear a thing."

"Well, that's not quite true," his wife said.

"I told you, honey, that was just lightning."

"And I told you it wasn't raining."

"It doesn't have to be raining here to see lightning out at sea."

Jane folded her arms over her chest. "Well, I've never seen green lightning before."

"When was this?" Riga stilled, her heart bumping against her ribs.

"Around three-thirty AM," Jane said.

"Late night?" Riga asked.

"Not at all," Jane said. "Something woke me up, and then I saw that strange flash out over the beach."

"You told me it was over the water," Dirk said.

"Well, they're both in the same direction," she said tartly.

Riga and Donovan glanced at each other. They needed to learn the time of death.

"But you didn't hear gunshots," Riga said.

They shook their heads.

"I'm thinking of buying Dennis's hotel," Donovan said. "We were in negotiations before he was killed."

"How wonderful if you did buy it," Jane said. "We'd be neighbors."

Riga sipped her drink and felt it go straight to her head. She should have eaten something before coming.

"It's a lovely hotel," Jane continued. "We go there quite often for brunch. Of course, it's horribly haunted."

Riga shifted forward in her chair. So stories of their ghost had gotten around. The ghost likely had nothing to do with Dennis's death, but her skin twitched with remembered unease. "Haunted?"

"Or cursed," Jane said.

"Honey," Dirk said warningly.

"I'm just repeating what others are saying. There was that fire, and all those other little accidents. And things going missing."

"What sorts of things?" Donovan asked.

"Guests' things. Things no one could have possibly taken because the guest was right there in the room when they went missing."

"If there's a ghost or a curse," Riga said, "there must be some sort of story behind it."

The Rogins looked at each other. Jane pressed her lips together.

Dirk laughed shortly. "Who knows how these things get started? I suspect old Dennis was just trying to stir up business – haunted Kauai, that sort of thing. Ghosts are hot now."

"If there are ill-feelings toward the hotel," Donovan said, "I'd like to know before I buy. One businessman to another."

Dirk scratched his cheek. "They renovated five years ago or so. There was some kerfluffle with the environmentalist group, but it seemed to blow over after Dennis joined it. Aside from that, I don't think anyone has a problem with the place. It's a nice hotel. Provides jobs."

"Did you know someone was on the beach that night, guarding the seal?" Riga asked.

Jane rolled her eyes. "Oh, yes. I was out walking that night and got too close to the precious darling. Dennis really let me have it."

"You didn't tell me that," her husband said. "He knew damn well you'd never harm a seal."

"It was nothing, and a moot point now that the poor man is dead." But there was something rehearsed about Jane's words, a carefully lanced truth.

"Do you remember what time you ran into him?" Riga asked.

"Oh, it was late. Past midnight, I think. I couldn't sleep, and there's something about the feel of the sand between my toes I can't resist."

"How well did you know Dennis?" Riga asked.

"He's what I'd call a casual acquaintance," Dirk said. "We saw him around, invited each other to parties. But I never really knew the man. He kept busy with his hotel and that Aquatic Protection Society."

"I believe what my wife is asking," Donovan said, "is do you know who might want to kill him?"

"I have no idea," Dirk said. "I'm afraid if you're hoping we'll expand your suspect list, you're barking up the wrong tree."

Riga smiled to hide her disappointment. That was exactly what she'd been hoping. "We had to try."

Donovan's lips bent in his lopsided smile, and he rose. "Thank you for your time and for your hospitality. I'm afraid my bride and I have dinner reservations and need to be going."

Jane exhaled, deliberately quiet.

Donovan pulled a silver case from his breast pocket and handed Dirk a card. "Call this number when you're planning your next trip to Vegas."

The women kissed each other's cheeks. Riga and Donovan departed.

Donovan revved the engine of the Ferrari and executed a quick turn in the driveway. "What did you think?"

"I think there's something they didn't want to tell us." Her stomach growled.

"I got that impression too. Interesting about the haunting. It sounded a lot like sabotage. We know the hotel has at least one ghost, but I'm not ready to blame her for the fire."

"Agreed," she said.

"And the green flash?"

"Could be magic, could be lightning. We'll have to check the weather reports for that night. And find someone who knows Dennis's time of death."

"If the police even have that information yet."

"You're right," she said. "It's unlikely the autopsy has even been finished."

She leaned her head back on the leather seat. The sky was an unremitting mass of darkness, the stars obscured by clouds. She'd never solved a murder in two days, and her impatience was unfair. But already she was beginning to feel trapped on the island by this case.

They pulled into the hotel driveway. Donovan tossed the keys to the valet.

"I thought we might have dinner at the hotel tonight," he said.

"Two birds with one stone? Interrogating the waitstaff over mahi-mahi?"

They strolled up the walk, through the open hotel doors. "We'll have to spend a lot more time at the hotel if we're going to sort this out," he said.

"Yes, and not in our bungalow." She gave him a mock severe look.

"We can interrogate the pool attendants. And this hotel has an excellent spa. The masseuses may have intel."

By unspoken agreement, they'd been edging around tackling the grieving wife and brother. But it had to be done, and soon.

"Think of the possibilities at the hotel bar," he continued. "I can see why you became a detective."

"Oh, yes. Ever since you've entered my life, detecting has been a never-ending whirl of champagne and resorts."

"Do I detect sarcasm?"

"No. You detect regret you didn't come along sooner."

CHAPTER 9

ARM IN ARM, THEY walked to the hotel's restaurant. Its exterior walls slid back on tracks, leaving it open to the cool breeze. They wound past gas-fueled heat lamps and crowded tables.

Heads turned, conversations died at their approach and rose in their wake. Riga stiffened, her cheeks warming. It wasn't the first time this had happened and wouldn't be the last. She had thick skin when it came to her own reputation, but not when it came to Donovan.

Last year he'd been accused of financing terrorism through his casinos. He'd been cleared, but the media which had so gleefully reported his downfall had been strangely silent after he'd been proven innocent. Anger at the unfairness smoldered in her chest.

He murmured something to the hostess. She hooked a quick left turn, depositing them in a booth.

"Someone will be right with you, sir," she chirped and hurried off.

Riga snapped her napkin open. "It's moments like these when it's a good thing my magic is on the fritz." She tried to keep her voice light, but even she heard the edge.

"Riga." Donovan laid his hand over hers. "Does the gossip really bother you? Being recognized?"

She gazed down at their hands, entwined on the table, and flushed with shame. *Selfish.* She was being selfish. Her snit might have blown off steam, but it couldn't have made Donovan feel any better. "I'm sorry. I don't know what's gotten into me."

"It's only talk. This business will blow over."

"I've never cared what people said about me. But I have an irresistible urge to punch people who say bad things about you." She looked up at him. "Bear with me?"

"That goes both ways. Though no one has been stupid enough to say anything but good of you in front of me."

A waitress in khaki shorts and a white blouse materialized before their table bearing thick paper menus and glasses of water tinkling with ice. "Can I get you something to drink to start with?"

"Can you do a mango martini?" Riga asked.

"Sure."

Donovan gave the waitress a smile that could melt a polar icecap. "Brandy, neat."

The young woman left, and Riga said, "You really are the perfect partner."

"In life?"

"That too, but I was thinking as a metaphysical detective. I'll bet you could charm a confession out of Lucrezia Borgia's ghost."

"Never met her."

"You wouldn't have liked her," Riga said. "Spoiled. Petulant. Rather childish."

"And where did you meet Lucrezia Borgia's ghost?"

"Rome. She swore she was no killer – just trapped in her father's schemes. I believed her. Still didn't like her."

"So why is she haunting Rome?"

"Wouldn't you if the Borgias were your relatives? Imagine the family dinners."

The waitress returned to take their orders, and Riga sat back while Donovan joked with her, making small talk. By dessert – a Hawaiian bread pudding – the smiling waitress had relaxed enough to lean one hip against Donovan's side of the booth.

"I've heard your hotel has some ghosts," Donovan said.

The waitress laughed. "There are tons of ghosts on these islands. Why would this hotel be any different?"

"But not all of them are malicious," Riga said. "We heard yours is a fire starter."

She shrugged. "It's easy to blame ghosts when things go wrong. But sometimes, you just get a string of bad luck."

"Too bad," Riga said. "We love a good ghost story."

"People have reported hearing a woman crying on the rocks out by the beach," the waitress said. "We think she's the ghost of a woman who drowned here."

"Oh?" Riga asked. "Who?"

She snatched the empty glasses from the table. "Before my time. Would you like another?"

"I would," Donovan said. "Riga?"

"Please." Riga had had enough but hadn't missed the waitress's reaction. Was she afraid of the ghost? Or was there something else to the tale she didn't want to reveal?

The waitress hurried away.

"Next time we're interviewing a pretty girl," Riga said, "I'll keep my mouth shut and let you do the talking."

"We're not finished yet," Donovan said.

When the waitress returned to their table, Riga said, "I'm sorry. Talking about ghosts must have seemed ghoulish so soon after the murder of the hotel's owner."

"No." The girl's smile stiffened. "I mean, yes, it was terrible. But one thing doesn't have to do with the other."

"Oh?" Riga asked. "What have you heard about Dennis's murder?"

Donovan's gaze shifted to the restaurant entrance. "Riga, we have company."

Paul Glasgow, his red-splotched face wreathed in misery, approached, his hand on the lower back of a tall, model-thin blond. The two stopped beside their table, and the hotel owner nodded. The waitress stepped back, the tray clutched to her chest.

"Donovan, Riga. I hope you're enjoying your stay. This is my sister-in-law, Deidre."

A chord of grief thrummed in Riga's heart for the new widow, and she resisted the urge to reach across the table, take her husband's hand. But she couldn't think of Deidre as Dennis's widow, as someone to sympathize with. She was a suspect.

"Please, join us," Donovan said. "We were just having drinks."

"I could use one," Deidre said. To the waitress: "A vodka martini. The bartender knows how I like it." She slid into the booth beside Riga, her blue sarong skirt twisting around her legs, and she lifted herself up, adjusted her skirt.

Her hair was pulled into a bun, and her eyes were the color of green sea glass. She smelled of key lime and coconut and sea salt, making Riga think of margaritas.

"Beer for me," Paul said. He sat beside Donovan. The waitress hurried away.

"I'm very sorry about your husband," Riga said.

Deidre twisted her hands, her long fingers heavy with gold rings. "The police told me you found him." She swallowed. "It was a terrible shock."

Riga felt a twinge of sympathy. *Suspect. She's a suspect.* "How are you doing?"

"I'm still in a daze," she said. "One moment I was married, now I'm a widow."

"Deidre." Paul reached across the table and grasped her hand.

Her eyes softened, lit with an inner glow. And then she bit her lip and turned to Riga. "I never thought, never, that his work with the seals was dangerous. He was so passionate about them."

"And you?" Riga asked.

"Me? I didn't grow up here. When I first arrived and married Dennis, it seemed like paradise. Now... I'm ready to leave."

"Leave?" Paul said. "Why would you leave? You're being ridiculous."

"No, I'm not," she flared.

Paul adjusted the gold wristband of his watch. "I just don't think you should make any decisions now. You're not thinking clearly."

"I hope you're not feeling pressured about the hotel sale," Donovan said. "Of course, you can take all the time you need."

Deidre touched her throat, her mouth making an O of surprise. "But it's not mine to sell. The hotel is all Paul's now."

Riga processed that, impassive. She understood why Paul wouldn't want a new partner, but surely Dennis's wife would have inherited his share. "Did you two have buy-sell insurance on each other?" she asked Paul. The insurance would ensure that Paul could quickly buy out the widow's share.

A muscle throbbed in his jaw. He nodded tightly.

"My brother-in-law is a CPA," Riga explained. "His hobby at family dinners is regaling us with horror stories of estate planning gone wrong."

Donovan smiled. "He says not having a will is a form of spousal abuse."

"Dennis was very well-organized." Deidre blinked rapidly. "He was thoughtful and didn't want to put anyone out. He would have been horrified that..." She cleared her throat.

"That his body littered the beach," Paul finished for her. He smiled apologetically at Riga. "I know how it sounds, but it's true."

The waitress dropped off their drinks and scooted away.

"It was hardly his fault," Donovan said. "Who could have done this?"

"One of the seal-haters," Paul said. "That's what the police think."

"But what do you think?" Riga asked.

Paul took a swig of his beer. "It's obvious, isn't it?"

"Well, no," Riga said. "The two bodies were found lying close to each other. So the question is, who was killed first – the seal or Dennis? I can't imagine a random person accidentally or in a fit of anger killing Dennis and then coolly sticking around to kill the seal. And why would they kill the seal if Dennis was nearby? Or if he wasn't nearby, if he came running from a distance to confront the killer, why would they hang around to shoot him instead of running away?"

"They probably didn't see him in the darkness," Paul said.

"Maybe," Riga said. "But both you and your brother are wealthy and carry some weight on this island. If I were the police, I wouldn't limit my investigation to seal-haters."

"But you're not the police." Paul's face darkened.

"Riga is one better," Donovan said. "She's a private investigator."

Deidre glanced up at her brother-in-law then down at her drink. She rotated the glass in her hand.

"I've heard you've been asking questions," Paul said. "Are you investigating my brother's murder?"

"Would you like me to?" Riga asked.

A young woman in a hotel uniform, with dark skin and black hair cascading down her back approached the table. She blinked at them through eyes glazed red. "Mr. Glasgow, there's an urgent phone call for you in the office."

"At this hour?" Scowling, he checked his watch.

"Yes, sir." She fiddled with her kukui nut necklace. "It's Mr. Hampstead."

Paul hesitated, watching Deidre. She gave a quick nod.

"I'd better take this." He edged out of the booth and stalked from the restaurant, the woman following on his heels.

Deidre watched them go. Her lips pressed into a flat line.

"Who was that?" Riga asked her.

"Sarah, my husband's... Paul's assistant now."

"She seemed upset," Donovan said.

"Did she?" Deidre took a sip of her martini. "So you're a private eye. I thought I'd read somewhere that you were a psychic."

"It would certainly make my job easier," Riga said, "but no, not a psychic. A metaphysical detective, and a licensed PI."

"And you really think there could be more to Dennis's murder?" she asked.

"It's too early to think anything," Riga said. "But there are a lot of questions outstanding."

"Such as?"

Riga leaned against the back of the booth. "When did Dennis get to the beach? What was he doing before that time? Who might have a grudge against him?"

"Midnight. He left our rooms at midnight, to take over for another one of the seal responders."

"Do you know who?" Riga asked.

Deidre closed her eyes. "A woman. Her name is Petra, I think. Petra... Singleton. I was annoyed with him. He woke me up, and I'd just fallen asleep. It had been a long day. My last words to him were... unpleasant." She put her head in her hands. "There were so many things I should have done differently."

"I'm sure he understood," Donovan said. "None of us are at our best when we're sleep deprived."

She raised her head. "*Did* he understand? I'm not so sure. And it wasn't just..." She gnawed on her lip. "I should go. I'm not fit to be out. Thanks for the drink and for the company."

Deidre walked a few steps away, then turned back to them, her face expressionless. "You're wrong though. My husband didn't have any enemies. So I'm quite certain he was killed because he was protecting the seal."

They watched her cross the restaurant.

"She's lying, though mostly to herself," Riga said. The thought was depressing. What was Riga lying to herself about?

"About which part?"

"I don't think she's at all sure that her husband was killed over a seal. And I don't believe her husband didn't have any enemies. Everybody has enemies."

"Who's she trying to deflect us from?"

"Did Deidre and Dennis have any children?" Riga asked.

"No."

"I'd like to talk to Dennis's wife and brother again."

"Then I'll make sure we do."

Riga laid her hand on his. "You're spoiling me. How will I go back to my practice as a lone metaphysical detective?"

"I thought you wanted to take your niece on?"

"Good God, no. I want to keep an eye on her, but Pen needs to walk her own path. Besides, she wants to be a film director."

There was a crash from the kitchen, raised voices. Tension rippled through the restaurant, and Riga's shoulders drew together defensively.

Donovan pointed to the kitchen, his mouth twisting with disgust. "If I do take this place over, that sort of thing will not happen."

He signaled for the check and signed for the bill. "Let's get out of here," he said.

Hand in hand, they strolled onto the deck, leaving the shouts behind, and walked onto the beach. Riga kicked off her sandals. The sand was damp, the air cool and oppressive with humidity in spite of the breeze flowing from the north. It teased at Riga's blouse, and she hugged her arms, cold.

Wordlessly, Donovan draped his blazer over her shoulders.

A crack in the clouds appeared, a growing crevasse. Moonlight slivered across the water, illuminating a slim female figure on the beach. Her skin shimmered with pale light, and for a moment, Riga saw the weeping ghost. And then the image resolved to a live human, staring at the endless rhythm of waves, her long dark hair tossing in the wind.

"Isn't that the young woman we met in the restaurant?" Riga asked.

"Dennis's personal assistant, Sarah," he said in a low voice. "Yes, I met her briefly earlier. She had a nice, quiet efficiency."

"She's crying." Riga stamped out her empathy. "We should talk to her."

Donovan frowned. "Now?"

"As the murdered man's personal assistant, she'll know things. And when people are upset, truths slip out." She tugged Donovan toward the woman.

"You're sexy when you're ruthless."

"I know. I'm a terrible person, and you have a soft spot for damsels in distress."

"You say that like it's a bad thing."

"Just imagine she's a man. And a rival."

He screwed up his face. "Not seeing it."

Sarah turned at the sound of their footsteps. Tears streaked her face.

"It's Sarah, isn't it?" Riga asked. "Are you all right?"

The woman blinked and didn't respond.

"Riga Hayworth." She extended her hand. "We met in the restaurant earlier. And you've already met my husband, Donovan."

Sarah didn't wipe away her tears. One dripped off the end of her chin. "Oh, yes. What can I do for you?"

"We thought we might be able to do something for you," Riga said. "You're upset."

"I'd prefer to be alone," she said.

"Of course." Donovan lowered his head and took Sarah's hand. "We've all been shocked by Dennis's death. He built something remarkable here, and I admired that. Our condolences on your loss."

Sarah bit back a sob. "Then you're one of the few. No one really appreciated him. Not his brother, not his wife. It hurt him badly. And now he's gone. Why would someone kill such a good person?" She burst into tears and buried her head on Donovan's chest.

Donovan rubbed her back and looked over her head at Riga, a panicked look on his face. "I don't know who killed Dennis," he said. "But I'd like to find out."

Sarah took a step back and shot an embarrassed glance at Riga.

"Donovan, do you mind if I leave you for a moment?" Riga asked. "I'd like to get my jacket from the room." Without waiting for a response, she headed down the beach. Sarah was responding to him, and Donovan would get more out of her alone.

She clenched her jaw and stamped her feet harder into the sand. Donovan was turning out to be a damned effective detective. The rhyme made her smile, then laugh out loud. What kind of bride was completely unconcerned with her husband's effect on the ladies, but jealous of his professional skills? The former was pathetic, the latter ridiculous.

The hotel rooms on the bank above dimly lit the beach. She skirted a piece of driftwood, a twisted lump in the half-dark. Stones rose before her, the final obstacle to the little beach and the path to their bungalow.

The noise of the waves grew, as if agitated by a passing boat. Then silence fell. The moonlight brightened, limning the clouds with mercury. Hair lifted on the nape of her neck. The skin on her arms tingled.

One of the rocks shifted, stood. "Aloha, my young friend." The tiny kupua removed his fisherman's hat and ruffled his thick white hair. "Peppermint?"

"Sure." Slowly, she came closer. "Thanks."

He pulled a blue, foil-wrapped candy from his hat and handed it to her with a flourish.

"Got any rabbits in there?" She unwrapped the candy and popped it in her mouth.

"No rabbits. But I hear they're good eating."

"I wouldn't know," Riga said.

"There's a lot you don't know. You're a beautiful woman, but willful ignorance is not attractive."

"That's the first time I've been accused of it. Of course, you could always enlighten me. I'm an excellent listener."

He laughed. "You're not listening to anything. The trees, the birds, the flowers, the water, they are all speaking to you, trying to tell you their story. You listen to nothing."

"Is that why you sent me to the Kalalau trail? I didn't see anything there."

"You saw what you needed to see. Why are you so scared of admitting it?"

"I've got xenomagicusphobia."

His brow wrinkled. "What's that?"

"Fear of strange magic. Though technically, a phobia is an irrational fear, and there is nothing irrational—"

"Pah!" He waved his hand dismissively. "And now you hide behind jokes. If you don't understand what's going on, it will swamp you."

"You said sacrifice had been on the island before, that kings used the deaths to increase their power. Is that what's happening now?"

"This was not the first place where rulers used murder to make themselves more powerful. And it won't be the last. The First World War fueled the rise of the Second. The Second World War fueled the great Russian bear—"

"Stalin? Do you mean Hitler used necromancy?" He'd been known for an interest in the occult. But Stalin, too? He'd been a genocidal maniac, but the occult angle was new to her.

"You sound surprised."

"Is that why this necromancer is killing? Just to develop personal power?"

"You haven't been listening."

"I'm listening now. Please tell me."

"Don't be so lazy. Listen. Watch the waves, read them. Your future is written there. Mine too. Read the stories they write on the sand. Look."

Riga looked. The waves left quicksilver trails. She studied the lines of foam, the ebb and surge.

"Now see," the kupua said.

She relaxed her gaze. The barrier of her skin seemed to fall away, and she saw. Each line of foam was a sentence, each droplet gleaming on the sand a universe of ideas.

And she was underwater, moving smoothly with the ocean current, hair streaming behind her. Dreamlike, she didn't question her ability to breathe, or her command of the element. One flick of her powerful tail thrust her along the reef, past schools of nighttime fish and jellies and octopi.

She was free, flying beneath the water, the tiny adjustments of her fins effortless. The sea caressed her skin, flowing across her scales. And her sisters waited, calling to her, voices low and musical. Their song thrummed in her blood.

She rounded a bend, and they were there. *Seals.* Coats lustrous, pale gray. Twisting effortlessly in the water. And then reality shifted again, and they were women with long, green tails, hair cascading behind them in the ocean current.

A thunderous rumble, and the reef broke apart, rocks tumbling toward them, coral splitting. Fish darted past, panicked.

Her sisters bolted in opposite directions, their songs turning to shrieks. Lava seeped from the newly formed cracks, fluorescent orange. The ocean boiled. Her skin peeled, blistered.

Abruptly, she was sitting on the beach, alive and human. Hands trembling from the vision, she pressed her palms against the cold rocks beneath her. Yes, this was real.

The little man looked up from his seat on the rocks. "You see now."

"The dead seals are mermaids?" Her voice cracked. She knew the answer, should have known it sooner.

The kupua was right. A part of her was still avoiding this case, letting Donovan take the lead. She'd told herself that sharing the load was a part of being married, when she'd really just been pushing the magic away. Why? No, the why didn't matter. What mattered was that she'd done it and had to stop.

"The wahine hiuia, what you call mermaids, are precious to water. And their murder is angering the water elementals. They are acting up. Now they're rubbing up against other elementals." He sighed. "Angry elementals are not good for people."

"I know," Riga said grimly, remembering another time, another place.

He chuckled. "Yes, I suppose you do know."

She looked out at the waves, their blackly glittering surge and swell. "The visions I've been having – the earthquakes, the tidal waves... Those aren't symbolic. They're prophecies, aren't they?"

"Those are just the beginning."

"What else...?" Reality shifted, panes of glass sliding past each other.

The sky darkened, and he was gone. Wind blew her hair into her face, and she clawed it back with her hands, shivering.

Riga stood, brushing the damp from the back of her slacks. She picked her way across the tumbled rocks.

The path beside the banyan tree was ghost and menehune-free, but she hurried by, the lights in the bungalow urging her forward to warmth and safety. She came to a sudden stop, rooted to the spot. The glass door on the deck was open.

But she'd left Donovan behind on the beach.

Someone was inside their bungalow.

Her muscles grew taut, her body ready to run. The smart move would be to watch and wait. Whoever was in there would come out eventually, and she'd identify the enemy.

But Riga wasn't feeling smart.

She was feeling angry.

CHAPTER 10

HEART THUNDERING, RIGA CREPT toward the patio. She kept to the shadows, brushing against birds of paradise. The leaves stabbed at her hands, and she jerked her fists away.

Donovan passed before the open window, cell phone pressed to his ear, and Riga's shoulders relaxed. She blew out her breath, willed her heart rate to slow.

He must have taken a different path to the bungalow. Riga shook off her irritation with her own stupidity. Putting on a smile, she ran lightly up the patio steps.

Donovan turned, his expression mingled surprise and relief. "Never mind. She's here now," he said into the phone and pocketed it. "I was starting to worry."

"Why? It's only been..." She looked at her watch. "Twenty minutes."

"Your watch must have stopped. It's been over an hour."

"What?" Riga checked her watch, its second hand ticking away. It read 10:17. She looked at the digital clock on the nightstand: 11:49.

Paling, she sat heavily on the bed. *Missing time. Freaking missing time.*

"What's wrong?" he asked.

"I was on the beach, on that pile of rocks, talking with the kupua. It seemed like just a few minutes. But it wasn't. My watch... I experienced missing time. Which means he's not a human kupua." She covered her mouth with her hand.

"Riga, what is it?"

"He's a fae. A Hawaiian faery. I've been taking advice from a menehune." And she hadn't even been able to tell the difference. She wanted to scream with frustration.

Donovan rubbed the back of his neck. "I can't believe I'm saying this. And if you tell anyone I'll deny it. But maybe it's time you got past your issues with faeries."

Her jaw slackened. "After everything... Are you kidding me? You know how horrible they are. They have no sense of right or wrong. It's all about what's in it for them at the moment, which is terrifying when you think about how much power they wield. And they're faeries."

"So what did this one do?"

"He taught me how to read the waves and warned me that we're in much bigger trouble than I thought."

"So he taught you something useful and gave you a warning we can use. Definitely the work of an arch nemesis."

"Do you know what's worse than a faery who's out to get you? A faery who's out to help you."

He grunted. "How much bigger trouble are we in?"

"I feel like such an idiot. The seals aren't seals. They're mermaids."

Donovan's eyebrows shot skyward. "Mermaids? They exist?"

"Think of them as a sort of water fae – in other words: dangerous. I should have guessed. Cultures around the world have myths about mermaids turning themselves into seals."

"But they're not myths?"

She got up and paced across the bamboo floor. "Apparently not. I glimpsed the truth when I saw the dead seal on the beach but didn't understand it. Once the mermaid was dead, her magic went with it. And then I saw it in my vision, and the kupua – or menehune, or whatever he is – confirmed it."

"At the risk of sounding callous, why are mermaids getting killed big trouble for us?"

"Mermaids are closely connected to water elementals," she said. "The dark magician must be killing the mermaids to set off water, which is in turn agitating the other elementals. And which is why I've been seeing earthquakes and tidal waves in my visions."

"But what's the necromancer's game? What does he gain from this?"

"I don't know. Is triggering the elementals part of a larger spell? Does he want to kill lots of people for one massive necromantic sacrifice?"

She twisted the wedding ring on her finger. Necromancers could control the dead, and necromancy used blood or death to fuel spells. If a necromancer was trying to kill people on a mass scale... She blanched.

Riga whirled to face Donovan. "No more playing tourist. We need to track down whoever's doing this fast. We've got two good leads – the woman, Petra, who handed off the seal watch to Dennis, and Kimo, the Hawaiian who's been agitating against the seals. We need to talk to them tomorrow."

"We've got an appointment with Petra in the morning," he said. "She lives in old Koloa, and Kimo's restaurant isn't far from there."

"How did you...?" When had he had the time to track them down, much less nail appointments? She shook her head. "Never mind."

He ran his hands up her arms. "I thought you'd be pleased."

"I am. Wait – we're meeting with the kupua tomorrow morning." *Ha.* Mr. Perfect Detective wasn't so perfect after all.

"And we're meeting with Petra after we meet the kupua."

"Oh."

"Riga..."

"It's just..." She began to laugh. "Half the time when I try to meet with a witness or suspect, they tell me to get lost. And you just snap your fingers, and voila. Date set. It's making me feel insecure."

"We have an appointment with Petra – not Kimo. He may still tell us to get lost."

She smiled. "Something to look forward to. So what did you learn from Sarah?"

"She's distressed by Dennis's murder. It seems they were quite close."

"How close?" Riga asked sharply.

"You're thinking an affair? It's possible."

"But if Dennis was cheating on his wife, why is his wife feeling guilty?"

"Sarah told me that Dennis and his wife were estranged."

"But still living together." This was sounding more and more like the my-wife-doesn't-understand-me bit. There was a good reason why it was a cliché, and Riga had heard it far too often. "Did she tell you what the problem was?"

"Only that his wife didn't understand him."

Riga rolled her eyes.

Donovan's smile broadened. "It does happen, you know."

"What about the brother? Paul?"

"According to Sarah, he's not as engaged with the hotel and left most of the work to Dennis. Now he's shifting it to Sarah, and she's struggling."

"This is all so vague. Does the hotel have a business center?"

"Of course. Why?"

"I'm going to do what I should have done yesterday – research. All we have now are vague hints. Was Dennis having an affair? What does his wife have to feel guilty about? I need to build a dossier on everyone involved."

"I might be able to save us some time." Donovan strode to the closet, pulled out his small leather case, and unlatched it. He rummaged through the compartment in the lid, and pulled out a thick file, handed it to her. "My background research on the hotel, as well as on Dennis and Paul."

Riga thumbed through it. "This is great. But we need more on the minor characters – Sarah and Deidre and the folks at the Aquatic Protection Society. What do you think? Split the work? You go through these files and see if there's anything relevant to the investigation, while I do online research?" It was nearly midnight, but she'd never get any sleep with these questions bumping through her brain.

"I already know the files, and there are two computers in the business center. Why don't I tell you about the files on the way, and we'll do the research together?"

"Is the business center even open at this hour?"

He nodded, rueful. "Twenty-four hours, just like the gym. It's a global economy, and business never sleeps."

She tucked her arm inside his. "Lead on, MacDuff." They locked the glass door to the deck behind them and strolled around the bungalow to the river-rock path.

"Profits at the hotel have been down for the last two years," Donovan said. "The mystery is why. When I talked to Dennis, he chalked it up to increased competition. And it's true, one of their competitors completed a major upgrade last year. But my analysts can't confirm that's the cause. Expenses have been bumping up as well, and unexplainedly. I'm starting to wonder if sabotage and work slowdowns are to blame."

Something rustled in the darkness of the banyan tree. Riga flinched, extended her senses, and felt... nothing. A mongoose darted from the tree and raced down the path.

She cleared her throat. "So the brothers might have good reason to want to unload the hotel."

"Mm. Combine that with Paul's gambling problem... He could use the cash."

"Gambling problem?" she asked. "Not in your casinos?" They passed a clump of ginger plants, lit from below.

"As far as I know, he's never set foot in Vegas. His debts are closer to home."

"To whom?"

"He's in to a loan shark in Lihue for over one hundred grand."

"Ouch. Lihue... That's where the airport is, right?" All the Hawaiian names were starting to sound alike.

He nodded.

"And what about our murder victim?" she asked.

"Dennis? Clean, as far as I could find. And no rumors of philandering." He stopped to open a heavy wooden door to the main section of the hotel.

They strolled to the business center and spent the next two hours researching their other suspects. Eyes burning, Riga arched her back, stretched her hands high in the air.

Donovan made a note on a piece of hotel stationary. "Had enough?"

"I had enough an hour ago."

"Why didn't you say something?" he asked.

"Why didn't *you* say anything?"

"Are we competitors now?"

"No." Yes. Riga's skull buzzed, and she rubbed her temple. She was being petty. What was wrong with her? "What did you find?"

"The Aquatic Protection Society was founded ten years ago but didn't accomplish much until its most recent executive director, Townsend, began running the place three years ago. I couldn't find anything on Jay, the kid we met there. Townsend grew up in Minnesota, moved to Kauai not long before he took over the society, and his mug is plastered all over the papers for charity events he's either attended or hosted."

"Big fish, small pond?"

"Something like that," he said. "One of the articles alludes to a tragedy in his past, but I'll be damned if I can find any mention of what it was, exactly. What did you find?"

"Not much," she admitted. "Dennis's widow, Deidre, used to be a model. The two met when she was on a shoot in the islands. Love at first sight. Some hints of drug use in her modeling days, but nothing concrete, and it's probably not relevant. I got nothing on his assistant, Sarah. A few pictures of her at hotel events, but that's all."

He stood and extended a hand to her. "We're not much further ahead, are we?"

She took his hand and rose. "Of course we are. There was one thing – I checked the weather for the night Dennis died. Whatever Jane saw on the beach that night, it wasn't lightning. We already pretty much knew necromancy was involved in his murder. If that flash was magic, it gets us closer to a time of death."

He opened the wooden door, and Paul sprang away from it. The hotel owner blew out his breath. "Wow. You startled me. I didn't think anyone was here."

"Neither did we," Riga said. What was he doing lurking outside their door? Not *their* door, she corrected herself. The business center was a public area.

"You're working late," Donovan said easily.

Paul ran a hand through his hair, and the red birthmark on his face darkened. "You know what they say, no rest for the wicked."

"That would explain why we're always so busy," Donovan said.

Riga laughed. "Speak for yourself."

"Well." Paul shifted his weight. "I don't want to keep you two."

Donovan nodded to the hotelier. "Goodnight."

"Yeah, you too."

Donovan led her off. "That door isn't exactly soundproof," Riga said.

"Think he was listening?"

"I know he was."

CHAPTER 11

RIGA HAD OVER-INDULGED ON macadamia nut pancakes at breakfast. Now, as Donovan rocketed around the bend in the Ferrari, they settled unpleasantly in her stomach.

The hillside road was narrow, the foliage thick, allowing occasional flashes of the Pacific, sparkling in the morning sunlight. She rested her hands on her stomach and willed it to behave. Donovan shot her an amused glance.

"I know, I know," she said. "But the coconut syrup was so good. Do you think they sell it on the mainland?"

The wind tossed his raven hair, ruffled his white-linen shirt. "If they don't we can always order some."

"Good, then I can stop over-eating."

"Are we getting any closer?" He sounded like a bored kid on a long car ride.

Riga bit back a smile. "According to my map, the kupua's house is the next turn on the left."

Donovan turned the car up an even tighter path. They wound up the narrow road, its hairpin turns hugging the steep mountainside. Chickens pecked at the red dirt in the drainage gully.

They hit a pothole, the Ferrari scraping the ground, and he winced. "Is it much farther?"

A green-painted wooden house surrounded by wide-leafed plants appeared around the bend. "That must be it," Riga said.

The car ground to a halt in front of wooden steps leading up to a porch. A dream catcher hung behind a window. Iridescent whirligigs hung from the rafters and spiraled lazily in the warm breeze.

Riga got out of the car. Donovan did not.

She stuck her head in. "You coming?"

He held his cell phone, looking at it with loathing. "I'm sorry. I need to make a call first. Do you mind going on without me?"

"Nope."

She walked up the porch steps. Two surfboards lay tilted against one wall.

The screened front door swung outward, and a bearded man emerged. He was tanned, fit, and Riga figured he probably ate only raw food and did yoga at sunrise. None of which was such a bad idea. Her muscles twinged. She really needed to get back to her hapkido workouts.

"Mrs. Hayworth?" The kupua extended a hand, and she took it. "I'm Mark Harrison."

"Hi, I'm Riga. My husband, Donovan, is in the car. He had to make a call."

He gave her a pitying look. "It's hard to get away from work."

"He's actually been doing a pretty good job of it, until now."

"I meant you, actually."

She laughed. "Is it that obvious?"

"I can see it in your aura. So, no, it's not that obvious. Would you like to come inside? Or shall we wait for Mr. Mosse on the porch?"

"I think we can go in," she said.

He stepped back, and Riga caught the screen door, following him inside. A wide space opened before her. Low benches had been built into two walls in an L-shape, and they were cushioned with natural-colored fabrics and throw pillows.

Behind the benches, open square windows, their blue-painted shutters wide, revealed lush trees framing an ocean view. A colorful throw rug lay on the wood plank floor. In an empty corner, a rolled yoga mat stood propped against a wall.

"This is a great space for yoga," Riga said. With a view like this, she could almost imagine herself stretching for the sunrise. *Almost.* "Do you practice regularly?"

"Yoga, surfing, a little running... Very little running. You?"

"Some martial arts, but I recently moved and haven't practiced much lately. I need to find a new dojo."

"Don't put it off."

She sat on one of the benches, turning her back on the view.

"So, you say you're interested in Hawaiian magic?" He sat on a meditation cushion on the rug, his legs folding easily beneath him.

"Yes. Three things."

He laughed. "Only three?"

"Two are fairly wide-ranging issues. I'm a metaphysical detective, and I practice ceremonial magic. So I have a basic grounding in magical theory." She shifted uneasily. Riga didn't like to advertise. Or was it that she didn't like to advertise her recent failures?

"More than basic, I suspect," the kupua said.

"Donovan and I have been having some unusual experiences on the islands. That's the first thing, and I'll wait for him to finish his call, if you don't mind, before I ask you more about it."

"And the second thing?"

"Under the Hawaiian system, how would one go about affecting the elements? Water, specifically."

"That's a big question, and there are lots of answers. But speaking to you, I find that I want to tell you about grokking. Are you familiar with it?"

Mentally, she tabbed through libraries of magical journals, came up empty. "No."

"Then you're not a science fiction fan," he said. "It was coined by Robert Heinlein in his book, *Stranger in a Strange Land.*"

She raised a brow. "And it's part of Hawaiian magic?"

"It's the easiest English-language word to describe this type of healing. Grokking means to understand something or someone from the inside. To be so sympathetic, to walk in their shoes, so to speak, that you can enter the spirit body of the person or the thing being grokked, merge with it, and help it change."

"Isn't that somewhat manipulative?"

"It's not intended to be. Perhaps I haven't explained it well enough. All the kupua, or the grokker does, is share the dream of what the grokker wants to happen. It's completely up to the grokee if he or she or it wants to accept or reject the dream."

"How exactly does grokking work?"

"Think about it," he said. "Everything is energy. So everything is vibrating, and that vibration creates a broadcast, a pattern. Patterns can be changed."

It was a common magical theory, and one that she herself had experienced. But she knew that each tradition had its path to manipulating that energy. "That's the theory – but the practice?"

"It's quite simple. You close your eyes, connect with the energies around you, and then merge with all the bodies of the grokee – spiritual, mental, emotional, and physical. Then visualize your dream of change. Become it. Change your own behavior as if you were the grokee, because in a sense, you already are." He held up a warning finger. "But you can't completely become the grokee. You need to be able to remember why you're there, and who you are, so you can accomplish your mission. Then when you're finished, you unmerge."

She raised her brows. "Mm. Simple," she said, wry. They were getting off track, she knew, but she could never resist a good rabbit hole when it came to magic.

"It is, and it isn't. The grok will only succeed if you can banish your own negativity, fill yourself with unconditional love. For many people, this is the greatest barrier."

"And with grokking you can control the elements, such as water?"

"You can't control nature, but you can influence it. Unlike man, nature is open to multiple possibilities. In a way, this makes it easier to grok, because it can be influenced to do something it might have done anyway. The wind may blow in any direction, so any direction is possible."

"So one would try to become the spirit of the water, imagine oneself as the water, to grok it?"

"Not try, do." He smiled wryly, stretching his arms across the back of the cushions.

Seated with the lush jungle behind him, sunlight winking off his golden hair, he presented a Buddha-like picture of contented goodness, of alignment with the world. But in her gut she felt an odd twist of... disgust wasn't quite the word for it. Superiority? Was this her natural cynicism raising its treacherous head? Or something worse?

I don't have to be the wrong kind of necromancer.

Yes, you do.

I don't need to use blood. I can choose my own way.

Dark laughter echoed through her mind.

"Is something wrong?" he asked.

"No. Yes," she said, feeling like a worm. Mark was helping her, freely sharing knowledge. Where were these crummy thoughts coming from? "I'm sorry. Things have been—"

"Hello?" Donovan called.

"Back here," Mark said, twisting in his seat.

Donovan walked into the room, and Mark's eyes widened. He turned to Riga. "Wow," he mouthed.

Her mental darkness evaporated. A bubble of laughter rose in her chest. Donovan had eclipsed her again.

"Sorry about that," Donovan said. He sat beside Riga and draped his arm behind her shoulders, over the back of the cushions. "What did I miss?"

Lips slightly parted, Mark studied Donovan.

"I wanted to ask him about what I saw on the Kalalau trail," she said. "May I?"

He shrugged. "You saw it. I didn't. Go ahead."

"Kalalau trail is a special place," she said. "Isn't it?"

Mark nodded.

"We saw many Hawaiian spirits walking the trail," she said.

Mark tore his gaze from Donovan. "Then you are fortunate to have such a gift."

"Is it a sacred place?" she asked.

"An old place."

"When we were on the trail," she said, "Donovan seemed strangely energized, unnaturally surefooted. So I checked his aura. It seemed like the auras of the plants and of the trail itself were reaching for him, blending with his own."

"I'm not surprised," Mark said. "You have powerful mana, Mr. Mosse."

Donovan's lip quirked. "Mana?"

"Your spiritual energy," he said. "It's remarkable."

"And the trail might react to that?" Riga persisted. Why had the menehune wanted her to see this? Or had there been something else on the trail, something she still didn't understand?

"Of course," the kupua said. "As I mentioned, everything is energy, and everything resonates. If your husband's energy field – his aura – was resonating at a sympathetic frequency to the land, it would be attracted to him."

"But I haven't seen the land connect with him at home, where we live," Riga said.

"Perhaps, Mr. Mosse, your resonance has changed recently. Your state of mind will determine which energies will resonate with you. A negative state of mind will attract negative, and vice versa."

"From a magical perspective," she asked, "is there anything else special about that trail?"

The kupua's white teeth flashed. "You want more magic than spirits and natural auras?"

Was that greedy? "One more question," Riga said. "What can you tell us about the menehunes?"

"The little people?" Mark laughed. "Never met them. Some of my friends swear they exist, but I haven't had an opportunity to study the phenomena. There is much to learn from the Hawaiian philosophy of huna. It's a lifetime of study, a path, a journey. Menehunes are not an avenue I've explored yet."

Riga nodded, disappointed. The menehune had wanted her on that trail, had told her she'd seen what she needed to. But what had she seen?

Her discussion with Mark had been fascinating, but she remained baffled. "Thank you."

Donovan snuck a look at his watch.

"I wish we could stay longer," Riga said, "and learn more. But we're on a schedule."

The kupua tilted his head. "Life is long. Perhaps you'll return some day, and we can talk about the mysteries of the menehune."

They stood, and Mark walked them to the door. As she passed beside him, he leaned toward her. "Lucky girl," he said, under his breath, darting a look at Donovan.

She smiled. "You got that right." She wasn't sure what she'd done to deserve it though.

Riga and Donovan got into the car and drove away. "What are you thinking?" Donovan asked after a long silence.

"That I'd rather be a kupua than a necromancer."

"Riga, you can be whatever you want to be."

"Yes, but there's no use denying one's natural... talents."

The highway opened up, unfurling like a wave, and the Ferrari cut through clefts in the flattening hills. They swung inland and soon found themselves driving beneath a canopy of Eucalyptus trees. The trees arched over the road, a living cathedral.

A sign indicated Koloa, and Donovan turned onto a smaller, residential street. More turns and they were in the center of the town. Neatly painted wooden buildings with sloped, tin roofs lined the main street.

They cruised past a shop with a fifties-era Texaco pump and a life-size wood carving of an attendant, oil can in hand. A family picnicked in an open, park-like area across the street, beneath what appeared to be a ruined Norman church.

Riga did a double take. The island could not possibly have a ruined Norman church.

Donovan pulled behind some shops and parked in a lot beneath a monkey puzzle tree. "We're meeting that seal responder, Petra, at her gallery," he said, and hopped from the car.

Riga's heel caught on the floor mat, and she flipped it free, stepped out. "The last person to see Dennis alive. Except for the murderer. Unless she's the murderer." Reaching behind her, she unpeeled her damp tank from her back. The air was humid, unmoving. A bead of sweat trickled down her chest.

"Let's think positive," he said.

"Would thinking positive mean she's the killer?"

"Thinking positive would mean getting some clarity."

Riga laughed hollowly.

They passed a dive shop and paused before a green-painted wood building. A sign in the window declared: *Hawaiian Arts and Crafts*. The window was filled with wooden carvings, paintings, jewelry.

"See anything you like?" Donovan asked.

She tilted her head, admiring the curve of his muscles beneath his slacks. "Yes, but not in the window."

"Mmm... For that, I may let you join me in the shower when we get back to the hotel."

"Let me?"

He grinned at her then leaned forward, his attention caught by what appeared to be a flattened wooden mallet studded with sharks' teeth. A leather thong was strung through one end. "Now that's a helluva weapon."

Riga preferred her Kimber .45. If she had to put holes in someone, she'd rather do it from a safe distance. Alas, the gun didn't fly well. She nodded. "Looks deadly. And beautiful."

"My kind of girl."

They walked inside, setting the bell over the door ringing. A gust of frigid air blasted them, and Riga's skin shivered beneath the air-conditioning. More Hawaiian art and shark-teeth studded weaponry lined the walls. On a square island in the center of the shop, racks overflowed with hair sticks and cheap jewelry.

Behind the cash register, a woman looked up from her magazine and brushed a strand of ash blond hair behind one ear. Her eyes blinked a startling shade of dark blue. "Aloha!" She was long and lean and tanned to leather.

"Hello, I'm Donovan Mosse," he rumbled. "And this is my wife, Riga Hayworth. We have an appointment with Petra Singleton."

She closed the magazine. "That's me. Welcome to the islands, Mr. and Mrs. Mosse."

"I have to ask." He pointed at the flattened mallet in the window. "What is that?"

"That is a leiomano." She went to the window and gently removed it from its stand, handed it to him. "As you've no doubt guessed, it's a traditional Polynesian weapon. But it's really a piece of art. The teeth are tiger shark. Here."

He grasped it in one fist.

"You loop the cord around your hand," she said. "That way, you can release the leiomano and swing it if necessary. It's sort of a mix between a club and a dagger."

He swung it experimentally. "Nice balance."

"It's a beautiful piece," Petra said.

"Take a look at this." He handed Riga the weapon.

The wood was smooth and felt right in her palm. Gently, she touched one of the teeth and a drop of scarlet welled from her finger. "Ouch."

"Careful." Petra laughed weakly. "I guess that warning came a little too late."

"My fault." Riga handed the leiomano back to Donovan and sucked her fingertip. She'd expected sharp, but not these jagged little razors.

"Now that you've bloodstained it, we'll have to buy it," Donovan said.

"Was that your plan?" Riga asked.

"Rubbish. You absolutely do not have to buy it." Petra smiled impishly. "But I'd love it if you did."

"Then buy it we shall." He handed it back to her. "Can you box it for us?"

"Certainly." She scurried behind the counter and dove for boxes and tissue paper.

Riga leaned against the counter, watching. "We understand Dennis Glasgow took over your seal watch the night he was killed."

Petra jerked, fumbling with the leiomano. She caught it before it could fall to the glass counter. "You do get right to the point, don't you?"

Right after Donovan bought an expensive piece of art, Riga thought wryly. "What time did you leave him on the beach?"

Petra shoved some jewelry stands aside and spread tissue paper on the counter. "It was a bit after midnight."

Riga prowled around the counter, watching her jerky movements, her stiff posture. Was the woman naturally uptight or was this a reaction to the questioning? She relaxed her gaze and Petra's aura unfolded, hot pinks and snapping blues. *Naturally uptight.* "Did you talk at all?"

"I suppose we did. The usual chitchat." She laid the leiomano down and folded paper around its teeth.

"And what was the usual chitchat?" Riga asked.

"Oh, you know. How's it going, has anyone approached the seal, seen any unusual activity?"

"And had you?" she asked.

"No," Petra said. "The beach was dead quiet."

"Was anyone around when you left?" Riga pushed on the edge of her magical senses, expanded outward. A weathered paddle hanging high on a wall tugged her closer.

"Sorry," the shop owner said, "I didn't see anyone. And I certainly wouldn't have left if I'd known someone was lurking, waiting to harm the seal."

Riga tore her gaze from the paddle. "Not to mention Dennis," she said dryly.

"Him too, of course."

"Did you hear anyone?" Riga asked.

"Nope. Sorry," she said cheerfully.

Donovan handed her his credit card. "How well did you know Dennis?"

"Not very well. We only knew each other through the Society, saw each other at meetings, at seal watches. I liked him. He was always cheerful. He got along with everyone."

"And the Aquatic Protection Society?" Donovan asked.

Petra beamed. "Oh, they're marvelous. They really get it. And they have teeth. Townsend has completely transformed the place. Before it was all about public awareness. Now they're actually doing something real.

That's why I got involved. And if I catch the person who killed that seal..." She drew a finger across her neck.

"And killed Dennis, of course," Riga said.

"Of course." Petra handed Donovan the package.

"That paddle on the wall..." Riga jerked her chin toward it. "What's its story?"

"Oh, just some old paddle," Petra said. "I found it at a garage sale, but it has great energy, don't you think?"

"I do," Riga said slowly.

They walked out of the shop, the package under Donovan's arm. "We're no closer to a time of death," Donovan said. "Between midnight and three-ish, assuming that green lightning was magic."

"Yes, when 'alone in bed' makes a perfectly reasonable alibi. Did you notice how little she actually told us? And Dennis may have been a great guy, but Petra seemed more concerned about the seals than him."

"Did you detect any dark magic?" he asked.

"No, but we can't rule her out as a suspect. We need to learn more about her."

"Lunch first. We passed a barbeque place on the way into town that looked interesting."

"You're on." In spite of her ginormous breakfast, Riga was hungry again.

CHAPTER 12

THEY SAT BENEATH SLOWLY turning fans on the restaurant porch and watched Koloa laze past. Sweating tourists snapping photos. Teenagers clustered, laughing and gossiping. Chickens scratched in the dirt. A breeze stirred the trees and Riga stretched, tried to catch some cool.

The waiter brought them pulled pork sandwiches and Riga dug in. She looked up. Donovan watched her with a bemused expression.

"No, I'm really not pregnant." She dabbed barbeque sauce from the corner of her mouth. "It only looks like I'm eating for two."

He smiled, took a bite, and closed his eyes. "Heaven. Why does food taste better on vacation?"

Raised voices, male and female, caught Riga's attention. Across the street, a young couple emerged arguing from a shop. A gust of wind blew the woman's long, orange dress against her legs, and the man pointed at it, shouted something. An ache crept up the back of Riga's neck.

They finished their lunch and strolled hand-in-hand from the restaurant.

"Kimo's place isn't too far from here," Donovan said. "How do you want to approach him?"

A fly buzzed past, and she swatted it away. "Directly. The latest seal killing – and Dennis's murder – was about necromancy, not about irate locals protesting environmental regulations. But if Kimo is involved in the anti-seal movement – or whatever it's called – he may have heard something about the latest killing."

"Maybe," he said, noncommittal.

She smiled. "Pull every thread, until we learn the truth."

"Is that one of your metaphysical rules?"

"No, just plain detecting. And Kimo was put in our path. We need to find out why, even if he's only a dead end. But I agree that we need to take more direct action to find this necromancer, and the best way to do that is with magic. Tonight." She paused. "I've been putting it off, and we can't afford that anymore."

"Putting it off? Why? You're not still worried about your own magic?"

"A bit. I'm a beginner again, trying to feel my way through."

He paused. "Oh. You mean you're going to use necromancy," he said, his voice flat.

"I may have to use the in-between energy. Why? Does it bother you?"

His face cleared. "No. Of course not."

"Donovan—"

The woman in the orange dress stormed out of a shop in front of them, jostling Riga. The man followed close behind.

He grabbed the woman by the arm and whirled her around. "Listen to me when I'm talking to you."

Donovan handed Riga the package. He stepped in front of her.

The woman in orange shook the man off. "I'm sick of listening. All I do is listen. And all you do is talk, talk, talk, talk, talk."

The man punched her. Riga gasped.

In one swift motion, Donovan grabbed the man by the neck and arm and shoved him against the building. "Cool off."

The woman shrieked, one hand clapped to her bleeding nose. "Let go of my husband!" She flung herself scratching and clawing at Donovan.

Riga cursed under her breath, heat flooding her body. Her brain hummed with fury. "Oh, no you don't." She dropped the leiomano and came behind the woman, grabbed her forehead and pulled the woman's head against her chest. She walked backwards, hauling the woman, off-balance, with her.

"Let me go! Let me go you old witch." The woman's arms flailed.

Old? Since when was mid-forties old? "Since you've asked so nicely..." Riga jammed her foot into the rear of the woman's knee and took another step. The woman folded, sat down, and Riga laid her full weight against the woman's back, Riga's toes pressing into the hot cement, her arms wrapping the struggling woman in a headlock.

She looked up. Donovan still had the man jammed against the wall. A crowd was gathering.

"Don't. Hit. Women." Donovan ground out. "It's not polite."

A woman in the crowd applauded.

"Now," Donovan said, "do you think you can calm down?"

Purple-faced, the man nodded. Donovan released him, and he sagged to the ground.

Riga let go of the woman, levering herself upright and taking a quick step back, her hands trembling. She didn't regret her actions, but the rage that had exploded inside her had left her shaken. The woman might have attacked Donovan, but she was also a victim.

The woman clambered to her feet and turned, scowling, on Riga. "Mind your own business."

Donovan took Riga's arm. "Let's go."

She bent to pick up the dropped package, and they walked back to the Ferrari. Donovan's muscles were loose, his smile easy, but she knew he was hyper-aware, half-expecting the couple to return, to attack.

They didn't.

"Unbelievable," Riga said once they were in the car. The man who'd elbowed her into the river. The brawl outside the cave. The argument in the restaurant. The domestic dispute. The angry drivers... What was going on?

"Sorry," he said briefly. "I know better than to get into the middle of a domestic dispute."

"Oh, Donovan. It wasn't a criticism of you." Of course he'd stepped in. That was who he was and damn the consequences.

"Oh. Well, don't be so hard on the woman," Donovan said. "First her partner knocks her around, then you did. All in all, she's had a rough day."

"No. I meant, it really *is* unbelievable. Think of all the fights we've witnessed in the last few days. It's not normal. It's not natural."

His lips pursed. "You think it's supernatural? Part of a spell?"

"Maybe. I don't know. But I've felt this odd buzzing in my head whenever we've been around it. I thought it was just a headache – the sun frying my brain, but..." But she'd been angry too. Irrational, short-tempered. "Have you sensed anything?"

"No."

"No unusual feelings of annoyance or irritation?"

"No. Why? Have you?"

Her cheeks burned. "Yeah. When that guy knocked me into the river. I wanted to kill him."

"Well, that's perfectly natural. I wanted to have words with him."

"Donovan, you wanted to have words with him." She hunched her shoulders, ashamed. "I wanted to kill him. I had the spell in my head. I was ready to use it."

"But you didn't."

"But I wanted to."

He drummed his fingers on the wheel. "Okay, that's not normal. But why haven't I been affected? We've been in the same places, experienced the same things. Do you think you're more sensitive to whatever's going on?"

"No more sensitive than those two we just left in Koloa. And I've been warding myself." She set up magical protection as a matter of course. So why *hadn't* Donovan been affected? Was it something to do with the strange magic he carried?

They drove to the rocky shore, and Donovan pulled into a dirt driveway to a blue-painted restaurant beside a pier. The restaurant stood on stilts, the sun lighting its wide veranda and glaring off the corrugated roof. A faded wood sign above it: *Kimo's*.

The scent of cooking fish drifted to them, along with laughter, and the sizzle of oil. Against the dock knocked a battered fishing boat.

A Hawaiian nearly as wide as he was tall clambered from it onto the pier. He put down a cooler and squinted at them. Bare-armed, he adjusted the straps on his overalls. "Hey, Magnum," he shouted to Donovan. "You're on the wrong island!"

Donovan chuckled and gave him a casual wave.

Paul Glasgow, in his denim hotel shirt and khakis, emerged from the boat. He turned to shake hands with a figure hidden behind the pilot-house. Pulling his sunglasses off the top of his head, Paul ruffled his sable-colored hair and slid the glasses into place atop his nose. He leapt off the boat to the dock and strode to a black BMW parked on the side of the lot.

"What's he doing here?" Riga asked.

"Good question. Let's see if he wants to sell the hotel badly enough to answer it." Donovan hopped out of the car and walked to the BMW. "Paul!"

The Hawaiian approached the Ferrari and leaned over the driver's side. "Tell me the truth. This has got to be a rental."

Riga slid out of the car. "Nice detective work. I heard there's only one Ferrari on the entire island."

He grinned, exposing a chipped tooth. "You're a hard lady to impress. Is your man going to let you drive it?"

"He'd better."

"Is he going to let *me* drive it?"

"Doubtful. And I'll be back." She walked over to Donovan and Paul.

"Then what are you doing here?" Donovan was asking.

Paul folded his arms across his chest. The birthmark on his face darkened. "That's really none of your business."

"No," Donovan said, "but Kimo came up as a suspect in the seal deaths, and—"

"And I'm suspected in my brother's death?"

Donovan shook his head. "I didn't say that."

"How do you know Kimo?" Riga asked.

"It's a small island," the hotel owner said. "Everyone knows everyone."

Riga lifted an eyebrow.

"Look, I don't know who told you Kimo was involved in the seal killings," Paul said, "but they're wrong. We've known his family for years, and he supplies fish to the restaurant." He yanked the door open and got inside. "Leave him alone." He slammed the car door. The BMW roared off, kicking up clouds of dust.

Riga waved it away from her face. "I don't care if this is a small island. This is too big a coincidence."

"Agreed."

"Let's see what Kimo has to say." She turned on her heel and walked to the car.

The large man leaned against the Ferrari and looked less friendly. "Doesn't look like Mr. Glasgow wanted to talk to you."

"I seem to be having that effect on a lot of people," Riga said. "Is Kimo around?"

He straightened off the car, and it rocked. Silent, he walked to the boat.

Donovan and Riga looked at each other. Waited. Riga extended her senses. Not a whiff of magic.

A man appeared on the boat's deck and clambered down the short ladder to the pier. He ambled toward them, his feet ringing hollowly on the dock, his white chef's jacket sagging on his thin frame.

He slowed to a halt and looked Donovan up and down. "You looking for me?"

"If you're Kimo. My name's Donovan Mosse. This is my wife, Riga Hayworth."

He scratched his moustache. "What do you want?"

"I'm a private investigator," Riga said. "We're looking into the murder of Dennis Glasgow."

"What do you want?"

"Information. I understand you're a friend of the family's," Riga said. "Any idea who might have wanted to kill him?"

The back of her neck prickled. Casually, she glanced over her shoulder. Young men dressed in cutoffs and torn t-shirts emerged from the restaurant and leaned against the porch railing, watching them.

"No," Kimo said.

The big man stepped off the boat, a gaff in his hand. Slowly, he walked toward them, swinging the wicked-looking hook.

"What about the seal?" Riga asked. "Who do you think might have killed it?"

"Did Townsend over at the Protection Society tell you I did?"

"No," Riga said. "He told us you had strong feelings about the seals. Which seems rather strange, you being friends with Dennis."

"Why is it strange I'm friends with Dennis? Because I'm just a fisherman?"

"No, because he was president of the Aquatic Protection Society. It's no secret you wanted them to stop roping off the beaches for the seals."

"I don't care about the beaches. Every time a seal steals food off my hook I'm supposed to report it now. If a seal shows up where I'm fishing, I'm supposed to leave. I got nothing against the seals, and they got nothing against me. It's the people who are driving me crazy. So Glasgow and I agreed to disagree."

The big man came to a halt behind Kimo. He clenched the gaff and stared hard at Donovan.

Donovan didn't blink. "Whoever met up with him on the beach that night wasn't as accommodating. Where were you the night he was killed?"

"Home in bed. Look, all I know is I didn't do it. And you can tell that freak at the Protection Society that I'll sue him for slander if he keeps dissing me."

"I believe you," Riga said. "Evidence suggests that whoever did this killed the seal – and Dennis – for his own reasons. We need to find him before he hurts anyone else."

"Good luck with that." Kimo turned and stalked into the restaurant. His friend shot them one last suspicious look and followed.

"Interesting that he knew Townsend Murray was the person who'd sent us to him," Riga said.

He slung an arm over her shoulder, and they walked back to the car. "Is that meaningful?"

"Maybe not. And I didn't sense any magic on Kimo or in the boat or restaurant. Did you feel anything?"

He opened the door for her. "Me? Why would I sense anything?"

"It seems like you've got more of a connection here. To the island, to the magic." She slid onto the seat.

He grinned. "You sound jealous."

"A little." Hawaiian magic sounded so... *nice*. Why did she have to inherit necromancy? "Are you sure you don't have a dash of Polynesian in your blood?"

He shrugged. "Unlikely, but who can tell? In any case, our problem is the necromancer, and we don't seem any closer to finding him."

Riga tipped her head back on the seat. Clouds scudded across the sky. She exhaled slowly. "Tonight. I'll scry for the magician at midnight."

He grasped her hand and said nothing.

CHAPTER 13

RIGA STRETCHED OUT ON an Adirondack chair on their private beach, her toes digging into the sand, her mind racing. In the not-too-distant past, her magic had broken, pushed just out of reach, out of phase. She could manage the basics, and in unexpected moments, her old magic surged through. But she couldn't count on it.

An ocean breeze toyed with her hair. She rolled her head, enjoying the play of tropical air across her skin.

She tapped her pen on the open notebook in her lap. Her last attempt to use locational magic, to scry for a necromancer last month, had worked. Sort of. The connection had been rocky, dangerous, and the return trip painful.

Her heart beat faster at the memory, and something unpleasant clutched beneath her throat. She'd been using the wrong kind of magic that night – the wrong kind for her. Riga's magic was necromancy now, and she needed to get comfortable with this inheritance. But she hadn't missed the look on Donovan's face when she'd mentioned it earlier.

Necromancers traditionally used blood in their spells, and it was the blood that had odd effects on her. But she didn't need to use it. There was another way, a way she'd only just begun to figure out.

Blood was a conduit to death, death a conduit to the in-between, that zero point of non-existence. And that was where the power existed. She could access that in-between energy directly. Sometimes.

Her grip on the pen tightened. She'd spent a lifetime detesting necromancy. A part of her still did. But the blood worked. It was quick. It was dirty. And she might need it soon. And Donovan... She shifted in her chair. Donovan was right. For her, using blood was dangerous. Also, disgusting.

He emerged dripping from the ocean, his black swim trunks clinging to his muscular thighs. Donovan rubbed the water from his face with both hands, walked up the beach, and collapsed into the chair beside her. "What are you working on?"

"A spell. My best chance to find whoever's doing this is by using necromancy to find our necromancer. Like calling to like."

He stared out at the bay. It glittered in the sun. "Ah."

She frowned, studying her notebook. Its pages were wrinkled from its submersion at the Kalalau trail. "It's only scrying, a basic spell, and I'll use the in-between energy to power it. I doubt I'll need blood."

"Ah." His voice was carefully neutral.

She put the notepad down and looked at him. His chiseled face was a polite blank. "That's the second time you've said that. You're not comfortable with this."

"Riga, the last time someone used necromancy around me, it killed me."

She winced at the memory. Just before their wedding, Riga's aunts had attempted a simple spell manipulating the spirits – a wedding gift. Due to the interference of an outsider, it had gone horribly wrong.

Donovan seemed to have bounced back from his "death" fairly easily. Now she wondered if it had been too easy.

"I haven't forgotten," she said miserably. Unwilling to meet his gaze, she looked at the water. "I don't know what to do. Brigitte and I had talked about creating a magical system just for me – God knows I've theorized about it enough. But that sort of thing takes time."

"And time is something we don't have," he finished for her.

"The problem is, I can't promise you things won't go wrong." And she wouldn't let him suffer for it again.

He grasped her hand and twined his fingers in hers. "Well. I don't expect you to be happy with every move I make."

She furrowed her brows. Riga knew that this was the reality of marriage – the honeymoon couldn't last. Couples had conflicts. But she felt a twinge of disappointment.

"Ultimately," he continued, "we'll both do what we think's right. It's who we are. And that's why we love each other."

"Are you saying you'll accept me going ahead with this?"

"I'm saying I'll stand well back. Which means you'll need Brigitte. How long will it take her to get here?"

"She is here," Riga said, grimacing. "She arrived when she sensed the necromancy."

He dropped her hand. "Why didn't you tell me?"

"I'm sorry, Donovan. I was trying to keep her out of our honeymoon. This is supposed to be our time."

"Riga…"

There was a scrabbling sound, and Brigitte emerged from the pile of rocks. She bobbed her head. "At last. I was growing weary of lurking in ze shadows. Now that we are out in ze open, we must have a plan of attack."

"Brigitte," Donovan said, smoothing his expression, "this is a surprise."

"I am full of ze surprises. What have you learned about ze necromancer?"

Riga glanced at Donovan. His expression was neutral.

"He's killing mermaids," Riga said, "not just seals. And he's stirring up the elementals to create a natural disaster, a mass killing. Also, it's broad daylight. Someone might see you."

"The beach is private," Brigitte graveled.

"Not that private," Riga said. All she wanted now was to hash things out with her husband. "We can talk about this later."

The gargoyle tilted her head. "A mass killing, and you wish to talk about this later?"

"Fine." Riga slapped her notebook shut. The sooner she satisfied Brigitte, the sooner this would be over with. "What have you found out?"

"Me? It is not my job to find out. It is my job to support your magic."

"Then you can support me when we scry for the necromancer at midnight."

"And what will you use as a sacrifice?" Brigitte asked.

Donovan gave a minute shake of his head.

"Nothing," Riga said. "I don't need one."

"You are right to make necromancy your own, to blaze your own trail. It is ze mark of an artist. But can you afford to experiment now?"

A muscle beat in Riga's jaw. "Blood, death, is just a conduit to the in-between. I don't need it to get there. I've done without it before."

Brigitte looked skeptical.

"Fine. If I need to," Riga said, "and only as a last resort, I'll use my own blood."

"Your blood is not as powerful as an animal sacrifice—"

"Animal sac... I will not sacrifice animals."

Brigitte ruffled her stony feathers. "Why not? You eat them."

"I will not sacrifice animals," Riga ground out.

"Faugh! Lives are at stake, and you are being morally inconsistent."

"No animals." A pulse beat in her temple. "For God's sake, Brigitte, you know how crazy necromancy can make people. If I start killing animals... I don't want to go there. A finger prick is fine."

"You've given up on using the in-between energy pretty quickly," Donovan said.

"No," Riga said. "I haven't. That's exactly what I'll be using. I don't even know how we got talking about blood. No blood."

Brigitte's head swiveled toward Donovan. "I was not aware Riga had spoken to you about ze in-between?"

"Donovan knows about it because he's involved in this too," Riga said.

"Yes, of course. But I am your familiar. That is *my* role."

"He's not involved in the spell. He's involved in my life. And he's—"

"I'll be there," Donovan said.

"But... Donovan," Riga protested, "you were right. I don't know where this will lead, and if you're close—"

"I'll be there," he said firmly, rising from his chair. "So, midnight at our bungalow? I assume you know where our bungalow is, Brigitte."

"Of course. It is very nice." Brigitte sniffed. "If you like small places."

His lips flattened, twitching suspiciously at the corners. "Ladies." He nodded to them and strode in the direction of the hotel.

"I still don't see why you need *him*," Brigitte said.

There were thousands of reasons, and none Riga could articulate. "No," she said. "You wouldn't."

"Hmph." Brigitte rose into the air and flapped over the kukui trees.

She cursed, hoping no one looked up. Riga stuffed her towel and notebook into her satchel.

"Riga," a woman shouted. Deidre strode along the beach toward her and waved. The sea breeze fluttered her sarong dress, teasing strands of blond hair from her bun.

Riga slung the bag over her shoulder and stood, shifting impatiently.

"Hi," the widow said. "I hoped I'd find you here."

Deidre smelled of key lime and coconuts. Despite herself, Riga found herself relaxing at this hint of tropical drinks.

"How are you doing?" Riga asked.

The woman's laugh was shaky. "I never knew widowhood came with so much paperwork. The curse of being married to a successful man. Thank heaven I have Paul to lean on."

Riga glanced toward the bungalows. "Oh?"

"He's been amazing." Deidre bit her lower lip. "He's actually why I wanted to talk to you. Paul told me about your encounter at Kimo's earlier. He thought he might have left a bad impression."

"And he sent you to clear it up?"

Deidre flushed. "No, of course he didn't. He's been very upset by his brother's death. Kimo is an old friend of the family's."

"He mentioned that. How did Kimo know your husband?"

"Oh, who knows how these things begin? Dennis told me they were almost like brothers growing up. I think his father was best friends with Kimo's father. There's nothing sinister."

"I'm surprised Paul didn't just tell us that."

"He's a proud man, and he doesn't like to have to explain himself. You understand, don't you? I know you're investigating Dennis's murder, but you're wasting your time if you think Paul had anything to do with it." She placed her hand on Riga's arm, her blue eyes beseeching. "He's a good person, and he loved his brother very much."

Riga just stared, wondering who else he loved, wondering why Deidre seemed more concerned about Paul's good name than her husband's murder.

As if reading her thoughts, Deidre snatched her hand away. She turned her face toward the ocean.

"Why would someone kill your husband?" Riga asked.

"I don't know. It makes no sense. God help me, I don't know." She walked back the way she'd come.

Riga watched her scramble across the rocks. She could go after her, press her. But she didn't have the heart for it, and Donovan...

The temperature dropped when Riga stepped off the beach and into the shade of the banyan tree. She draped the rough towel around her shoulders and rubbed her neck, thoughts tumbling through her head.

Donovan wasn't happy about this. But she wouldn't use blood. The scrying spell might take a little longer, but that was okay. They weren't on a deadline. Although Donovan would have to get back to his casinos sometime.

She'd need salt for the scrying – extra protection. Hawaiian salt? No, too expensive. Then she remembered too *expensive* didn't apply to her anymore, and her brain hamster wheeled back to Donovan.

He lay in a hammock stretched between the porch post and a palm tree. His eyes were closed, but he reached out a hand to her as she approached.

Dropping bag and towel, she took his hand and rolled into the hammock. His skin was damp and warm. They swayed gently.

"So," he finally said. "Brigitte."

"It was wrong of me to keep it from you. I'm not sure why I did."

"I forgive you," he said, his tone self-satisfied.

"I don't know what's gotten into her," Riga fretted.

"Separation anxiety, I expect."

"What?"

"Of all the magicians she's worked for, she's only liked three and you're one of them. And you're the first female magician. She's wondering about her place now that we're married."

Riga blew out her breath. Insecure was not how Riga would normally describe the gargoyle. Brash. No-nonsense. Annoying. Not insecure. But could he be right?

"And there's something else." He opened his eyes. "Ellen's here."

Riga sat up. The hammock swayed dangerously. "Your personal assistant?"

"It was the only way I could manage it. I've been meeting with her in the morning, before you woke up, to take care of any urgent business. She's been managing things, so I haven't had to take calls."

"You've been cheating!"

His eyes widened. "What? Riga—!"

She brushed away his objection with one hand. "Not on me, on the detecting. You've been pulling all these meetings with suspects out of your hat and letting me think it was you. Ellen's been doing the work."

"I told you I had help."

"Not here. That makes a huge difference. Where is she? At our hotel?"

"I'm not that dense."

"Ah, ha. So you know what you did was wrong."

"I didn't want work to interfere. I wanted to give you a real honeymoon, with my undivided attention. I didn't want to be one of those guys with his nose in his phone while sitting next to a gorgeous, half-dressed woman."

Riga folded her arms. She laid back down and stared at the tree branches.

"You're not really angry, are you?" he asked.

"Honestly? No. We agreed we wouldn't keep secrets from each other that might affect our relationship. These don't. And I'm kind of relieved you're not a super-detective in addition to being a super-businessman. Being married to perfection would get annoying fast."

He snorted with laughter. "I'll keep that in mind."

"Where is Ellen staying?"

"I got her a condo not far from here. We've been meeting in the hotel business center in the mornings."

"I hope she's getting a chance to enjoy the island."

"She's not punching a time clock, so I'm sure she is."

"I'm jealous. I could use a detective's assistant."

He grinned. "You've got me." The phone rang inside their bungalow. Donovan swung out of the hammock. "I'll get it."

His heat gone, she shivered, and pulled a towel over her chest.

A shadow flitted beneath her. She twisted, and the hammock lurched, threatening to deposit her on the patio tiles. Riga gripped the sides, steadying herself. The breeze swayed the branches above, sending their shadows dancing. She was getting jumpy, seeing things.

He returned a few minutes later, his brow creased. "That was Kimo's friend, Mana."

"Mana?"

"The big fellow we met at the dock. He says he has some information for us – for a price."

She sat up. "You believe him?"

"No. He seemed over-protective of Kimo. Selling him out would be something of a turnaround."

"Unless he's not selling Kimo out. Unless it's a trap. What's his price?"

"Nothing we can't afford."

They eyed each other.

"It's probably a set up." Riga rubbed the back of her neck, unhappy.

"I don't think we've got much choice. We're low on leads, and if he does know something... I want to play this out."

"Where does he want to meet?"

"The parking lot by the lighthouse in one hour," Donovan said.

"Can we get there early?"

"We can."

"It hasn't been the most peaceful start to our marriage," she said, regretful.

"You're right," he said. "I'll bring the shark-tooth club."

CHAPTER 14

RIGA STEPPED FROM THE Ferrari into the deserted parking lot. Wind whipped her hair, and she clawed it back. She walked to the cliff and peered over the metal rail. Far beneath her stretched the blue Pacific, tipped by whitecaps. The sun lay low on the horizon, making her squint.

She looked north to the green spit of land jutting like a crooked finger into the ocean. Rising like an explanation point from the end of the peninsula stood a bone-white lighthouse. Its shadow spilled over the eastern cliff's edge and tumbled to the rocks below. Her thoughts followed the tumble, and she imagined the horror of such a fall, the swooping in her stomach, the rocks rushing toward her.

Riga shuddered, and turned her back on the ocean, leaned against the metal rail. It wobbled. Hastily, she straightened away.

Donovan came to stand beside her, a loosely wrapped brown package under one arm, and whistled cheerfully. She was quite certain it was only in her imagination that the wind howled along to Donovan's tune.

Riga wasn't squeamish, and speak-softly-and-carry-a-big-stick seemed a sensible philosophy. However, she eyed the package beneath Donovan's arm askance. He'd ripped one end off and put the leiomano inside for easy access. It was one thing to hang it on a wall. The bloody prospect of actually bashing someone with the shark-toothed wonder was another matter entirely.

"You could really hurt someone with that," she ventured, nodding to the package.

"I certainly hope so."

Riga shut up.

"Looks like Mana chose a good spot for the meet after all," Donovan said. "Are you sensing anything?"

The wind pressed against her, tickling her blouse against her skin. She dropped her barriers, extended her senses. The world tilted, dissolving into a sea of particles, dabs of color, gold threads connecting all. And she was a part of it, everything and nothing. *Nothing.* Did she exist at all? Fear clutched her like an anchor. She gasped, grabbed his arm, and the asphalt was firm again beneath her. "No dark magic." Her voice quaked.

"Is something wrong?"

"No. I'm fine." How to explain it? She'd had moments like that before, moments where the mountains seemed to breathe, the rocks to sing to her. They'd been fleeting, beautiful, terrifying – a glimpse of the world's true nature. "For a moment, I saw the universe as a web of energy."

He rubbed his jaw. "According to quantum physics, that's exactly what it is. What did it look like?"

"A painting by Seurat – tiny dots of color, and only when you step back can you see the whole." But how to step back when you're a part of it? She changed the subject. "If you were going to set up an ambush, where would you do it?"

"I'd block off the driveway, bottle us in."

"Which would push us onto the path to the lighthouse."

"Mm. I'll move the car." Donovan hopped into the Ferrari and drove it from the lot. He parked it on the side of the road and strode back to her.

She turned to the ocean. An oil tanker lumbered across the horizon.

Donovan placed a hand on the small of her back. "He's late."

A seagull screamed above them. A battered Honda sputtered into the lot. Mana unfolded himself from it, a giant in blue overalls.

He nodded to them and ambled across the pavement. "Hey, Magnum."

"Mana," Donovan said. "You said you had information."

"You said you had money."

Donovan waited a beat. He handed Riga the package. Reaching behind him, he drew a wallet from his back pocket. Counted out five bills. Folded them in half around one finger.

"No money, no talkie," Mana said.

"First, I'm curious." Riga tried to loosen her grip on the hidden leiomano. "Why are you doing this? I thought you and Kimo were friends."

"We are."

Donovan extended the money. "Then let's have it."

Mana reached for the cash and opened his mouth. His broad face contorted. He clutched his throat, choking.

Riga's stomach lurched, and a wave of nausea rose through her. Dark. Sweet. Cloying.

Blood bubbled at Mana's lips. He bent, and something red and white and triangular fell from his mouth. Another. One by one, the triangles hit the black pavement with dull clicks. Mana fell to his knees, his shoulders convulsing.

Swearing, Donovan yanked out his cell phone, and dialed 9-1-1. Mana curled onto the ground.

Riga dropped the leiomano and scrambled in her bag, dark magic battering her, scattering her thoughts into darkness, a seductive tide. *The salt, the salt, where was the salt?* Triumphantly, she pulled out the plastic bag of red salt they'd purchased earlier. Ripped a hole in it with her nail. Chanting, head spinning, she poured it in a circle around them.

The circle closed. There was a snap, like a rubber band breaking. The magic seeped away. Gone.

Her shoulders collapsed forward, and she took deep breaths. Her hands steadied.

Donovan knelt beside the fallen man and pressed his fingers to his neck. "He's alive."

Riga bent and retrieved one of the white chips on the ground. "My God. It's a shark's tooth."

"We don't have time to wait for an ambulance. We need to get him to a hospital. Get the car." He tossed her the keys.

Riga grabbed the leiomano, raced to the Ferrari, and tossed the Hawaiian weapon onto the seat beside her. A cold horror crept over her as she looked at the box. Fingers trembling, her chest weighted, she peered into the open package and pulled out the weapon. Where sharks' teeth had once studded the leiomano, there were only empty loops of twine.

"Oh, my God," she said faintly. She jammed the weapon back into the box and shoved it under her seat, then drove to the two men.

Donovan was on the phone. He shook his head, hung up. "New plan. The nearest hospital is in Lihue. He'll need to be choppered out if he's going to have a chance. What the hell just happened?"

She knelt beside Mana, the pavement digging into her knees, and took Mana's hand. It was calloused, the nails short, uneven. A working man's hand.

"It's called allotriophagy," she said in a low voice. "I've read about it but have never seen it before. Black magic, causing someone to throw up objects, usually sharp."

"The salt circle – it broke the spell?"

"Yes, but…" She looked up at him. "Sharks' teeth, Donovan." They were like razors, and her counter spell too little, too late. Helpless frustration raged in her chest. She was no healer, never had been. Her first-aid skills were limited to puncture wounds and breaks. And Mana's punctures were internal.

Mana's face grayed, his life draining out.

"Come on, Mana." Gently, she squeezed his hand. "You can fight this. Help will be here soon."

The wind blew the salt, streaking pale red across the pavement. An ambulance wailed in the distance. Donovan placed a hand on Riga's shoulder, and warmth spread from his touch.

Mana's lips moved, his voice a soft wheeze. Riga bent her head to hear. "I don't want to die."

She placed a hand on his chest. "You're going to be okay, Mana." But she knew it was a lie.

The siren grew louder. Finally, an ambulance rolled down the driveway, and a police car screeched to a stop behind it. A uniformed man and woman sprang from the ambulance. Donovan pulled Riga away. The male paramedic knelt beside Mana.

The woman strode to them. "What happened?"

"He approached us and began vomiting up those." Donovan pointed to the sharks' teeth scattered on the asphalt.

She blinked and pursed her lips, blowing out her breath. Finally, she said, "Wow. Sounds like pica disorder. I never thought I'd see that." She hurried back to her partner and said something to him and the police officer.

The paramedic shook his head and stood. *Too late.* Riga's vision blurred, and she bowed her head.

Donovan went to speak to them then returned to Riga. "They've canceled the chopper. He's gone."

"Donovan, there's something I need to tell you. The leiomano – the sharks' teeth are missing."

Donovan looked back toward Mana, then at her. His face darkened with anger. "You mean those are the teeth... How?"

She raised her hands helplessly.

"Let's get out of here," he said.

The police officer walked over to them, and Riga cursed beneath her breath. It was the same cop who'd taken her statement on the beach. His brows lowered when he saw them.

"I know you." He snapped his fingers. "The couple from the beach. What happened here?"

"The man was sick," Donovan said. "We called 9-1-1."

"You know him?"

"Slightly," Donovan said slowly. "We were at the beach near Poipu this morning. He worked on a fishing boat there with a man named Kimo."

"So you knew Mr. Glasgow, who you found dead, and you knew this man, who you also found dead. What was he doing here?"

Riga's heart sank. This conversation could not end well.

Donovan folded his arms across his chest. "He called us at our hotel, said he had information about Dennis Glasgow's murder, and asked to meet."

The cop's face darkened. "Right. You two follow me down to the station. And don't even think about running. This is an island. I'll find you."

Riga and Donovan got into the Ferrari. They waited for the police car to pull out in front of them.

"What did Mana say to you at the end?" Donovan asked.

She looked out the open window and swallowed. "He said he wanted to live."

"You did everything you could," he said.

But it wasn't enough. They watched the policeman say something to the paramedics and get into his car.

"We don't tell the police about the leiomano," he said.

"Agreed."

"On the bright side," Donovan said, "he didn't put us in handcuffs."

Riga snapped on her seatbelt. "He's probably only got one pair."

They spent the next three hours at the police station being questioned separately in cinderblock interrogation rooms that smelled of disinfectant. In the end, they were admonished not to leave the island and set free.

They peeled away from the police station, gravel spinning beneath the Ferrari's tires. "How'd you do?" Donovan asked, making a hard-right turn.

"I stuck to our story, though I'm not sure it helped us. We would have been suspects no matter what we said." She drew the denuded leiomano from under the seat. "And speaking of which, the police let us off too easily." They'd been at the sites of two suspicious deaths in a week. That had to put them at the top of a suspect list.

Donovan glanced at the weapon. His jaw tightened. "Who knew we had that?"

"The woman who sold it to us, for starters."

"Petra Singleton, the responder with the Protection Society," he said, "coincidentally also the last person to see Dennis alive."

He wedged an earpiece in his ear and tapped a screen on the updated Ferrari. "Connect me to Petra Singleton in Koloa." After a moment, "Petra, this is Donovan Mosse. I bought a leiomano from you... Yes, we are... Actually, no, the leiomano was stolen..." He glanced at Riga.

She nodded to herself. If questioned, it would be hard to disprove the weapon had been stolen, though she hoped to hell they'd never have to.

"No, no... No," he said. "Did you tell anyone that I'd bought it...? Of course not... Yes, I understand. Say, have you spoken to anyone from the Aquatic Protection Society lately...? I see... Thanks."

He tapped the screen and yanked the piece out of his ear. "She denies telling anyone," he said. "There's another possibility. Someone who worked for the hotel could have gotten inside our bungalow."

"And Deidre, Dennis's widow, may not work at the hotel, but I'll bet she wouldn't have any trouble getting her hands on a master key."

Donovan pulled into a gas station. "I think it's time we ditch the murder weapon."

Riga began to protest at this destruction of evidence, but he was right. They'd never be able to explain how the sharks' teeth from Donovan's leiomano had gotten into Mana's stomach.

He got the gas pumping, then tucked the leiomano into its package and strolled with it around the side of the building, towards the restrooms. When he returned, his hands were empty. He paid for the gas, and they drove off.

"Feel better?" she asked.

"Throwing the damned thing in a volcano would have been more satisfying, but beggars can't be choosers. Dinner?" he asked.

She thought of Mana, leaning on the Ferrari that morning and joking, and her fists clenched. Dinner. Drinks. And then she'd scry for a killer.

CHAPTER 15

"Mr. Mosse." Sarah hurried down the garden path toward them, her long, black hair trailing over one shoulder. Donovan paused, plastic key card in the slot. She stumbled to a halt, panting. "I'm so sorry."

"Sorry about what?" he said.

"The police searched your room. They had a warrant. I couldn't stop them, but I assure you the press will not learn of this from any hotel staff. They're gone now. And the maids have been inside your bungalow to put things back in order as best they could."

Donovan's lips flattened into a grim line, and Riga guessed what he was thinking. Sarah couldn't really control the hotel staff. And surely more people than the maids knew the police had searched their rooms.

"Thanks for letting us know," Riga said.

Sarah knotted her fingers together. "They wouldn't tell me why—"

"We witnessed a death," Riga said. "Two in one week struck them as suspicious."

"A death? Who?"

"A man named Mana," Donovan said. "If you'll excuse us." He placed a hand on Riga's lower back and guided her inside. Once the door was closed behind them, he said, "The police didn't let us off so easily after all."

"We look guilty." Riga paced the living area, caged between the couch and the dining table. This was exactly what their adversary had wanted, and they'd played into his - or her - hands. "Dammit."

There was a scratching at the glass door, and Riga opened it. Brigitte hopped inside. "What have I missed?"

"We're prime suspects in a murder," Riga said bitterly.

"Again? Tell me everything."

Riga did, while Donovan made phone calls to his lawyer and his publicity agent.

"This necromancer is a devious one," Brigitte said. "But you could not have ignored ze poor Mana's call. Still, you have been playing his game. It is time he plays by your rules."

Donovan ended the call and looked down at the drying tarot cards Riga had laid out on the bungalow's low coffee table. Their submersion in the creek had left the cards wrinkled. The sitting room's hanging lamp highlighted their streaked and faded colors.

He sniffed, wrinkling his nose. "They're molding. I think you need a new deck."

Brigitte chuckled. "Especially since she has not been playing with a full one." She reached behind her neck with one claw and scratched, the grating sound of stone on stone.

"You're a laugh riot." Riga swept the cards off the table and dropped them into a round garbage bin. Donovan was right. They were ruined.

Donovan's shoulders twitched. "Mind if I turn down the A/C? It's freezing in here."

"Go ahead," Riga said. "In fact, I could use some fresh air. Would you open the doors?"

Donovan drew back the floor-to-ceiling shutters and slid open the doors to reveal their small, private pool, set into the tile patio. A salt-water breeze flowed into the room and rattled the palms outside.

A measure of Riga's tension eased away. Brigitte was right. It was time to take control of the game. "Shall we scry?" Riga asked.

Donovan stared into the darkness without answering, then turned. "What do you need from me?"

"Help clearing a space, for starters."

Brigitte watched them shift chairs, toss colorful red, white and orange cushions to the side. Together they lifted the matching chaise lounge. They moved the table to the patio outside, and rolled up the sisal carpet, exposing the bamboo floor.

"Where are we going to sit?" he asked.

She looked down.

Donovan rolled his eyes, strode outside, and grabbed two cushions from the chairs. He tossed them onto the floor.

Riga retrieved her supplies from the other room. Candles. Matches. Salt. She hesitated then grabbed the knife.

She frowned as the breeze caressed the back of her neck. The air might be too much to keep the candles lit. But it felt good, and she needed that.

Her last scrying for a necromancer had left her with a healthy fear of the breed. She told herself this was different, she was better prepared now. Still, she was uneasy. Which was ridiculous. This was her heritage. And this was a simple spell, a spell she knew, and the only alteration was that it would be powered by the in-between.

Outside, a patter of rain carried a cool draft of air into the bungalow. Riga's chest tightened.

Brigitte squawked, wings flapping. "Something touched me."

"A bug?" Donovan asked.

"It was not a bug," Brigitte snapped. "I know what a bug feels like."

"Then what was it?" Riga asked.

"I do not know," the gargoyle said. "Something cold."

Riga relaxed her vision, extending her senses. Something translucent, irregular, fluttered outside the open glass doors and disappeared. Unease rippled through her. She'd spent so much time around ghosts, that she'd come to take them for granted. They couldn't hurt her.

"Spirit, show yourself," she said loudly.

Nothing did.

Feeling foolish, she rubbed the bridge of her nose. "There's nothing in the room. Not anymore, at least. There was something on the patio, but it's gone now."

"What was it?" Donovan asked.

"There's so much magic on the island I'm having a hard time differentiating," Riga said. "But it seemed like a ghost."

"Seemed like?" Brigitte said. "Seemed like? Do not seem. *Know*. You are a necromancer. Ze other magic should not matter. Feel for what calls to you."

Riga bit back a retort. Blood called to her. The local magic appealed to her. But half-hearted necromancy was what she was stuck with. "Thanks for the advice."

"Are you going to start ze spell, or not?" Brigitte asked.

Riga arranged the cushions in the center of the room. "Get comfortable," she said to Donovan. "This may be a bumpy ride."

He folded himself easily onto the cushion and watched while she conducted a banishing ritual and cleared the room. When she was finished, she poured a circle of what was left of the red, Alaea salt around them, muttering an incantation.

"Question," he said. "If the salt stops magic, will it keep your magic inside the circle?"

"It's a protective circle. It doesn't trap my magic inside – just harmful magic from coming in."

He shifted uneasily. "And we're both safe in here from outside interference."

"Just don't break the circle. Donovan, if you're not comfortable with this—"

"I'm trying, Riga."

Brigitte said something under her breath.

Riga ignored her and sat on the cushion across from him, inside the circle. Her knees cracked, and she winced at the sound. Every day she was a little older, and no wiser.

Her back was to the open door, blocking the white pillar candle from the breeze. She lit it and blew out the match.

"Now what?" Donovan asked.

She took his hands. "Now I cast, and you focus your energy on supporting my spell."

He didn't ask how. She'd never explained the process to him. Somehow, she knew she didn't need to.

Closing her eyes, she took a long breath and focused on her own center, the still point that was nowhere and everywhere and felt... butterflies. Riga rolled her shoulders and focused on her breathing. *Centered, just get centered.*

Nothing.

Brigitte cleared her throat. "Any day now."

Riga opened her eyes and glared at the gargoyle.

Brigitte shrugged. "I'm simply suggesting that you shall miss ze midnight hour if you do not hurry things along."

"This is still a new method for me, okay? Give me a minute."

She closed her eyes. Breathed. There was energy and there was non-energy, the in-between. Riga thought of Hecate, the goddess of magic, of death, the goddess who came before. Her center, still and powerful.

Energy flowed through her, cool and dark, hot and light, there yet not there. She let it fill and empty her and focused on what she needed: like calling to like. Necromancy to necromancy. Blood to blood.

The barriers of her skin fell away, and she was flying. Out the open doors, over the hotel. The world beneath was a sea of energy, sparkling light rising and falling, an ocean wave connected by gold filaments.

The chaotic masterpiece was dazzling. She tried to make sense of it all, and gradually, glowing patterns emerged. A burning woman sleeping beneath the earth. A blue bird, gigantic, its wings spanning two mountaintops. A triggerfish, orange and black and white, shimmered along a beach. And Riga was the in-between, the nothingness between it all.

Layers on layers. She shifted her focus, and those patterns sank beneath new ones. The dots of energy resolved into roads and jungles and buildings.

Magic. Find the magic.

Something fishhooked beneath her breastbone and pulled her southward. A speck in the distance, a dark sun, a missing piece of the pattern. A lizard spouted water, roaring. Suddenly, it swelled, flaring ultraviolet, engulfing her, and she was falling, spinning.

The room was shaking.

"Riga."

She blinked, back in the bungalow. Something crashed to the floor in the bedroom next door. The candle tipped over, its flame winking out. She sat frozen, unable to speak. The ground lurched.

Donovan hauled her to her feet, pulling her away from the windows and into the doorframe between the sitting room and bedroom. He clasped one arm around her waist, braced another against the frame. She clutched him, her heart slamming against her ribs.

And then the earthquake was over.

Eyes wide, Riga looked up at him. "I didn't do it."

Brigitte hopped into the salt circle. "Well, someone did it. I felt ze magic. Did you at least discover who was responsible?"

"No, but I think I know the origin." Riga stepped around a splintered ceramic lamp and dug a travel guide out of her suitcase. She flipped the pages. "In my vision I was headed south. I saw a lizard spitting water. It must refer to the legend of the Spouting Horn."

"The lizard monster that got stuck in the blow hole?" Donovan asked. "Let's go."

Sirens wailed in the distance. Riga slipped on her sandals. The blood thrummed in her veins. They were close. They would find him. The earthquake had been triggered by a big spell, by necromancy.

And someone else had died.

CHAPTER 16

THEY WERE BACK ON the darkened highway, Riga's hair streaming behind her in the open convertible. They'd only been on the island a few days and already the road was familiar. In a strange way it reminded her of their home at Lake Tahoe, but here they endlessly circled the same mountains rather than a lake.

Though in Kauai, they couldn't actually circle the whole island. Not by car, at least. And though the island was small, they'd been on the road over forty minutes. They drove past a fire truck, lights flashing, going in the opposite direction.

Brigitte's shadow passed before the crescent moon. It glowed weakly through the clouds smothering the stars above.

Donovan swerved to avoid a boulder in the middle of the road. Riga grasped the door handle to steady herself, her jaw tightening.

"Let's hope the earthquake didn't do any serious damage," he said.

Aside from the aimless and wide-eyed people standing in the road, things had seemed normal when they'd left the hotel. Riga, a native Californian, estimated it was a five on the Richter scale. The damage would depend entirely on how well the buildings were constructed.

Donovan turned the Ferrari down a residential road lined with palm trees and large houses. The lights of their car illuminated a green sign for the Spouting Horn.

"How far from the Spouting Horn do you think the spell was cast?" he asked.

"Not far, but I'm not sure in which direction."

Another sign for the Spouting Horn, an arrow into the parking lot, dark and empty. Donovan pulled in and killed the ignition. Quiet crept into the Ferarri, broken only by the ticking of the car's metal contracting and the far-off crush of waves.

"Give me a minute." Riga closed her eyes, broadened her senses. Something tugged her to the left, and she turned her head. "That way." She pointed.

They crossed the parking lot and snapped on flashlights. Riga's beam passed over a warning sign. They strode past it and scrambled down slick rocks.

There was a hollow, gurgling sound, like water in old pipes, and then a whoosh. Vapor danced across Riga's bare arms.

Donovan skimmed the light across the rocks. "There." He darted forward.

She didn't see anything but followed, stumbling across the uneven ground. Her light bobbed over the jagged rocks, casting weird shadows.

Another gurgle of water. Closer. Louder. And then a gusher roared up before her. She swore. Water drenched the front of her tank.

"Careful," he said.

She muttered another curse. She'd nearly fallen into the blowhole. Would have fallen in if the water hadn't chosen that moment to spout. She steadied her breathing and crept forward more carefully, eyes straining. A rock skittered from beneath her sandal.

And then... silence. The sound of the waves, the gurgling in the blow hole, Donovan's footsteps, all fell away. The blanket of stillness disoriented her, and Riga stopped, swaying, her ears straining.

A chill rippled up her spine. They weren't alone.

Someone was watching.

"We're too late," Donovan said, breaking the spell.

The sound of waves rushed back, and something loosened inside her chest. Heedless of the uneven stone, she hurried to Donovan's side.

His flashlight illuminated a mournful gray figure on the beach. Another seal, its skull shattered by a gunshot wound.

She relaxed her gaze, and for a moment it was there, a woman, bare-chested, staring, a bloody hole in her temple. And then the image flickered, and it was only a seal.

The gargoyle landed neatly on the rocks beside them. "Ah, ze poor thing," Brigitte said. "What harm did she do anyone? Who is this monster who stole her life?"

"Let's find out," Donovan said in a low voice. "Brigitte, we're being watched. Can you find him?"

"He shall not hide from me." Brigitte crouched and sprang into the air.

Something gleamed white at the corner of Riga's eyes, and she angled her flashlight. A symbol had been chalked on the rocks. She dug her phone from her pocket. "Donovan, would you shine your light over here? I want to get a picture of this." She snapped a close-up.

"There's another," Donovan said.

They found five in all, roughly equidistant from the body, as well as traces of melted wax and ferns. Riga hesitated, then forwarded the pictures to her aunts Peregrine and Dot. Experienced necromancers, they might have some insight into the symbols.

The lights in the house above them switched on, lighting the rocks. They looked up, startled.

"Let's go." Donovan took her elbow. "I don't think we need the police to find us here."

He stayed by her side as they hurried back, Riga scanning the night sky for the gargoyle. Donovan helped her up the small hill to the parking lot. She didn't relax until they were back on the highway.

"He was there, Donovan, watching us."

"I know. And now he knows we're onto him. We can flush him out, if Brigitte hasn't already."

The phone in her pocket vibrated, and she dug it out.

A message from her aunt Peregrine: "U?"

Riga picked her way across the tiny keyboard: "NO."

Peregrine: "Nasty. AVOID."

Riga: "Can't. Tell me more?"

Peregrine: "Avoid AT ALL COSTS."

Riga: "URGENT."

No reply.

Riga made a sound of disgust and jammed the phone in her purse. "I hate texting."

"Why don't you just call her?"

"Because then I'd have to talk to her."

Donovan grunted.

Disquieted, Riga searched the sky, and tugged her jacket more firmly into place. Where was Brigitte?

"Did she tell you anything about the symbols?" he asked.

"Just that they're trouble. Hopefully, Peregrine will send more detailed information later."

"Do the symbols tell you anything?"

"I wish I could profile spell casters the way the FBI profiles serial killers. Theoretically, the way he's configured this spell might give me a better sense of what we're dealing with. But in reality, I'm just taking the pictures to be thorough. Maybe Brigitte or one of my aunts will see something." Riga leaned forward, craning her neck, her head almost pressed to the windshield. "Brigitte should have been back by now."

"You're not worried about her, are you?"

"Of course not." She tied her hair in a knot, but strands whipped from it, snapping her cheeks. "Brigitte can handle herself. She's probably following our watcher back to his lair." Wind buffeted the small sports car.

"Lair?" he asked.

"It's a good word," she said defensively.

"It's an excellent word. Why don't we have a lair?"

They rounded a bend in the road, the beams of the Ferrari spotlighting palms. Abruptly, the trees flattened. The wind rose to a scream. The car swerved as if struck, its front tires lifting. It dropped hard, and Riga was wrenched forward, gravity tugging at her stomach.

"Hold on." Donovan corrected course. The wind fell, and they rolled to a stop on the side of the highway. "Are you okay?" he asked.

Riga released her grip on the door handle and swallowed. "Yeah. Were we... airborne?"

Donovan grinned. "I've never flown a Ferrari before." He sobered. "I'd better check the car." He jumped out and walked around the bumper, examining it with his flashlight.

She exited more slowly, letting her heartrate return to normal. "Any damage?"

"Not that I can see. You feel anything?"

She cast about. Magic tingled at the edges of her awareness then faded to nothing. "Past magic."

"Hm. No surprise. That wind wasn't normal. But if it was an attack on us, it was badly timed. This is a nice, flat stretch of road. Why not wait for a windy cliffside, where he could do real damage?"

Her stomach churned. "Unless the attack was meant for Brigitte."

"Can you contact her?"

"I can call for her, but it's like sending up a bat signal. She'll know she's wanted but not why. And if she is in the middle of tracking, I don't want to call her off. If she's been disabled by that spell, my call won't help."

"Doesn't it work the other way?"

"She can't call me."

"But you're connected to each other. There must be a way for you to find her."

"I'd need supplies..." Her lips puckered, and she hissed an indrawn breath. But she had supplies. She dove into the car and rummaged through her bag, pulling out her mint tin. "I knew this was a good idea."

He leaned over the car door. "Breath mints?"

She opened the tin, exposing a white tea candle, a rolled scrap of paper, a tiny bottle of oil, and matches. In the top of the tin, she'd affixed a drawing by her niece, Pen, representing the four elements. "Mini altar kit. Waterproof, fortunately. This will help me focus, though it would be better if we had something that belonged to her." Better still if they had a piece of Brigitte, but unlike other familiars, Brigitte wasn't in the habit of shedding fur or feathers.

"She lent me a book before we left. I've been carrying it around with me." He went to the other side of the car and dug behind the seat, pulled out a scarred paperback. "Will this do?"

Riga took it from him. "Tami Hoag – this is one of her favorites." She smiled. "Brigitte must like you."

He cocked a brow. "What's not to like?"

Her movements quick, jerky, she drew a circle and pentagram in the soft dirt along the roadside, sheltered from view by the car. She emptied out the tin and set the candle in the center of the drawing on the tin lid, placed the book in the center of the circle. Riga sat down beside it and lit the candle.

A Jeep blasted past. The tiny flame flickered.

She closed her eyes and centered, empowering the circle with the in-between. After her earlier spell, it seemed to come more easily to her now.

Riga chanted. It was a simple rhyme, but at the last minute she altered it, calling to the four elements. Here in Kauai, where the elements seemed closer, it just seemed right.

She held the book over the candle flame, envisioning smoke and heat curling about it and imprinting on its essence, and then rising into the air to find its owner. She thought of Brigitte, of the gargoyle crouching, springing impossibly lightly into the air, her stone-feathered wings spread wide. No, Riga didn't need to bleed to make magic.

Brigitte, where are you?

She called the elements, imagining them flowing from earth and air and water and fire through her. With a breath, she sent them racing outward in search of Brigitte, following the trail the book had lain.

Her vision fragmented. It wasn't happening. She wasn't connecting. The spell was failing. Had failed. Riga raked her hands through her hair, cold spreading through her belly. Something had happened to her familiar, her friend, and she didn't have time for a systems failure.

"May I borrow your knife?" she asked.

Frowning, Donovan unlatched the knife from his belt. He snicked it open and handed it to her, handle first. He edged away from the circle, his expression unreadable.

Riga took the knife and pressed it into the pad of her finger. A droplet of blood oozed out. She squeezed it into the pool of melted wax.

A sigh in the wind. From the corner of her eye, Riga caught the flutter of a Hawaiian shirt, the menehune turning his back on her.

Power surged through her, hot and enticing. Images flashed. Brigitte, tumbling through the sky. The gargoyle staggered on a rock wall, one wing dragging behind her.

Riga's nails bit into her palms. Which rocks? Where was she?

Twin waterfalls. A river winding below, through a verdant valley. And stones, stones, sacred stones covered in snow, sacred to a goddess.

Swaying, Riga blew out the candle. She packed up her miniature altar kit, dropped the candle, fumbled with the oil. The world was spinning, and she gripped her head to steady it. "Wow."

"Did you see anything? Where is she?"

"Who?" she asked. Donovan was frowning at her. Even annoyed he was cute. Warmth radiated throughout her body.

"Brigitte," he said.

"Oh." God, she hadn't felt this good in ages. The world felt fuzzy around the edges, and she liked it.

"Where is she?"

"She's at some heiau to a snow goddess, on a hillside." Her words slurred. She spoke slowly, with the dignity of a drunk. *Brigitte*. They had to find Brigitte. She was in trouble. "There's a waterfall nearby. The guidebook is in my bag."

Donovan stared at her, his lips compressed into a thin line, then went to her bag, found the guidebook, and flipped to the index. "Here. The Poliahu Heiau by Opaeka'a Falls. It's not far."

He jumped into the car and waited while she fumbled her seatbelt, then they roared down the highway. Donovan leaned forward, reaching between his legs, and pulled a first aid kit from beneath his seat. "Here.

There may be some disinfectant inside for your finger. I'm not sure how clean that knife was."

She laughed shakily. "Now you tell me." Her stomach twisted, heaved, and she clamped her lips shut.

They crossed a river. "How are you feeling?" he asked.

"Go left here." Riga's head was clearing, thanks to the pounding of a ferocious headache. "It's only a few miles in, according to the book."

He made a hard turn, pressing Riga against the door. "I ask because your pupils are dilated, and you're slurring your words."

"Still?"

"No," he admitted. "The slurring stopped two turns ago."

"The spell affected me, but I'm feeling steadier now."

"It's not right for you, Riga. Using blood."

There hadn't been a choice. But something niggled at her. She wanted more. "I needed to do it." But she wondered if that was true and looked away.

Donovan didn't respond. They drove inland, up a windy road, and soon he slowed the car, looking for the site. "If we reach the waterfall, we've gone too far," he said.

Their headlights struck a metal historical marker sign – a white-robed King Kamehameha wearing a sweeping headdress.

"There," Riga said.

Donovan pulled into the dirt parking lot, illuminating cropped, browning grass, stunted palms, and a low, lava stone wall with raised ground, wild grasses behind it.

"See her?" he asked.

The Ferrari bumped to a halt. The moon emerged from the clouds, and the river below turned silver, an eel writhing through the dark valley.

"No," she said, "but this was definitely the spot." She flicked on her flashlight and got out of the car. A sense of despair washed over her. She shouted. "Brigitte?"

No answer.

A chill swept through Riga. She turned up the collar of her jacket.

Donovan came to stand beside her and nodded to the right. "This way."

"We'll go quicker if we split up."

He scratched the faint scar on his jaw with his thumb. "Are you sure you're feeling all right?"

"I am," she said. "Really." The lightheadedness and nausea were almost completely gone. The headache remained. But she deserved that.

"Then you take left. I'll take right."

She walked beside the wall of the heiau, her shoulders stooped, swinging her flashlight. The metal felt slippery in her hands. Scalp prickling, she stopped and turned to look behind her. "Donovan?" she shouted.

"I'm here. You find her?"

"No." Feeling foolish, she continued along the uneven wall.

Footfalls pattered past, and she started, her flesh pebbling. She swept the beam. Red dirt, a stone dislodged from the wall, a palm, its shadow long, spiky.

A child's giggle. *Menehunes.* She did not need a fairy encounter now.

She swung in a circle. "Brigitte!"

Light footsteps, dozens, running in the opposite direction. She spun toward the sound.

"Brigitte!" She cursed. *Forget the footsteps.* They were just menehunes. *Little people. Happy, harmless little people.* (Fae that scared the hell out of her). Brigitte was here, and they were a distraction.

Blowing out her breath, she turned her back on a giggle. She strode toward the end of the clearing and a tangled kukui tree, its moonlit leaves silvery spearheads.

Donovan's voice echoed. "Brigitte?"

Her sandaled feet crunched over loose dirt and stone. A car drove past on the highway, slowed, and sped onward.

Something squeaked, low and rhythmic. The cone of light from Riga's flashlight arced back and forth, a miniature lighthouse across the dirt and grass. The squeaking grew louder.

A breeze kicked up, rustling the leaves. Riga tightened the belt on her safari jacket.

The branches of the kukui tree creaked. The squeaking was louder here and faster. She shined her light in the branches, thick with leaves.

No Brigitte.

She moved on, and the squeak was behind her. Slowly, she turned, walked beneath the tree. What was that sound? It was like something hanging. A dead man.

She turned the beam of her flashlight upward, dreading what she'd find. Something gray and shaped like a teardrop hung from the tree. It reminded her of a giant insect pod she'd seen once in Thailand, and she recoiled.

Something shifted beneath the gray matting, and she stifled a yelp, her heart clenching. An eye – dark and stony – glared from the pod.

"Brigitte." She put her hand to her chest, willing the thundering to ease. "How did you...?" She stepped closer, squinting. The gargoyle had been wrapped in ti-leaves and tied with vines, enveloped in a neat ball.

"Donovan! I found her! Over here!" She turned to Brigitte. "It's okay. We'll get you down." Her light followed the trail of the vine that suspended the gargoyle. It had been hung over a main branch and then looped and tied off around a lower branch, just out of Riga's reach. But it wasn't out of Donovan's.

Nice. He should be able to lower Brigitte to the ground without dropping the gargoyle. She studied the knot and shook her head. They'd need a knife to get that undone before daybreak. Donovan's blade was getting a workout on this vacation.

She started in his direction, thinking to find him. The beam from her light mirrored back at her.

Riga halted, baffled. Slowly, she walked forward, the reflected light growing larger, flatter. She reached out her hand, fingertips tingling, and felt something solid and unyielding. Anxiety pressing her chest, she pushed harder, felt with both hands, stepping sideways, circling.

A barrier. It wrapped around the tree. They were trapped. She snarled in frustration.

Above her, Brigitte growled low like an angry cat. The gargoyle spun slowly, her visible eye accusing.

"I'll figure this out," Riga snapped. "Just give me a second."

She'd been an idiot. Brigitte had been the bait, and she'd walked right into the snare. And Donovan was outside it. Was that intentional? Meant to divide and conquer? Or an accident that would work in their favor?

She walked around the tree again, her hands gliding over the barrier, probing for a weak spot. There was none.

Riga pressed a palm to her brow. *Think, think, think.* Anything could be happening outside the barrier. What if Donovan was hurt, or... Her heart clenched. *No, don't think of that. Think of how to get out of here.* First – what was this invisible wall? Riga blew out her breath and extended her vision.

That strange web of light sprang into being, a burst of color netted by gold, and she staggered, momentarily blinded. Riga lowered her lids, shielding her eyes through her lashes. She could see the barrier now, a shimmer of iridescence, sunlight on snow and hard as ice, surrounding the tree. And above it...

The colors changed. So the barrier was a wall, not a dome. She blinked, returning to normal sight, and shined her flashlight above her. The branch Brigitte hung from extended over the barrier.

"Ha!" She tucked the flashlight, still on, into the waistband of her shorts and found the lowest tree branch. Riga scrabbled onto it, scraping her bare legs and dropping a sandal to the ground. Swearing, she kicked off the other sandal and climbed higher to Brigitte's branch. She wormed along it, the wood creaking.

Brigitte made strangled sounds.

"No, I'm not going to cut you free," Riga said, inching past the gargoyle. "You'll just drop to the ground. There's a barrier around the tree, but the branch goes over it. I'll get Donovan, and—"

A crack split the night air.

"Oh, shi—"

The branch plummeted, and the ground rushed to meet her. Riga hit hard, elbows and knees jarring. She rolled to her back, the wind knocked from her. "Ow."

A light shined in her face. "Riga?" Donovan knelt beside her. He took in the branch, the thrashing gargoyle. "Did you try to get Brigitte down by yourself? Why didn't you call me?"

"Because the trap..." No, *no, no*. The barrier would spring back into place now that he was here. "Get out! Get out!" She scrambled to her feet and grabbed his hand.

He let her pull him away from the tree, his face creased with amusement. "We're not making Brigitte happy."

"It was a trap. Ow." A cold, knifelike pain stabbed her side, and Riga bent, one hand pressed to her aching ribs. "When I stepped beneath the tree, a magical barrier came down. It blocked everything – light, sound. That's probably why you didn't hear me calling."

"Well, it's not there now." He strode inside and knelt beside Brigitte.

"But..." Riga reached out a hand to him then let it drop to her side. If the trap snapped into place, at least one of them would be on the outside to effect a rescue.

He cut the last vines free from the gargoyle with his knife. In the moonlight, the gargoyle seemed speckled white and gray, as if lichen-covered.

Feathers ruffling, Brigitte hopped outside the circle of the tree. Her head twisted back and forth. "Never! Never have I been so humiliated." She loosed a string of French expletives.

Slowly, Donovan followed, folding his knife, and Riga felt a flare of irritation. Why hadn't the trap reset itself?

"What happened?" Riga asked the gargoyle.

"He discovered me and conjured a storm. I crashed here."

"He?" Riga said sharply.

"I do not know. He, she, it, whatever it is has powerful skills. And my wing!" The gargoyle lifted her wing and blinked. "My wing is fine."

"How did you get in the tree?" Riga asked.

"Menehunes." The gargoyle hissed. "I injured my wing when I crashed into that stone wall. I could not fly, and then they were on me. Nasty, giggling little creatures. They trussed me up like ze Christmas goose. Riga, you must do something about them."

"But your wing looks fine now. Did they repair it?" Donovan played his light over the gargoyle's back, revealing rows of tiny white handprints. "What the—?"

Riga nudged him. The gargoyle was angry enough.

"But you were following whoever did this," Riga said. "What did you see? What kind of car did they have?"

"Car?" Brigitte spat. "From my height – my safe height – I saw only two headlights in ze darkness. Bravely, I swooped lower. I knew it was ze first chance to learn ze identity of ze evil doer. And then he hit me with his spell."

"So you didn't see anything," Riga said flatly.

"I was nearly killed. You have no idea ze trauma I have been through. Falling, and then ze nasty, little menehunes."

"Considering you crash-landed on a sacred site, I think we can count ourselves lucky," Riga said.

The gargoyle screeched, flapping her wings. "How was I to know where I was crashing? I was crashing! It... What is on my wings?" She craned her neck, rotating her body. "What have they done?"

"Donovan, she was dangling like bait," Riga said. "And when I went to her, the trap closed, and we were trapped. But it doesn't make sense. What was the point?"

He shrugged. "You told me the menehune are tricksters."

"Did anything happen out here while I was in there?" Ignoring the gargoyle's indignant squawks, Riga motioned toward the tree.

"No. Just an old woman walking down the road. She stopped to ask what we were doing here. I told her, and then I went to look for you."

"You... What exactly did you tell her?"

He rubbed his jawline with his knuckles. "Ah..." His lips parted, his face carved in horror. "Riga, I told her everything."

CHAPTER 17

THE MOON SLIPPED BETWEEN two slivers of cloud, casting the uneven ground in a chiaroscuro of shadows and light. The wind rustled the tree branches, and they groaned in response.

Riga stared at her husband. "What do you mean you told her everything?"

"What have they done to my so beautiful stone feathers?" Brigitte wailed.

"Everything." Donovan ran a hand through his hair. "That the earthquake had been caused by a necromancer we were pursuing. That your familiar had crashed here, and we were searching for her. About the seals, the suspects. Everything. What the hell?"

The gargoyle sat on the ground and scraped at the white handprints with one talon. "Cretins! Visigoths! Menehunes!"

"It was magic," Riga said, shaken. "It had to be. That's why we were separated. What did the woman look like?"

Donovan paced. "I can't... It was like a dream. Talking to her made so much sense. And now it's all slipping away. I remember she was old. And Hawaiian. But I couldn't tell you what she was wearing or if she was fat or thin."

"Did anything stand out?"

Brigitte howled, rolling in the dirt.

"Not a damn thing." He clenched his jaw. "And now whoever we're following knows everything."

"If it was the necromancer, and he or she's as badass as we think, why didn't he try to take you out?" She rubbed her eyes, suddenly tired. "There have always been other players in this – the menehunes, the mermaids. We don't know who that woman was."

He pursed his lips. "You're right," he said. "There's no sense second guessing ourselves. Let's get out of here. Brigitte, can you fly?"

"I have been tagged. By faeries!"

Donovan went to examine the damage. "It looks like some sort of powder. It should wash off."

Brigitte launched into the air and flew towards the black expanse of ocean.

"Come on, Riga." He tugged her toward the car, and she followed.

But her limbs felt curiously heavy, her hands clammy. Depression washed over her. "Donovan, do you sense something here?"

"It's a lonely sort of place."

"What else do you know about this heiau?"

He froze, and she stumbled to a halt behind him, her hand in Donovan's tightening.

A glowing, rectangular tower, narrowing at the top, now stood behind the rock wall of the heiau. Faintly translucent, the poles that made up its infrastructure were visible, as was the thing that swung inside it.

Feet dragging, Riga walked toward it.

"Riga," Donovan said sharply.

Something swinging, hypnotic... Her gaze followed the sickening arc of the body, hung upside down. Riga wanted to shut her eyes, to run, to make it go away, but horror rooted her to the spot. And the more she looked, the more detail she saw. Details she'd rather not see.

But the rotting corpse was only a ghost, a memory. She swallowed, and the movement, slight as it was, affirmed she still had power over her body. Riga shuddered. Yes, she could move. "You're right," she said. "We should go."

Glowing figures rose from beneath the tower and streamed from it. Riga took an involuntary step back, but the marchers ignored them and walked down the hill, towards the ocean.

Riga and Donovan returned to the Ferrari. He drove slowly down the winding road.

"You asked what else I knew about this heiau," he said. "I read about this place in our guidebook. They believe it was once used for human sacrifice, after the Tahitians arrived."

"That's what the little man told me, that sacrifice had come to these islands before." She thought of the hanging man, dangling by his ankles, the sacrifice. Necromancy was old here.

They made it their own. The thought echoed like laughter in her head. She pressed her knees together and rubbed her mouth, feeling sick.

He frowned. "Dark things may have happened here once, but the old woman who appeared to me – she seemed benevolent. Was I fooled by a spell?"

"Maybe not," she said. "There are stories of the local goddesses appearing on the road as old women. If you're respectful to them, they respond in kind."

He shot her an amused glance. "I thought you didn't believe in gods and goddesses."

"I don't. They're archetypes brought into being by human consciousness or some other form of consciousness, reappearing over and over in different forms. The trickster god, Maui, isn't so different from Hermes or Loki."

"Mm. Still looking for that grand unifying theory of magic, are you?"

"Everyone needs a hobby. Besides, if I can crack it, I may have that magical system I've been looking for." Something fully her own, something that had nothing to do with death and blood and necromancy. She tightened her jacket around her.

"Are you any closer?"

She re-tied her hair, whipping in the wind. "No. But I have to say, Hawaiian magic seems an interesting synthesis."

The need to sleep beat at her. The clock on the dashboard read two thirty, AM "If I could figure it out..." She might not need necromancy. The image of the gently swaying corpse appeared before her, and she closed her eyes. She wouldn't make necromancy her own. She would find a different path to the in-between.

"Why is it that we're always looking for unifying theories? Why can't there be more than one answer? What about chaos? What about nature?"

She closed her eyes, smiling, and rested her head against the seat. "That's your bailiwick." Her brain caught a spark, struggled toward it, and she fell asleep.

Riga woke as they pulled into the hotel driveway, and she sat up with a start. "Sorry." She yawned. "Did I miss anything?"

"Not at all. And you're adorable when you snore."

She frowned. If he could hear her over the roar of the Ferrari's engine, there was nothing adorable about her snoring.

"I was joking," he said. "You weren't snoring."

"That's a relief."

He snickered. "This time."

In their bungalow, they tumbled into bed and fell asleep to the sound of each other's breathing.

⁂

When Riga awoke, sunbeams slanted along the bamboo floor. Donovan was gone, a note left on his pillow that he was at the business center. Brigitte perched on the dresser.

"I see the handprints washed off," Riga said.

"Those menehunes are lucky they did." Her eyes narrowed. "They do not want me for an enemy. Where is the remote?"

Riga rolled out of bed. "It's in the drawer beneath you." She stumbled to the bathroom, showered, and changed into a crisp, cotton blouse and wide-legged slacks. Fiddling with her collar, she exited the bathroom and walked through the ghost, dripping in her bathing suit.

"Gagh." Riga shivered.

The ghost flit sideways and disappeared through a wall.

"Dammit." It was the first time she'd seen the ghost in their rooms. Had this once been the ghost's bungalow? Were her habits changing? Or had she come to Riga on purpose?

"Did you notice the ghost earlier?" Riga asked the gargoyle.

"Forget ze ghost. We have more important business to discuss. What is our next step?"

The door opened, and Donovan walked inside. He drew Riga to him and pressed her against the wall, kissing her. His broad hands drifted to her hips.

"Mm." His voice was a rumble against her neck. "We have some unfinished business."

"That is what I told her," Brigitte said.

He jerked away from Riga, releasing her. "Good morning, Brigitte," he said heartily. "I didn't see you come in."

"Riga was about to tell me of our plans for ze day."

He cocked a brow. "Were you? I'd like to hear them."

"We should talk to Kimo again," Riga said. Hero, villain, or bit-player, Kimo was a part of this story. "He knew something, and his friend's death might shake it loose. And we should circle back to Townsend at the Protection Society. He was the one who put us onto Kimo. There's likely more he's not telling us."

"What about me?" Brigitte asked.

"We need to know more about Hawaiian magic. Can you do some research?"

"Why Hawaiian? You should be studying necromancy. Are you avoiding it again? You know you cannot do Hawaiian magic. And furthermore—"

"Hawaiian magic, Brigitte." She grabbed her bag and gave Donovan a get-me-outta-here look.

He clasped Riga's hand and tugged her out the door. "Don't work too hard," he said over his shoulder.

The door closed behind them. "Alone at last." He nuzzled her ear.

The pool man walked past, net over his shoulder.

"Relatively alone," Donovan amended.

❧❧❧ ❧❧❧

They drove down the coast, catching the morning traffic in Lihue before escaping onward to Kimo's restaurant in Poipu. They turned down the narrow, rutted road to the rocky shore, Riga's shoulder lurching against the door when they hit a pothole.

Donovan winced and pulled into a spot beneath a palm tree. Kimo's boat bumped against the deserted dock. They walked up the steps to the crooked shack.

Riga inhaled, smelling breakfast, remembering she hadn't eaten. Her stomach rumbled.

Donovan laughed. "Since we're here, we may as well eat."

A smiling waitress escorted them to a booth, and Riga slid across the torn Naugahyde cushion. The waitress handed them plastic menus, and they ordered orange juice.

Behind the counter, Kimo peered at them through a window to the kitchen and scowled. Half a dozen men, their skin roughened by sun and sea, sat on a row of barstools. They followed his gaze and stared at Riga and Donovan.

"Kimo's friends?" Riga asked under her breath.

"They do look familiar." Donovan looked over the menu. "He's got your favorite, macadamia nut pancakes."

She closed the menu, and Kimo ambled toward them. He wiped his hands on the stained apron that sagged about his narrow hips.

Donovan stood. "Hello, Kimo. We hoped to find you."

Kimo's gaze darted between the two. A breadcrumb was snagged in his moustache. "What are you doing here?"

"It's about your friend, Mana," Donovan said.

"What about him?"

"Maybe you should sit down," Donovan said. "It's bad news."

"What kind of bad news?"

"Mana's dead," Donovan said.

"Dead?" Kimo paled. "What do you mean, dead? He's not dead. I saw him yesterday."

"I'm sorry," Riga said. "It happened in the parking lot overlooking the lighthouse."

His brown eyes looked dazed. "Was he hit by a car?"

"Sharks' teeth. He vomited them." Riga gestured toward the space beside her. "Please, sit down."

"Shark..." Kimo placed a hand on the table. "How?"

Riga scooted, and Kimo sat beside her. "We think someone put them inside Mana," she said. "That it was murder."

"But... how?" His eyes narrowed. "Why are you two telling me this? Why not the police?"

"The police seem to think he swallowed the teeth himself," Riga said. "Something called a pica disorder."

"That's stupid. Why would Mana do that?"

"He wouldn't," Riga said. "He asked us to meet him. He said he had information about Dennis's murder."

Kimo's face clouded. "He couldn't."

"Did Mana live alone?" Riga asked.

"No. He has a girl. Damn. I wonder if she knows?"

Riga rolled a butter knife between her fingers. "Where does she live?"

He gave them an address.

"How well did Mana know Dennis?" Donovan asked.

"Dennis was around a lot. They joked together, but they didn't know each other – not well. At least, I didn't think so."

The waitress returned with their orange juice. Kimo waved her off.

"Dennis was more than just a family friend, wasn't he?" Donovan asked.

Kimo put his face in his hands, fingertips jammed into his black eyebrows, and sighed. He laid his hands on the table. "We're half-brothers." His lips twisted. "I'm the bastard son. Quite the cliché, eh? The dark-skinned outcast."

"Were you? An outcast?" Riga asked.

"I didn't find out about my father – none of us kids did – until after he died. He was like Washington with his slaves – knew it was wrong, but only set them free in his will." He folded his arms across his chest. "But dear old Dad didn't remember me in his will. Sure he stayed close, was always around to help my mother out. That's how Paul and Dennis and I knew each other growing up. But then he left it to my mother to tell us the truth after he was gone."

"How did Paul and Dennis react to the news?" Riga asked.

"How would you react?"

Donovan glanced around. The stained wood floor, the peeling paint, the cracked linoleum counter. "I take it Paul and Dennis decided not to share the wealth."

"I don't want his money. This restaurant, the boat, they're mine. I built them. My sweat. My brains." He mashed his finger on the table, beating out his point. He slid from the booth and stood. "But Dennis and Paul are okay. They're my brothers." Kimo laughed harshly. "Were my brothers, and Dennis isn't okay. He's dead, and now you tell me so is Mana. I don't know what Mana knew, or what he thought he knew."

"Whatever it was," Riga said, "someone thought it was worth killing for."

Kimo swore. "I can't believe this. Why would Mana meet you without telling me? I don't know who anyone is anymore." His mouth twisted. "You know even Townsend and I used to be friends? He'd sit right where you are, ordering up the eggs and extra bacon. Now he's siccing the animal police on me. Things used to be good on this island. Now everyone's gotten all bent up, turned around."

"If you know anything that might have a bearing on these deaths," Riga said, "no matter how strange or unimportant it may seem, please tell me. Or tell the police."

"I wish I did know something. Though sometimes, I think I don't want to know. Enjoy your breakfast. It's on the house." He turned and shuffled to the kitchen.

"What do you think?" she asked Donovan.

"I think the banana macadamia nut pancakes look excellent."

Riga made a face.

He pushed his menu aside. "I think it takes a remarkable person not to feel some resentment over being cut out of your father's will."

"Can people even do that today? Usually children have some legal standing, regardless of the will."

"It depends on the state and on how the will was written."

"If Kimo fought it in court, that will be a matter of public record."

He rubbed his jaw. "I'll ask Ellen to check, but I doubt Kimo fought it in court. He doesn't seem the type. Which isn't to say he didn't resent what happened."

"That George Washington comment... I wonder if it was really his father he was thinking of? Because unlike Washington, his father didn't do the right thing in the end. Kimo said his brothers didn't share the inheritance, but I wonder if Dennis has, now that he's gone?"

"Dennis didn't have any children – at least not that I know of. He may well have left his half-brother something in his estate."

"If he did," she said, "it's a motive."

"I thought we were going on the murder by magic theory."

"We are. I am. Black magic killed Mana, and the seals or mermaids have been sacrifices. But... Why kill Dennis? Was he just in the wrong place at the wrong time? Or was there something else? And if Dennis was a random killing, then what could Mana have possibly known about it that threatened the murderer? Was he a witness? Mana lives on the other side of the island. It's unlikely he just happened to be wandering that beach when Dennis was killed. No, the murderer – our necromancer – is somehow connected to Dennis and Mana."

The waitress returned. The two ordered.

After her skirts whisked behind the counter, Donovan said, "All right. You've made a good case. We'll talk to Mana's girlfriend. Maybe she can tell us what he's been up to. It's a shame we can't talk to Dennis, but I haven't seen his ghost. Is it too soon to conjure it?"

"It usually takes weeks, or even months, before a ghost will manifest after its death."

"Usually, but not always?" His eyes glinted.

"Not always," she said slowly. "It's worth a try."

"I love it when you agree with me."

Riga laughed. "Is that the only time you love me?"

His eyes darkened. "No."

Mana and his girlfriend, Teresa, lived in a concrete apartment complex just far enough from the water to miss an ocean view. They learned from a neighbor that Teresa was a teacher and at work, so Riga and Donovan played tourist, returning to the Spouting Horn.

Leaning over the fence, Donovan's arm around her waist, she watched the water blast through the hole in the rocks. Below her, just beyond the geyser, yellow police tape fluttered, the only sign of the murdered seal. Cloying tentacles of the dark magic remained, and Riga shivered, turning away.

Donovan followed her gaze across the parking lot, where vendors had set up stands sheltered by plastic awnings. "Retail therapy?"

Riga checked her watch. They still had several hours to go before school was out. "It's that or the beach, and I didn't bring my suit."

"Which raises all sorts of intriguing possibilities."

She smothered a laugh. "Thanks for reminding me we're on our honeymoon."

"If my masseur was right about love and happiness being the same, I'll never stop reminding you."

"A honeymoon that never ends? That's a nice fantasy."

"We'll always have the real world to contend with, but let's face it, your connection to the other world isn't exactly dull. Why not make the most of it?"

"Magic excites me," she admitted. The mystery slowly uncovered, the surprises, the satisfaction of a job well done. And she'd never failed to solve a case. She thought of Mana and his words to her, his fear of dying. "But it comes with some dark baggage."

They walked across the parking lot together to the long row of stalls.

Heat radiated off the asphalt, baking her feet through her thin-soled shoes. She ducked quickly beneath the shelter of a plastic tarp.

"You're not responsible for Mana's death," Donovan said, turning her to him. "We'll find the person who is."

"I know."

"But I can see a part of you loves the hunt."

"The mystery of that woman you met, the magic of that trail... It's fascinating." She laughed. "And I'd pay good money to see Brigitte covered in tiny handprints again." She examined a rope of green-tinted pearls.

"You'll look better in violet," he said.

She shot him a look. The stand didn't sell violet pearls. "I'll take them," she told the vendor.

Donovan shrugged. "I know about these things."

They frittered away more time with a walk along the beach and a late lunch at a local resort hotel. Then they waited in the car outside Teresa's apartment until she came home, a heavy book satchel slung over one narrow shoulder. Her blue and white print blouse was untucked from her skirt, her head bowed, her mahogany hair tied in a loose bun.

They watched her trudge up the concrete stairs, unlock her door, and go inside. Reluctance fell like a wall around Riga, but she opened the car door, stepped out.

Silently, they crossed the patch of faded lawn, walked up the steps. Teresa opened the door before Riga finished knocking.

"Yes?" Her expression was wary, demanding, her eyes pink, the skin around them swollen.

"My name is Riga Hayworth. This is my husband, Donovan Mosse. We were with Mana yesterday, when he died."

Teresa bit her lip, appraising them.

Riga pulled out her investigator's license. "I'm a private investigator."

Teresa took the license and stared at it for a long moment. She handed it back. "Come in."

Inside the apartment, light filtered dimly through the drawn vertical blinds. A recliner in an indeterminate shade of neutral and with a wide sag in the middle sat angled toward a small television.

Teresa motioned them toward the nubby couch. She perched across from them, on the edge of the recliner, hands clasped on her knees. "You were with him? Was he...? Was he in much pain?"

Yes. Most definitely.

"It was quick," Donovan said.

Teresa looked down at her shoes, black and coated with dust. "I didn't know he..." She stood and shambled to the kitchen. "I'm sorry. May I offer you something? Some ice water?"

"Ice water would be great," Donovan said.

"This whole day – this whole week – has been terrible. Did you know I had to break up a fight at school today? It was an actual brawl." Theresa laughed shakily. "I've never seen anything like it. These are grade-schoolers." She returned with their drinks, ice tinkling in the tall glasses.

Theresa sat, tucking her skirt beneath her. "The police said it was an eating disorder. Pica? I had to look it up. He ate a lot." She smiled at this. "But I never saw him eat anything strange." She looked away, blinking rapidly.

Riga leaned forward, unconsciously imitating the woman. "Did Mana tell you why he wanted to meet with us yesterday?"

"No. He just said he had business. Why *did* he want to meet you?"

"He told us he had information about the death of Dennis Glasgow."

She blinked. "The man killed beside the seal? That's..." Her teeth pulled at her lower lip.

"That's what?" Riga prodded.

"He was upset by the seal killings. Worried. Mana wasn't a fan of the seals. He once told me that environmental group – the Protection Society – was a form of mainland oppression. But the killings disturbed him."

"Do you know why?"

"They disturbed me too. They're just innocent animals. I never asked Mana why."

"What else did he tell you about them?" Riga asked.

"Not much. He was worried. He said someone was stirring up trouble. But I don't know what information he'd have about Mr. Glasgow's murder."

"Did you ever meet Dennis Glasgow?" Riga asked. "Or his brother?"

"No."

Donovan's hands dangled between his knees. "Is there anything else you can think of? Anything Mana might have said about the seals, or Dennis Glasgow, or the murder?"

She shook her head.

He rose and handed her his card. "If you think of anything, please give us a call."

"Was there anything... Did he say anything before he died?" Teresa asked.

"He said..." Riga hesitated. "He told us he loved you."

Teresa wept.

They said their goodbyes and left. Riga and Donovan didn't speak until they'd reached the Ferrari.

Donovan started the engine. "That was kind of you."

"She shouldn't have to remember him dying in fear."

"If his girlfriend is being honest, Mana was a more nuanced character than I gave him credit for."

"Mm." Riga buckled her seatbelt. "I wonder if the seal killings worried him generally, or more particularly? He knew something. The killings must have touched someone in his circle."

They looked at each other. "Kimo," they said in unison.

"What isn't Kimo telling us?" Riga asked. "Mana seemed to be protecting him when we met with Kimo yesterday. Was he meeting us to rat him out, or did he know something else?"

"Whatever it is, he'll spit it out eventually. I know Kimo's type. He's thinking it over, weighing the pros and cons. But he'll make the right decision."

Riga's stomach tightened. She only hoped he made his decision in time.

CHAPTER 18

OVER HANALEI BAY, THE setting sun turned the clouds to orange and violet flames. The police tape had vanished. There was no sign that days ago, a murdered man and mermaid had lain together on this spot of beach.

With a stick, Riga drew a circle in the sand around the site. Other tourists had come to watch the sunset over the bay, but they stayed apart from Riga and Donovan, wanting their own private moments, or sensing the coil of death magic that Riga had begun to conjure.

A beagle ran past, and Donovan herded the small dog away from her circle. "Maybe we should have waited until midnight," he said.

"Sunset is an in-between time, and if Dennis's ghost is waiting to manifest, it's in the in-between. Besides, I'm getting impatient."

"No argument there. This necromancer is really pissing me off." He tilted his head, clapped one hand to his eye, and gazed at her work. "Your circle looks like Australia."

"Argh." She kicked some of the sand away, redrew the circle with her stick, and added protective symbols for good measure. They were misshapen in the uneven sand, but they'd work.

He rubbed his jaw. "You're not using blood this time, are you?"

"For a summoning?" She snorted. "No. I could do this in my sleep."

"Good. So what would you consider a safe distance?"

"Donovan—"

"Can you blame me? The last time I was involved in a summoning it killed me."

She grimaced. "No, I can't blame you." She rummaged in the bag at her feet and tossed him what was left of the red salt. "Make a circle around you with the intention that it will protect you. And make it a small circle. You don't want any breaks in it, and we're low on salt."

She closed her eyes and called to the ghost of Dennis Glasgow, pulling from the in-between, envisioning him inside her circle in the sand. Her eyes opened.

The circle was empty.

Donovan raised an eyebrow. "Hm."

"I did say it was early," Riga said. "His ghost might not be available yet."

She closed her eyes and thought again of Dennis Glasgow. Thought of him sprawled on the sand beside the murdered seal, imagined him alive, striding through the lobby in his hotel jacket. Riga extended her senses and summoned. Her hair lifted, as if stirred by a breeze.

"Now that was unexpected," Donovan said.

She looked. A figure glowed inside her circle, imprisoned by the symbols she'd drawn in the sand. Long, green hair. Pearlescent skin. Tail. The mermaid hissed, exposing pointed teeth. With a thrust of her tail, she surged, snakelike, toward the edge of the circle.

Riga took an involuntary step back, but the circle held. The creature swayed, head swiveling to see what had trapped her, tail lashing angrily.

Riga glanced toward the tourists admiring the sky. Unless one of them had the talent, they wouldn't be able to perceive the mermaid's ghost.

Donovan stepped from his protective circle and paced around the mermaid. "So that's what mermaids look like."

"Dead mermaids." She shouldn't have thought of the seal. Oh well, angry mermaid was what she got, and she'd have to make the best of it.

"Mermaid," Riga said, "I've summoned you to learn who ended your life. My intention is to bring your killer to justice. What can you tell me about the person who did this to you?"

The mermaid hissed. She clawed at the invisible barrier.

"Listen to me," Riga snapped.

The mermaid froze, head cocked.

Riga sighed. Before she'd learned about her necromantic heritage, she'd taken it for granted that the dead obeyed her commands. Now, she wasn't sure she liked the talent.

"I want to find the human who killed you," Riga said, "and stop him from killing any more of your sisters. Tell me what you saw the night you died."

Images flooded Riga's mind. She felt herself flying with the current, cool against her skin. Breaking the surface, saltwater streaming down her face. She wriggled onto the sand, and the sunlight on the beach turned to darkness.

The crunch of sand beneath heavy feet. Garbled voices, one high-pitched, one low. A departure, and silence. A new presence. Low voices. Malice. A soft popping noise, unnatural. She looked up, interested. A figure loomed. Then darkness.

Riga sighed. "She's given me all she can." To the spirit, "You can go." The mermaid vanished.

"Well?" Donovan asked.

"It was dark, and she wasn't paying attention until the end. Dennis was shot first, by a man, I think, and using a silencer. The mermaid hadn't understood their words, but their voices were masculine."

"That narrows the field."

"Not by much." She kicked the sand, breaking the circle, obscuring the symbols.

"Come on." Donovan pulled her against his chest. "Let's get dinner."

"The hotel?"

He nodded. "That's where our prime suspect is."

"Paul. He is the man with the easiest access, isn't he? I wonder where he was last night, when the second seal was killed?"

"Mr. Mosse?" a woman's voice called.

Trudging through the sand, Sarah, Paul's assistant, waved to them. She broke into a trot, her long, black ponytail bouncing behind her. "I thought that was you," she said, panting. She handed Donovan a file folder. "Here are the documents you requested. Paul said he could go over them in the morning with you, if you like."

Donovan frowned. "He's not free tonight?"

"No, he has to go to Kapaa to meet with a supplier."

"Mm..." Donovan flipped through the file and squinted at it in the dying light.

"How have you been doing?" Riga asked her.

Sarah swallowed. "Things are getting better. Paul had a meeting with the staff today and let them know that business was continuing as usual. I think it relieved some tension."

"I'm not surprised they're worried," Riga said. "A potential buyer, new heirs…"

Sarah's dark brow wrinkled. "There aren't any heirs. He explained about the insurance – that Mrs. Glasgow won't be a shareholder."

"What about Dennis's half-brother?" Riga asked.

Sarah pursed her lips. "I didn't realize you knew about Kimo."

So it wasn't a complete secret. "They were fairly close, weren't they?" Riga asked. "I can't believe Dennis would have left Kimo out in the cold."

She crossed her arms over her chest. "He didn't. Dennis left Kimo an annuity. He bought it not long after his father's death. Dennis knew Kimo wouldn't accept his father's money, so it's sort of like an insurance policy, paying out to Kimo after Dennis died. He was very generous."

"I told you Dennis had his financial affairs in order," Donovan said to Riga. "Sarah, is there anything you want me to know about these files before I go through them?"

"It's all in the notes on the first page."

"Perfect," he said.

"By the way," Riga said, "do you know where Paul was last night? We tried to get hold of him and couldn't."

"No. I left the hotel at eight o'clock. What Paul did afterward was his own business." She shot Riga a disapproving look and hurried away across the sand.

"She's protective of Paul too," Riga said.

"Don't tell me you think there's something between the two of them now."

"No," she said. "I think she's young."

"And?"

"And I don't know about you, but when I was her age, I wasn't half as smart as I thought I was."

"Hm. When I was her age, I'd just turned around my first casino."

"Ah," she said. "Right. You actually *were* as clever as you thought you were."

"Though I will grant you that I've improved with age."

"And you've never suffered from false modesty."

His brows drew together. "Why would I?"

She laughed. "No reason at all. Sexy, smart, successful. How did I get so lucky?"

"I wonder the same thing about myself. It doesn't sound like Paul has left yet. Shall we try to follow? Dinner and a stakeout?"

She threaded her arm through his, enjoyed the feel of his warmth pressing against her side. "It's a date."

CHAPTER 19

"WHEN I SUGGESTED DINNER, this wasn't exactly what I had in mind." In the Ferrari, Donovan balanced his paper cup against a bacon cheeseburger, wrapped in oily paper.

They were parked on a narrow road lined with warehouses. Twenty feet ahead, a streetlamp flickered.

Riga pressed the binoculars to her eyes. The lighted window of a cleaning company leapt into view.

Their car sat at the far end of the block, well away from their quarry. They'd put the top up, so it wasn't quite so obvious two people were seated inside. But they were conspicuous in the Ferrari.

But when they'd spotted Paul leaving the hotel, they hadn't had time to get a different car. He'd led them south to the town of Kapaa. Thanks to the darkness and Donovan keeping well back, Paul hadn't spotted them. Yet.

"Haven't you heard?" she asked. "Stakeout food is calorie free."

Paul crossed in front of the window, motioning emphatically with both hands.

"I'm not worried about the calories," Donovan said.

She rested the binoculars in her lap and grinned. "No, you certainly don't need to." But she should. The older she got, the faster time moved and the slower her metabolism.

"Is he doing anything interesting?"

"No." She handed him the binoculars. "Maybe it really is just a late business meeting."

Donovan snorted. "The supplier should be coming to Paul, not the other way around. Hold on." He leaned forward. "Kimo's in there."

Someone banged on the Ferrari's window. She jerked in her seat.

A broad, dark face scowled at her. He held a baseball bat in one hand and looked vaguely familiar. Keeping her eyes on the bat, Riga wracked her brain to remember where she'd seen him before. She cracked the window. "Yes?"

"What are you two doing here?"

"What are you doing here?" she countered.

"I asked you first."

"I don't think that should matter. We're just sitting here on the street, minding our own business."

"The hell you are. Get outta here."

"Haven't I seen you someplace before?" She snapped her fingers. "I know, you're—"

Donovan leaned across her. "Thank you. We'll be going now." He started the car, and they roared off. "Correct me if I'm wrong, darling, but isn't surveillance supposed to be covert? After that performance – entertaining as it was – that guy's sure to remember us."

"We're in a Ferrari. He'd remember us no matter what I said."

"And on that note, let's get a drink." He made a sharp turn, and they were back on the main road, cruising slowly through town.

"Was I wrong in thinking I'd seen that guy before?" she asked.

"He was in Kimo's restaurant."

"Ah, you're right. That's where it was." Having a partner with a memory for faces had its benefits.

Donovan parked the Ferrari in a lot behind a two-story, tin-roofed building. Blue paint flaked off the aging wooden boards. They walked up the back steps, music and light and laughter gushing from the open windows above.

Miraculously, a small table near the bar cleared up as they entered, and they found seats in the crush of people. Riga ordered a pineapple martini, Donovan a brandy.

"Do you remember that lighthouse keeper we met?" she asked. "The one who'd had too much to drink?"

"Yes, he said he was a friend of the Glasgows."

"He seemed torn up over Dennis's murder, and the lighthouse was where Mana was killed. I'd like to talk to him."

One corner of his mouth quirked upward. "Grasping at straws?"

"At straws, mermaids, menehunes... Anyone who'll talk to me. To us," she corrected. "And we should take another look at the Protection Society, find out what they know about the seal killed at the Spouting Hole."

"I don't suppose they can protect every seal that turns up on a Kauai beach."

"No," she said. "But if I wanted to kill seals, the Society would be a great place to infiltrate. They must be notified somehow when seals come ashore. I wonder where that information is kept and how it's disseminated."

"And the fellow who runs the place, Townsend, knew Dennis."

The waitress returned with their drinks.

Riga stabbed her pineapple wedge with the plastic sword. "Everybody knew Dennis. He was a regular man about town."

"So is his brother. It will be interesting to hear his explanation about this late-night trip to the cleaners tomorrow."

"If he gives you one."

"He will if he wants to sell this property." Donovan set his jaw.

"What do you think of Dennis's widow, Deidre?"

"She's obviously going through a difficult time."

"And she leans a lot on Paul," she said. "Too much?"

"You're not suggesting there's something between them?"

"I have no evidence of it," she said carefully. But Deidre was too eager to clear Paul's good name. And Riga saw guilt in the way Deidre avoided her brother-in-law's gaze as she reached for his touch.

"If something happened to me," Donovan said, "I'd hope my family would help you."

"Mm." She plunged the sword into the pineapple. Donovan's closest family was his cousin, Reuben. He tolerated her rarely and randomly.

"Have you talked to your niece yet?" he asked.

"No." She grimaced. She'd been so caught up in the murders she'd forgotten all about Pen. Riga dug her phone out of her purse. "Do you mind?"

"Go ahead."

Riga wound her way through the crowd, to the back door. She walked down to the parking lot and the roar from the bar fell to a dull rumble.

Pen answered on the third ring. "Hey, how's Hawaii?"

Riga jammed a finger in one ear. "It's... great. Brigitte is here."

"I told her not to bug you, but you know Brigitte."

"How are things on your end? Any problems?"

"Mom's being haunted by her teenage boyfriend," Pen said. "It's totally gross."

"Does she know?"

Pen snorted. "Puh-leese. Mom doesn't believe in ghosts."

They talked ghost management strategies, then Pen said, "Oh, I got a kind of weird message for you from someone named Sal."

Riga tensed. Sal was a shaman who worked with faeries. The relationship between the two women was challenging. If Sal was calling, it couldn't be good news.

"What did she want?" Riga asked.

"She said she'd been trying to call you, but it hadn't gone through. I didn't tell her that you'd changed your phone number. I wasn't sure who you wanted to know about it."

The noise from the bar rose, and Riga edged further into the parking lot. "Thanks. I am trying to keep it quiet, but Sal's okay. Did she say anything else?"

"She said, and I quote, 'shit's getting weird again, kinda like the last time.' And if you had anything to do with it, to cut it out."

Riga mouthed a curse. "And are things getting weird?" she asked lightly.

There was a brief silence. "You haven't been watching the news, have you?"

"Not on my honeymoon."

"Yeah, well, ignorance is bliss," Pen said.

"You see that on a t-shirt?"

"There was a riot in San Francisco yesterday. Two people were killed."

Ants crawled up Riga's spine. She looked up at the clouds obscuring the stars. So the conflicts were spreading. The spell was widening. "What started it?"

"No one can figure that out."

A barstool clattered to the pavement beside her. Riga yelped and skittered sideways.

"What?" Pen asked. "What's wrong?"

In the bar above, a woman screamed. A man tumbled from the open window and landed on the stairs. People poured out the door, down the steps, and he disappeared in a sea of feet.

"Nothing," Riga said. "I gotta go. Keep your head down."

She jammed the phone in her pocket and started toward the steps, knowing she'd never get through that crowd, up the stairs. But Donovan was inside and –

A hand grasped her wrist, and she spun around. Looked down.

The little man adjusted his fishing hat and tsked. "Bad dream. That's no place for you, sorceress."

Riga pinched herself. *No, not a dream.* She angled her wrist free. "My husband is in there, Menehune."

His face creased with pleasure. "Yes, and he wants you to stay here."

"How do you know what he wants?" she argued, knowing the mene-hune was right. Donovan wouldn't want her in that mess.

"Your husband has beautiful dreams. Powerful dreams. That's why he has such strong mana."

Three men struggled against the open window. Two fell out and into the crowd below.

"I have to help him," she said, starting forward.

"No."

Her feet anchored to the pavement. She struggled to lift them, failed. Riga twisted toward the menehune.

He was gone.

"Let me go!" she shouted to no one.

And then it ended. The flow of people from the restaurant stopped. In the parking lot, the crowd dissipated, faces filled with shock and confusion.

The spell released her, and she was running across the lot, up the stairs, into the empty bar. Tables and chairs were overturned. Spilled drinks pooled on the floorboards, drowning broken glass and paper umbrellas.

Donovan stood behind the bar, his hand on a waitress's shoulder. An elderly couple huddled beside him. Two other waitresses clutched a beefy man wearing a manager tag on his Hawaiian shirt.

Riga's legs wobbled. "Donovan."

He turned to her and smiled. "I knew you'd have the sense to stay in the parking lot. We're okay." He said something in a low voice to the waitress, and she nodded, her blue eyes wide.

Unsteadily, Riga walked to the bar. "What happened in here?"

"One minute I was having a drink, thinking about that leiomano, and the next minute, the bar exploded. I started grabbing waitresses and putting them behind the bar."

"And me," the old woman chirped up. She adjusted her muumuu, an orange and red bird of paradise pattern.

Her husband rubbed his head. An angry mark swelled on his temple, and he sagged against the counter. "I don't know what happened."

"I'll call an ambulance." One of the waitresses hurried away.

Riga raised her brows, her mouth dry. "You grabbed the waitresses."

"There were several nearby, and behind the bar seemed the safest place," Donovan said.

"You saved our lives." The old woman's voice quavered.

"No," Donovan said, "if your husband hadn't been sucker punched... Riga? Are you all right?"

Riga sank onto the single barstool that remained upright.

Swiftly, Donovan came around the bar. "You weren't hurt, were you?"

"No. But I saw our menehune friend. And did you know there was a riot in San Francisco yesterday? I thought whatever the necromancer was doing was limited to this island, but the conflicts are spreading."

"Pen wasn't involved, was she?"

"No. Pen's fine. I'm just..." *Confused, relieved, terrified.* "Glad you're okay. Can we get out of here?" *Before the police come.*

"Of course."

"Sir." The restaurant manager held out his hand. "Next time you're here, drinks are on me."

Hurry, hurry, hurry. Riga shifted her weight as the two men shook hands. The cops had to be on their way, and she did not want another encounter. Then the old man insisted on shaking hands with Donovan. One of the waitresses gave him a hug. Riga wanted to scream.

Finally, they were trotting down the restaurant stairs and getting into the Ferrari.

"You say a menehune was here?" He started the car and pulled from the driveway and into the street. A siren wailed in the distance.

"Not *a* menehune. *The* menehune." She looked behind her. Two police cars were pulling into the parking lot they'd just left. That had been close. "The one who keeps offering me candy, though he didn't offer me any tonight. He stopped me from going back inside."

"I'm glad."

"He said you would be. At the risk of sounding egotistical, I thought the menehune was appearing to me because of my magic. But I think he's here because of you."

"Now you're just feeding my ego."

"When you were attacked by something and suddenly let go – he was on the beach. He told me that you dreamed powerful dreams, that you had big energy. He stopped me from returning inside because it was what you wanted."

"For some reason Hawaiians love Vegas. Maybe he's a fan of the casino."

"Donovan—"

"If he's interested in me, I'm as much in the dark as you are as to why."

"Have you been to the islands before?"

"Yes, but not to this island. And we didn't sense any magic on the other islands. Or did you?"

"No. I mean, yes, there's magic everywhere, but nothing on the other island that involved us, nothing personal." She turned in her seat. "Grabbing waitresses? Really?"

"You know what brawls are like. The best thing you can do is get out of the way."

She gave him a look.

"The waitresses were in danger," he said. "And portable."

Riga laughed. "And the elderly couple?"

"Ah. The man got knocked down. I think someone kicked him in the head. They needed help."

"You really are a hero," she said, rueful.

"On occasion."

CHAPTER 20

THEY DROVE ALONG THE dark highway, Riga's jaw lit by the phone she held to her ear. If Sal was concerned enough to try to track her down through Pen, the faery shaman deserved a call.

"This is Sal."

"It's Riga. Pen said you tried to call me."

"Is this your new number? What – are you so high and mighty now you get a private number?"

"Sal..." The car rounded a tight bend, and she grabbed the door handle for balance.

"Sorry." Donovan eased off the accelerator.

"Everything's out of balance," Sal said. "Have you felt it?"

"I've seen it. Pen told me about the riot in San Francisco. And Donovan and I just escaped a bar fight. What have you sensed?"

"Water. All I see is water rising, churning. I've heard there's a whirlpool somewhere in the Pacific, but the news isn't reporting it."

"Then where did you hear it?"

Sal made an exasperated sound. "From our network. Or I should say *my* network? When are you going to join?"

Metaphysical practitioners tended to stick together, and in the internet age the network had become overwhelming. Riga avoided it. "I'm not a joiner. Besides, why join when I've got you to fill me in?"

"Now you're just being aggravating."

"We're tracking someone in Kauai who's been ritually killing mermaids. A necromancer. I can't see how it would reach as far as San Francisco, but it might be the cause of the water problems."

"You make it sound like a plumbing issue."

"Well?" Riga asked. "Could the spell extend that far?"

There was a long pause. "Yeah. If they've been murdered in a magical ritual, that might get the attention of a sea goddess. And goddess energy can go big, especially when combined with elemental energies."

"That's not good."

"No." Another pause. "You need help out there?"

"She asks with obvious reluctance." Riga smiled crookedly.

"Can you blame me?"

"No. I'll keep you posted." Riga hung up.

Donovan chanced a quick look at her. "What have you got?"

"I'm not sure. Sal says she's sensing a disturbance in the water element, which makes sense given the dead mermaids. She seems to think it's connected to the rioting, but I don't see it. Symbolically, water is traditionally connected to the emotions. And as humans we're composed mainly of water. But..." The explanation didn't satisfy her. There had to be more. "We're missing a piece of the puzzle."

They drove into the hotel's circular drive, and a valet hurried to help Riga out of the car. Hand in hand, Riga and Donovan walked the outdoor path to their bungalow.

Once inside, he tossed his room key on the bed. "I'm going for a swim. Join me?"

"After what happened at Na Pali?" She frowned. "I'm not sure that's such a good idea."

"We need answers. You said we needed to talk to everyone, including mermaids. You got something from the dead one – why don't we try some live ones?"

She blew out her breath and looked at the ceiling. He was right. The mermaids were potential witnesses. Dangerous potential witnesses.

"Assuming the mermaids were at Na Pali," he said, "they came to us there for a reason."

"They tried to drown you."

"They didn't try very hard."

"Under normal conditions, I would interview friends of the victim, and the mermaid was a victim. But they're water fae. We don't know how they'll react. It's a risk."

"A calculated risk."

Was it worth it? Two men were dead, the aggression was spreading, and they still didn't know the necromancer's end game. If mermaids were the real targets, they might have information she could use.

If they were targets. If they knew anything. If they could be trusted.

And if the spell continued to spread, then what?

If.

She nodded. "Okay."

"I think it's enough that one of us goes in the water. They approached me last time. It's best you stay on shore."

"If you go, I go. I'm not letting you out of my sight."

He unbuttoned his shirt and pulled it over his head. "You make me sound like one of your suspects."

"More like a riddle."

"Wrapped in an enigma?" He closed the gap between them. "At least you won't get bored."

She circled his neck with her arms. "With you? Never."

A dark object whooshed into the room. Donovan pivoted, putting himself between Riga and the open window.

Brigitte landed on the dresser. She scrabbled for purchase, scarring the wood, and Riga winced. That was going to cost them.

"I hope your day has been as productive as mine," Brigitte said.

Donovan's lips tipped upward. He strode to the other room, grabbing his swim trunks off the dresser as he passed.

"What did you learn?" Riga said, grinding her teeth.

"Ze elementals, they may be more dangerous than we thought."

Riga paused. "More dangerous than earthquakes and windstorms?"

"More dangerous to humans."

"How?"

"And well you may ask. I had to go to one of ze other islands and study ze petroglyphs there. Ze spirit of a..." Brigitte sniffed. "Is there a ghost in here?"

Riga looked around. "I don't see one."

"Hmph. Of course you know, I have a great sympathy with all things stone. It speaks to me. However, ze petroglyphs were unclear. In fact, it was very strange, because they seemed to indicate ze earth element controls humans."

"Earth? I just got off the phone with Sal. She said water was causing the problems."

"Who are you going to trust? Me? Or a shaman who consorts with faeries?"

"So how is earth dangerous?"

Brigitte shrugged, her stone feathers rippling. "Because it rules your nature."

Riga clawed a hand through her hair. "But how?"

"How? How? How should I know? That is what I am trying to tell you. Ze petroglyphs were vague."

"All right," Riga said. "But if that's true, it would have been nice if one of the Hawaiian shamans I've spoken with had mentioned it."

"Did you ask them?"

"Of course I asked about the elementals."

Brigitte tossed her head. "Riga. Everybody knows that ze Hawaiian shaman does not volunteer information. They will only answer ze questions you ask."

Riga's eyes narrowed. "Everybody knows?"

"Well, I have only learned of it recently, but you must have heard or read it in your research. It is their way of understanding if you are ready for ze information. Only those who are ready will ask ze right questions. And then they may have ze answers."

Logical. And annoying. Riga rubbed the bridge of her nose. "At least now I know to ask. That is good information, Brigitte."

"And what did you learn?"

"We have more leads, more suspicions, but no real idea yet who the necromancer is. But we're getting closer," she said with more certainty than she felt.

"That is all? You are losing your edge."

"I'm on my honeymoon. Besides, there's more to me than sharp edges."

"Yes, and your soft parts are all boring."

Donovan strolled into the bedroom, a towel slung over one bare shoulder. "I disagree. You coming?"

"Yes," Riga said, "just let me change."

"What?" Brigitte asked. "What is happening? Where are you going?"

Riga rummaged in the dresser for her swimsuit. "Swimming."

"Swimming? This is no time for swimming."

"It's been a long day." Riga found her suit and headed for the bathroom.

"Healthy mind, healthy body," Donovan was saying as she closed the door.

When she reemerged, the gargoyle was gone. "Where's Brigitte?"

"She went for a flight. Riga, there's something we need to talk about. When we go home—"

"Brigitte is banned from the bedroom."

"Thank you."

Riga followed him out to the beach, passing the ghost woman on the rocks. The spirit stared morosely toward the bay and the moonlit patterns in the sand.

Donovan plunged into the low waves, a gleaming arrow in the moonlight. Riga followed more slowly, shivering as she stuck her toes in the water.

"Don't," a woman said behind her.

Riga turned.

The ghost on the rocks reached toward her. Water streamed down her body, soaking her bathing suit. "Don't. He'll hurt you."

"Donovan? Why do you think that?"

"He'll hurt you."

"Did someone hurt you?" Riga asked. "What's your name?"

The ghost vanished, a mournful whisper in the wind.

Riga pressed her lips together. The ghost would reappear when she was able. But at least the ghost had reached out to Riga, which meant she was ready to talk. Soon Riga'd be able to put that mystery to bed.

She walked further into the water, flinching as it rose inch by inch, past her thighs, waist, chest. Riga stubbed her toe on a smooth rock and wobbled, fighting for balance.

Donovan popped up beside her. "Darling, you're torturing yourself. Just go under."

She slid her hands around his waist. He was warm, so warm. "We're here to find mermaids, not for aquatic therapy."

"I thought we were here, so they would find us." Donovan lurched backwards, taking her under with him. She came up laughing and spluttering.

"Stay here, close to shore." He knifed through the water towards a buoy, his strokes long and sure.

"Donovan!"

He didn't respond, probably couldn't hear her.

"I guess we're going deeper." She dove after him. The salt stung her eyes, and she wondered why she bothered trying to see in the stygian bay.

A bell rang. Had he reached the buoy? She plunged onward then stopped to look up and get her bearings.

Something brushed her leg, and her heart jumped. She hissed an indrawn breath. "Donovan? I really hope that was you."

"What?" He waved from the buoy.

"Something's out here." Scenes from *Jaws*, stories of night-feeding animals, flashed through her mind. "I really hope it's a mermaid. Sort of hope," she muttered.

A woman's head emerged from the water beside her, her hair a black cascade.

Riga blew out her breath. "Ah. You scared me."

The woman bared her teeth, jagged and animal-like.

Uneasy, Riga licked her lips, salty from the sea. Donovan had been right. The mermaids had come. Why didn't that make her happy? She treaded water, edging closer to the shore. "My name is Riga."

The mermaid licked her lips, as if mimicking her.

"We're here to help you," Riga said. "Someone's been killing your sisters on land. We're trying to stop—"

Hands grasped her ankles, dragging her under.

You killed our sisters.

Riga thrashed, helpless against the pull. Her muscles and lungs burned. She was going to die, to drown, just as the ghost had warned. She powered her legs, but the hands held her fast. Riga's torso twisted in the water. Sparks burst behind her eyes.

And now we'll take what you love.

Donovan? Where was he? Were they drowning him as well? Riga curled her fingers into claws, slashed downward, didn't connect. She jackknifed her body, tried to pry the webbed hands from her ankles.

Laughter burbled from the depths.

A wave of hot rage rolled through her, unreasoning and wild. Energy pulled from the in-between surged down her arms and through her hands.

A wrench, and she flew backwards, up and out of the water. She landed hard, sand and gravel scraping her flesh. Something jammed her shoulder blade, and she cried out in pain.

"Riga!" Donovan ran up the beach and dropped to his knees beside her. Lightly, he ran his hands over her body. He touched her shoulder and grimaced. "Where's your bag?"

She coughed. "Wherever we went into the water."

"Can you walk?"

"Yeah." She staggered to her feet.

He clamped his hand to her shoulder blade and pushed her forward. She hissed. Pain burned through her.

"You've got a puncture wound in your shoulder," he said. "We need to keep pressure on it. It might need stitches."

"Mermaids," she said, dazed. "They blame me for the deaths. Did you see them?"

"Not directly." He found the bag and slung it over his shoulder. Donovan pressed a towel from it to her shoulder blade. "Let's go."

"Water faeries." She wheezed. "Is no place sacred?"

"From now on, we'll stick to the pool." He steered her up the beach and into the hotel lobby. In low tones, he explained the problem to the desk clerk. They took Riga to the manager's office. Donovan sat beside her, keeping the towel pressed to her wound.

"I'm really starting to dislike mermaids," she said.

Paramedics. A stretcher. And she was on her stomach. A ride in an ambulance. The hospital. Burning antiseptic. Stitches.

But the wound – a gouge from driftwood she'd landed on – wasn't as bad as it had looked. It was still dark when they returned to the hotel. Half asleep, she stumbled into bed.

When she awoke, sun streamed through the open glass doors. The sheets rustled, and the bed shifted.

"She is awake," Brigitte said.

Riga sat up. Her shoulder ached and itched. She reached over her shoulder and found a thick gauze pad stuck to her skin.

Donovan, dressed in khakis and a loose black shirt, set an orange bottle of pills on the table by the bed. He sat beside her. "Three times a day with meals."

"Thanks," she said.

"For leaving you when I should have stayed by your side?" he asked bitterly.

She looked at him. Why had he left? And then the answer dawned. "You thought they'd come for you. You were drawing them away from me."

"Unsuccessfully."

"We took a risk."

"You warned me against it."

"But I don't regret trying. It was a risk. It went badly. It happens. What exactly *did* happen, by the way?"

"Brigitte drove the mermaids off after you flew out of the water." He sat beside her on the bed. "You?"

Riga ran her hand through her hair, thick with salt from last night's swim. "I'm not sure if the mermaids blame me personally for what's happening, or just all necromancers. One dragged me under and I... reacted."

He raised an eyebrow. "Some reaction."

"You were airborne," Brigitte said. "And you were not meant to fly."

"Yeah," Riga said. "I'll need to learn to control that someday."

"Some day?" Brigitte snarled. "You learned a spell that is useful and did not discuss it with me? I am your familiar. When you learn new things, it should be with me."

"I know lots of spells that are useful." Most just didn't work anymore.

"So what was it?" Brigitte demanded. "What was ze spell?"

"It's sort of... an expulsion spell?" Riga said.

Brigitte flapped her wings. "Why are you asking me? How should I know?"

"Look, whatever the spell was, I'm not going in the ocean again until this case is over." And maybe not after that.

She swung her legs out of bed and stretched, wincing at the pull of tape on skin, at the ache in her shoulder. "What time is it?"

Donovan checked his watch. "Nine o'clock."

"Late," Brigitte said. "You are supposed to be catching a necromancer, not frolicking with ze mermaids and lying about in bed."

"We were hardly frolicking," Riga said.

"Then what are your investigative plans for ze day?"

"I'd like to speak to that lighthouse keeper," Riga said. "And the ghost approached me last night. If she died at the hotel, someone here must know what happened, and it may be connected to what's going on now. I need to do some research. Knowing more about how she died and who she is might help me connect with her."

Donovan frowned. "It shouldn't be hard to find the lighthouse keeper. But are you sure you're up for it?"

"The doctor said I was fine, as long as I keep the stitches dry and avoid contact sports."

"All right," he said. "Why don't you get dressed, and we'll get some breakfast? Maybe we can get some answers on our ghost from the hotel staff."

"I love the way you combine business with pleasure," Riga said.

Brigitte huffed. "Yes, it is very convenient."

"And Brigitte and I can have a talk while I'm getting ready," Riga said.

Donovan winked. "I'll be back." He walked out the rear doors and disappeared past the banyan tree.

"You've been rather short with Donovan," Riga said.

"I? Short? I have no idea what you mean."

"Is something bothering you?"

"Let us see. A necromancer is trying to destroy ze world. Mermaids are trying to kill you. We are being menaced by menehunes... and you didn't even ask how long it took me to remove those terrible handprints."

"How did you get them off?"

"They were only powder, as Monsieur Mosse had suggested. But it took me quite some time in ze water, and as you know, I do not float. It was not a simple matter."

"You can hardly blame Donovan for that."

"No. But there is something different about him. You are both behaving strangely."

"Yeah. We're happy. We're on our honeymoon." She strolled to the closet and ran her fingers over the clothing. No tank tops, not with the giant gauze patch on her shoulder blade. She pulled out a lightweight blouse.

"Oh, please. You have always been happy, most especially when you were miserable. It is more than that," Brigitte said. "Your husband's magic is returning. Can you not feel it?"

"I don't think his magic ever really left," Riga said slowly. "We just never knew exactly what it was."

"So *he* says."

Riga turned, a pair of wide-legged slacks in one hand. "Brigitte, I'm starting to think you're jealous."

"Jealous? Me? Ridiculous." The gargoyle sniffed. "I simply have your best interests at heart."

"I know things have changed for us. But you haven't lost a magician. You've gained a... person with some very strong and mysterious magic that we don't understand. Instead of one magician, you have an entire family. Think of the possibilities."

"What possibilities?"

"Well, first to learn more about Donovan's magic. But then..." She trailed off, unsure of the then.

"I see," Brigitte mused. "Yes. He will need my guidance even more than you do. And then there is Pen, our brave young magician. She shall be a challenge."

"I'm confident you're up for it."

"Well, of course I am up for it. What have I not been up for? I supported you through enchantment, alchemy, shamanism..."

Riga started for the bathroom before remembering she couldn't get the stitches wet. She contemplated angles of water and realized there was no way she could wash her hair today. She knotted it at the back of her head and showered carefully. And though she wasn't head-to-toe clean, she felt better.

When she returned to the bedroom, Brigitte was gone. Riga wandered through the sitting room and spotted her husband lounging on a chair by their pool. She came to stand beside him. "Hungry?"

"Ravenous. By the way, what *did* the doctor mean when he said no contact sports?"

She slipped her arms around him. "I don't think the honeymoon is over quite yet."

CHAPTER 21

THE HOTEL DINING ROOM was packed with people and good smells – frying bacon, syrups, and a tropical breeze heady with sea air and vegetation.

"There's Sarah." Donovan nudged Riga. He pointed to a woman half-hidden by a potted palm. "Maybe she can give us some straight answers about our ghost." They walked toward the executive assistant.

Sarah pushed the remains of a poached egg and toast about her plate. Her hair was pulled into a knot, thicker and fuller than Riga's, held in place by two long, wooden hair sticks with carved tortoises on the end.

"Good morning," Riga said.

Sarah looked up, her eyes widening slightly. The skin beneath them was the color of a bruise. "Mrs. Mosse. I heard what happened last night. How are you feeling?"

"Embarrassed. It was clumsy of me." Riga pointed to the remains of her meal. "Not hungry this morning?"

Sarah pushed her plate away. "I thought I was. What can I do for you?"

"I need some information about a woman who drowned here a few years ago," Donovan said. "But I don't know the exact date."

"A woman who drowned?" Sarah's forehead creased. "It must have happened before I started here. Why do you need to know?"

"I heard a rumor there might be a lawsuit headed our way," he said.

She paled. "Oh. That's the last thing we need. I'll look into it."

"Thank you," Donovan said. "And enjoy the rest of your breakfast." They walked to an empty table near the open windows and sat.

"You heard a rumor?" Riga asked.

"One I just started. Now you've heard it too."

"Hm," Riga said. "How long has Sarah been at the hotel?"

"She started two years ago, I believe."

"Long enough to grow close to Dennis."

"You still think there might have been something between them?"

Riga spread her hands. "I have a nasty, suspicious mind. She was very upset by his death."

"Playing devil's advocate, I will note that murder is shocking, and they worked closely together."

They ate slowly, enjoying the feel of the breeze off the bay. When they finished, they drove to the lighthouse. Donovan maneuvered the Ferrari into a parking spot.

A warm breeze caressed her skin. The sky was brilliant blue. But all she could think of was the day before, the man vomiting shark teeth. At the end of the peninsula, the lighthouse winked.

She stepped from the car. The green spit of land reaching into the Pacific seemed brittle, buffeted by wind and ocean. "It's not quite as beautiful today, is it?"

"No. Our memory's been tainted."

They skirted the patch of red that stained the pavement and headed down the walk winding along the verdant peninsula. Rising ahead of them the lighthouse speared the pale blue sky. They passed other tourists, chatting, taking pictures.

Donovan snapped a picture of her with his phone. "We need to look the part." His smile was lopsided. "Besides, I don't have enough photos of you."

"As if I'd let you forget what I looked like." She tucked her arm under his. They strolled the grounds, the wind freeing strands of Riga's knotted hair.

Beside the yawning lighthouse door stood a man with his back to them, speaking with Townsend. The non-profit director's bald head had ripened to pink. Riga thought that adding a hat to Townsend's outfit – a blue Aquatic Protection Society windbreaker and khakis – wouldn't be amiss.

The second man turned. It was the lighthouse keeper, Grover, in a Dodger's cap, shorts and a green jacket. It strained across his gut.

At the sound of their footsteps in the gravel, Townsend waved. "Riga, Donovan! I was hoping we'd run into each other before you left the island."

"Oh, we're in no hurry to leave, are we, darling?" Riga smiled up at Donovan.

Townsend blinked. "That's wonderful news. I assumed you'd have to hurry back to Vegas. Have you had a chance to think any more about our organization?"

"I have," Donovan said, "and my assistant will be in touch with you about a donation."

"Wonderful." Townsend rubbed his hands together. "Does this mean you'll be buying the hotel?"

Grover's hand stilled on his jacket zipper. At least, Riga thought, his hand wasn't trembling. Though the lighthouse keeper had been blasted when they'd first met, he didn't show obvious signs of chronic drinking. No jaundice, no drinker's nose.

"You're buying Dennis's hotel?" Grover asked.

"The hotel and I are still getting acquainted," Donovan said. "I haven't made a decision."

Townsend wagged a finger at him. "Playing close to the vest. I'd expect no more from a card shark like you."

"I heard another seal was killed," Riga said.

Townsend clucked his tongue. "Terrible. Sometimes I think the planet would be better off without people on it. Unfortunately, we weren't there to protect the seal. We're a small organization, and the seals don't let us know when or where they'll be arriving on our beaches."

"How do you find out where the seals are?" she asked.

He rocked on his heels. "There are certain areas they tend to show up, of course. And people will call us and let us know, and then we'll put the call out to one of our responders."

"How exactly does that system work?" Riga leaned against the wall. The lighthouse was warm against her back, like a living thing, and for a moment she imagined she could feel the gentle swell of its breath.

"Why do you ask?" Townsend said.

"I wonder how many people knew that Dennis would be guarding that seal on that beach," she said.

The lighthouse keeper cursed, pointed to a group of young boys crawling over the cliff-side barrier. "Get off that." He raced toward the kids.

Townsend watched Grover, arms waving, chastise the boys. "I'm not sure where you're going with this, but anyone in the office could have found out. We keep our schedule on a white board in the conference room. That way, we know where everyone is."

"And how many people are typically in your office?" Donovan asked.

"Not many. Myself. My assistant, Jay. The responders when they come in, but their work is primarily on the beaches."

"Did any responders come into the office the day of Dennis's death?" Riga asked.

"I wasn't there the entire day, but I only remember Petra, the woman Dennis took over for on the beach."

"I imagine the whiteboard changes quite a bit," Riga said. "Like you said, you don't know when a seal is going to arrive or how long it will stay."

"That's true. In the case of Dennis, we had him scheduled maybe three hours in advance. Fortunately, his hotel wasn't far from where the seal turned up on the beach, so it was easy for him to get there on short notice."

"Was anyone in your office last night?" Donovan asked.

"Only Jay and myself. There's a board meeting coming up, and the two of us stayed late, preparing."

Riga looked down the trail toward the parking lot. "A man died out here yesterday. You might have known him. Mana."

He shook his head once, frowning. "Grover mentioned the death, but not the name of the man. Mana, you say? Doesn't sound familiar."

"He was a friend of Kimo's," Riga said.

"Ah. I heard it was a suicide. Remorse, you think? Perhaps he and Kimo both were behind the seal killings."

"Kimo told me he didn't have a problem with the seals," Riga said, "just with your organization."

"You mean with Dennis? With me? Do the police know this?"

"I don't know," Riga said. "But I'm not convinced Mana's death was a suicide."

Sunlight glinted off Townsend's round glasses. "If he was gobbling up things that weren't meant to be eaten, it might not have been a conscious act, but certainly it would indicate a subconscious self-hatred. Don't you think?"

"Mm," Riga said.

"You don't sound convinced."

"The options are limited," she said. "Suicide, accident, or murder."

"Murder?" His smile was supercilious, smug, and Riga felt the cords twanging in her neck. The man had every right to think murder by pica was ridiculous, and his reaction shouldn't annoy her. But it did.

"Now," he said, "I do know the police don't believe he was murdered."

"If the police were perfect," Donovan said, "we wouldn't need private detectives."

Grover huffed back to them. "Parents these days. Their kids get hurt because they're not watching, and we get sued. What'd I miss?"

"Mrs. Mosse was just telling me about her theory that the man who died in your parking lot didn't commit suicide."

Grover adjusted his baggy pants. "He died spitting sharks' teeth. There's only one way those are going down, and that's if he swallowed them."

"Wouldn't swallowing the teeth have done as much damage as regurgitating them?" she asked.

"But if it wasn't this Mana fellow who killed Dennis, then who?" Townsend tilted his head. "There are some other people you might talk to. Not suspects, but they hang about the beaches, they're aware of things."

"Oh?" Riga asked.

"There is a group of, er, young people who live out on the Na Pali coast," Townsend said. "They've got their own colony out there. They might be worth chatting with."

Grover snorted. "Come on. What would they know about it? They're not involved."

"Not involved, no. But they're more sympathetic with the rights of the so-called indigenous population than with the seals."

"So-called?" Donovan asked.

"No one is truly native to these islands," Townsend explained. "We're all immigrants. Some just came later than others."

"How simple life must be," Riga said, "when you can come down squarely on one side of a moral ambiguity." Though she'd chosen a side as well. Two men had been murdered. The seal politics were bound up in those deaths. But for Riga, the human murders came first.

"Er, yes." Townsend's phone rang, and he checked the number. "Excuse me, please. I need to take this call." He hurried away, into the shade of the lighthouse.

Riga gave the lighthouse keeper what she hoped was a sympathetic smile. "You were friends with Dennis Glasgow, weren't you?"

"Yeah." He rubbed his face, his hands making scratching sounds against his five o'clock shadow. "I want to apologize to you both. I made an ass of myself the other day. I don't usually drink much, but Dennis's murder threw me. I'm sorry."

"I'm a private investigator," Riga said. "I'm looking into his death."

"Are you?" He eyed her. "That might be a good idea. Everyone seems to think the murder was random – that he'd stumbled across the seal killer. But that doesn't make sense, does it? He was there, watching the seal. Wouldn't the seal killer have avoided him?"

"It was dark," she said. "Maybe the killer didn't see him until it was too late."

"Maybe. Dennis was a great guy. We grew up together. He helped me get this job. But some folks thought he was a little too active in the community, if you know what I mean."

"You mean his good works got on people's nerves," Donovan said.

"Exactly. He stopped new hotels from being developed, which I agree with. If we overdevelop the island then we'll lose the very thing that people come here for – paradise. Peace. Natural beauty. But let's face it,

Dennis already had his hotel, and there were plenty of people who would have liked the jobs new hotels would have brought. Some folks said what he was really fighting was competition."

"But there must have been people who agreed with him," Riga said.

"Most did," Grover said. "Dennis wasn't exactly swimming upstream with his views. But he rubbed some people the wrong way."

"Anyone angry enough to kill?" Riga asked.

Grover studied his tattered shoes. "I didn't think so. Fact is, the really angry people were the developers, and they're all from the mainland or other islands. Once they lost their opportunity, they left. But someone killed Dennis. Townsend might know more. They were both involved in the sustainable development hullabaloo." He nodded toward Townsend, still on the phone, his head bent, forehead creased.

Scowling, Townsend jammed the phone into his pocket. He returned to the small group.

"Problem?" Donovan asked.

Townsend rubbed his domed forehead. "Just the usual hassles of getting ready for a board meeting. Broken printer, that sort of thing."

"Grover was just telling us that Dennis annoyed some developers with his sustainable development push," Donovan said.

"Oh," Townsend said. "Yes, we did get under the skin of some people. The Aquatic Protection Society has always been the tip of the spear when it comes to sustainable development. Though if you're looking at that as a motive for murder, I suspect I'd be a bigger target than Dennis. His death hasn't changed anything on that score."

"He was president of the board, wasn't he?" Donovan asked. "Who'll be taking his place?" Donovan's phone rang, and he pulled it from his pocket, checked the number. "Sarah from the hotel. I'd better take this." He walked away from the group to stand beside a banana tree.

Townsend's gaze followed Donovan. "Cell phones are the devil's tool. They're supposed to be a convenience. I think I preferred the days when I was unreachable."

"Amen," Riga muttered.

"But you were asking about the board," Townsend said. "Carol Harding is the vice president. Dennis had just begun his two-year term, so she'll be completing it. But I don't see any change in the direction of the board with her ascension to president."

"Where does she work?" Riga asked.

"She owns the Pineapple Bed and Breakfast in Hanalei."

"Were she and Dennis friendly?"

"No more than with any other board member." Townsend's gaze drifted to Donovan. "We're all busy people. We get along, but we have lives outside the Protection Society. Or at least, they do."

Grover checked his watch. "Well, this has been fun, but I've got work to do. Let's talk later about that fundraiser," he said to Townsend.

Absently, Townsend clapped him on the shoulder. "Good, good."

The lighthouse keeper walked across the trail and into a whitewashed outbuilding.

Townsend tore his attention from Donovan. "For all my talk of the seals, you must think I care more about them than Dennis."

"Not at all," Riga lied.

"Dennis was a good man and a good friend. I want his killer to be found and punished."

"Then we share common ground."

Donovan put the phone in his pocket and strode to them.

"Word on your hotel deal?" Townsend asked.

"No," Donovan said. "It turned out the call wasn't that important after all. Are you ready to go, Riga?"

"I think I've seen everything I need," she said. "Goodbye."

They shook hands. Riga and Donovan walked up the trail.

"What did Sarah have to say?" she asked.

"That a woman drowned at the hotel three years ago, but she's been assured there's no chance of a lawsuit over it. Apparently the statute of limitations in a wrongful death lawsuit in Hawaii is two years."

"Did she tell you the woman's name?"

"No, oddly enough. Sarah couldn't get me that information, though she did tell me the woman was on her honeymoon. Apparently, she struck her head on the rocks near our bungalow, slipped into the water, and drowned."

"How is it that Sarah knows the details of the accident but not the victim's name?"

"I got the feeling she does know," Donovan said. "She just wouldn't tell me."

Her jaw set, a fluttery feeling expanding in her chest. "Interesting." The mystery was a pebble in her shoe, impossible to ignore. So she wouldn't ignore it. And she'd start with learning the victim's name.

CHAPTER 22

RIGA AND DONOVAN WALKED along a stone path. Spiky violet and green pineapple bushes brushed their clothing, snagging the fabric. Pineapple finials adorned the fence posts and gabled entryway. A pineapple door knocker hung beneath a pineapple stained glass window set in the top of the door.

"I'm starting to detect a theme," Donovan said.

A woman opened the door. Her hair was pulled into a long braid, and two pineapple earrings swung from her earlobes. "Mr. and Mrs. Wiederhauser?"

"No." Donovan's eyes crinkled in a smile. "Mosse. Are you Carol Harding? I'm considering a donation to the Aquatic Protection Society. Townsend suggested we speak with you. We were in the area, so we thought we'd just drop by. Is this a good time?"

Her return smile was forced, but she smoothed her pineapple apron over her pineapple print skirt and stepped back from the door. "Yes. I thought running a B&B would be a fun semi-retirement. Little did I know how much work it would be. But yes, I have some time."

She led them into a sitting room with a pineapple rug and needlepoint pineapple cushions. Riga smothered a grimace. If the woman wasn't a dark magician, she ought to be. Riga extended her senses and didn't even feel a whisper of magic.

Carol settled herself in a wicker chair and motioned them to the couch. "What can I tell you about the Aquatic Protection Society?"

Donovan sat, leaning forward, his elbows on his knees. "How will the direction of the Society change now that Dennis won't be at the helm?"

"I can't imagine it would," Carol said. "The Society has been running smoothly with Townsend's leadership as executive director. We're all in alignment on our goals."

"But what are your goals?" Riga asked.

"Personally, I'd like to recruit more responders. It's awful that we couldn't get someone out to the last seal that was killed. And of course, all the board members are responsible for assisting with fundraising."

"And why couldn't you get someone out?" Riga asked.

"Our assistant, Jay, tried, but no one was available. It happens sometimes. As I said, we're a small organization, though our goals are mighty."

"And what were Dennis's goals?" Donovan asked.

She blinked. "Dennis? Why, the same as everyone else's. You should understand that in many ways we're still a new organization. We went through a major transformation three years ago."

"Because of Townsend's stewardship?" he asked.

"Well, that and the bequest from Townsend's wife. Before, we were all about education and advocacy. Now we're much more directly involved in protection, and not just of the seals. Many aquatic creatures are endangered by overfishing, habitat loss, and pollution. And illegal shell trade, consumption of eggs, and beach recreation have all made sea turtles vulnerable. Though people consider this a paradise, in many ways, ours is an island in peril."

"We ask because it was Dennis who initially got us interested in the Society," Riga said.

Carol's eyes lit. "You knew him? Wonderful man. I mostly saw him at Society and Chamber of Commerce meetings, but he was such a caring, charming man. He will be missed."

"Who might have killed him?" Riga asked.

"Obviously, whoever is killing those seals." Carol stood and paced. "It's a short step from murdering an animal to killing a human. Isn't that what they say about serial killers? They start as children, killing pets? There is no one – no one – who would want to kill Dennis. He was absolutely dedicated to the environment. Everyone respected him. Everyone."

"Were there any conflicts on the board?" Riga asked.

"Of course not. Townsend manages the Society wonderfully."

Someone knocked at the door, and Carol leapt from her seat. "That must be the Wiederhausers."

Riga and Donovan rose and followed her to the door. "Thank you for your time, Ms. Harding," Donovan said. They squeezed past the Wiederhausers on the front porch and walked back to the Ferrari.

"How much do you know about non-profit board operations?" Donovan asked.

"Not much," Riga said. "I've never served on one."

He slid into the car. "Boards are managed by the president. The board typically has authority over the executive director – Townsend. But sometimes, especially with small organizations and all-volunteer boards, the executive director ends up actually running the show."

"You think that's what's happening with the Aquatic Protection Society?"

He started the car. "The way Carol talked, it sounded like Townsend was responsible for changing the strategy of the organization. But even if Townsend is running the board from behind the scenes, it's no motive for murder."

She filed away that nugget to turn over later. "Do you mind if we stop at the Society's office? There's something I'd like to check out."

Donovan turned toward central Hanalei. Soon they were pulling into the mini-mall parking lot.

In the office, Jay stood at the printer, stacks of printed paper piled high on the table. He shifted the memorial with the two glittering dolphins to the side and added another pile to the mess.

"Hello," Riga said.

He looked up and scratched at his wispy beard. "Hey. I heard you're making a donation. That's awesome. Thanks."

Riga nodded toward the table. "That's a lot of paper."

The young man stiffened. "It's recycled."

"I just meant it looked like a lot of work," she said.

His shoulders relaxed. "Yeah. I've been at it all morning. We've got a big board meeting coming up and a fundraiser. But what can I do for you?"

"What time did you leave work yesterday?" Riga asked.

"Why? I mean, uh... Seven o'clock, I think. Why?"

"Did Townsend leave at the same time?" she asked.

"No," he said, "I left him to close up. I don't know when he left. Why?"

"Just checking something," Riga said. "It's a shame you weren't able to find someone to watch that seal two nights ago."

"What? No, I mean, right."

"What do you mean?" Riga asked.

"Nothing. Yeah, it was a bummer we couldn't find anyone. So, do you need our tax ID number or anything for that donation?"

"My assistant, Ellen, will be in touch," Donovan said.

They turned to leave. Something crashed behind them. Riga started and whirled around.

Jay stood, papers clutched in his hands, staring down at the fragments of glass dolphin. "I didn't... It wasn't... It was an accident," he said shrilly. He dropped the papers and stooped, tried to fit two of the pieces together.

Riga just shook her head. She knew a lost cause when she saw one.

They left the Society and drove east on the winding highway. Ocean sparkled on Donovan's left. Green, conical mountains rose on Riga's right.

"You missed the hotel," Riga said as they sped past.

Donovan's teeth flashed. "That's because we're not going to the hotel."

"Then where, pray tell, are we going? To harass Kimo some more?"

"No, though that's not a bad idea."

The car slowed as the highway passed through a village of cinderblock buildings and chain link fences. A chicken pecked idly at the side of the road. Donovan turned on the narrow street to the lighthouse.

"Another question for Grover?" Riga asked.

"Nope."

"Then I give up," Riga said. "All our other suspects are behind us."

"I thought it would be helpful to take a step back from the situation, get more of a bird's eye view."

"Bird's eye..." She twisted to look at him, her shoulder pressed against the car door. "No. You didn't."

He grinned. "I've booked us a helicopter ride. That's the other reason Sarah called me from the hotel – to confirm our seats. You don't mind, do you? The tour only takes an hour."

Riga rummaged in her purse for a motion sickness pill. "Will we fly over Waimea Canyon?"

"Yes."

"What about the Na Pali coast?"

"That too."

"I wonder if the pilot can get us to that colony Townsend mentioned?"

"We can ask."

Riga chewed thoughtfully on the pill. It tasted like bitter children's medicine.

The fact was, she was dying to fly around the island and had never been in a helicopter. She'd intended to return to the hotel and organize her case notes, plot next steps.

But Donovan's plan held appeal, and it was only for an hour. Though she hadn't taken seriously Townsend's suggestion that someone at the colony might know about the seal killing, if there was a chance...

"You're brilliant," she said.

"True."

They drove to a small landing strip not far from the lighthouse, where a red and black and orange helicopter waited. The pilot, a tanned woman with long, blond hair tied in a ponytail and eyes hidden behind aviator sunglasses, settled them in the helicopter.

Soon they were zooming low over the water. Any thoughts of the case evaporated in the spray of waterfalls, cascading down the tall folds of emerald and burnt-orange mountains.

Riga leaned closer to the window, her lips parted, one hand pressed to her chest. Lush canyons and pinnacled cliffs dashed headlong to the multi-blued Pacific. No wonder magic had flourished here. It was an elemental place.

Wordlessly, Donovan grasped her hand. The helicopter lowered beside an arch cut in a cliff next to a sandy beach. Then it shot along the spines of mountains rippling outward from the mist-shrouded Waialeale Crater.

The pilot grimaced when they asked about landing near the colony. "Sorry. It's not worth my job to do it."

"It was a long shot," Riga said to him. And it was hard to feel disappointment in the face of Kauai's heart-stopping landscape.

"Whatever happened to follow every thread?" he asked.

"That thread is going to the back of the line. I'll ask Brigitte to check out the colony. She's been looking for a quest."

"She's not going to like it."

"What's not to like? The chance to play covert op, do some surveillance…"

"We'll see." He flipped a switch, so they could communicate through the headphones privately. "Let's talk about the case."

"I keep thinking of something a cop once told me. There's no such thing as hard evidence, only evidence. But there isn't a whole lot here we can take to the police. At first I thought Dennis had been killed because he was Dennis. Now it's clear the seals were the target. We won't be able to use the magical evidence in court, but if we can nail down means, opportunity, and motive – even an occult motive – the police might go for it."

He nodded. "I've been thinking the same thing. So who are we left with? Kimo could have killed the seals. He certainly spends a lot of time roaming the island. And he's connected with Mana. He might have had an inkling that Mana was going to talk to us."

"But Mana said he was friends with Kimo," Riga said. "It didn't sound like he was going to rat him out."

"Unless he thought he was doing it for Kimo's own good."

"Maybe," she said. "Both Paul and Deidre had opportunity for the first seal killing. We know they were close to the beach. And they could have gotten into our bungalow. As the owner and manager, Paul's got a master key to the entire hotel. Conceivably, Deidre could have gotten hold of one."

"And then there's the Aquatic Protection Society."

"Someone may be using it to find out where the seals are, where to strike."

"Townsend?" he asked.

"Maybe. The opportunities are there." The fact was, she didn't like Townsend and knew it was coloring her perception. "Mana's death is the key."

"It's also the only death we'll never be able to prove was murder."

Tour over, they set down on the landing pad. Donovan handed her out of the chopper. "Shall we go back to the hotel?" he asked as they got into the car.

She sighed. "I do need to organize my case notes."

"Finally, I get to watch the process in action."

"It involves a lot of mumbling and paper shuffling and staring out the window." Riga laughed. "It's not that entertaining."

They roared off. When they reached the hotel, Donovan paused the car at the edge of its circular drive. It was filled with emergency vehicles, their lights flashing.

A hotel valet hurried down the drive. "I'll park it from here," the valet said, terse.

"What's happened?" Donovan stepped from the Ferrari and dropped the keys in the valet's outstretched hand.

The valet looked down at his shoes. "There's been an accident." He jumped in the car and slowly drove away.

Riga took in the scene. Five police cars, an ambulance, a fire truck. "There are an awful lot of police here."

Donovan nodded. "Let's find out what's going on."

The lobby was filled with chattering guests. They approached an older woman in a baggy safari shirt and shorts. "What's happened?" Riga asked.

"A woman drowned in the fishpond," she said, her voice hushed.

Riga's heart sank. "Do you know who...?"

Two EMTs pushed through the crowd carrying a stretcher. The slim figure of the woman on it was hidden beneath a sheet.

"Come on," Donovan said. "Let's find Paul."

The office reception area was empty. Riga went to his name-plated door, knocked lightly.

After a moment, a strained voice called, "Come in."

Riga opened the door. Paul sat bowed over his desk, his head in hands. He looked up, his eyes dull and wet.

"Paul, are you all right?" Donovan asked. "What's happened?"

"It's Sarah. She's dead."

Donovan sucked in his breath. "I'm sorry," he said. "I didn't know her well, but I liked her. And I know she was close to you and your brother."

"She was like a kid sister," Paul said. "They said she must have slipped, hit her head."

"Where did it happen?" Donovan asked.

"Are you worried about liability?" His voice was high, reedy.

"No," Donovan said. "But we couldn't help noticing all the police cars in the drive. Are they treating this as a possible murder?"

"Murder? She hit her head and drowned in the damn fishpond. It was an accident."

"I hope you're right," Riga said. "If there's anything we can do, please let us know."

Donovan followed her out of the office. He closed the door behind them.

"We need to take a look at that fishpond," she said in a low voice.

"There are three at the hotel."

They hurried through the hotel grounds, along wandering paths lined with ginger plants and birds of paradise. The police turned them away from a trail that led to a secluded pond in the shade of banana trees.

They returned to their bungalow. Riga tossed her bag on the coffee table.

"We'll check the pond out after the police have left." Donovan shoved open the tall glass doors that lined the living area.

"Yes." Riga rummaged through a desk drawer and found a watercolor map of the hotel complex. "Sarah had her accident at the most isolated pond on the grounds."

"Making it a good place for a private meeting," he said.

"Or a murder." She spread the map on the table, pointed to the pond. "It's secluded, and there are two paths leading to that fishpond, leaving two good potential exits for a killer."

"You're right. If someone's coming down one path, he or she can escape down the other. But it's not completely private. There are bungalows near that pond."

"This map isn't detailed enough to tell if any of the bungalows have views. We'll have to see the pond for ourselves. At least in this case, time of death shouldn't be difficult to narrow down."

"Especially since I spoke with Sarah this morning."

"What time was that, exactly?"

He checked his phone. "Ten thirty-seven. If it was another murder by our necromancer, it's not part of the magical pattern. And killers generally keep to the same MO. Or so I've read."

"I won't know if magic was involved until I get down there. And if he's trying to make the deaths look random or accidental, he'd change the pattern." She put her hands on her hips. "But maybe he is repeating his MO. Didn't Sarah tell you that the other woman who drowned here also hit her head and went into the water?"

"That was over three years ago."

"Yes, but the ghost is appearing to us now. Often a ghost will manifest due to a trigger event. Maybe her killer's become active again, and that's why she's returned." Riga went to the desk and booted up her laptop. "We need to get that ghost's name, find out more about her."

But an hour of internet searching turned up nothing. Riga found newspaper articles about the death, but the victim's name was withheld at the family's request. She tossed her pencil across the table. "There's got to be someone who'll talk about that drowning."

"Paul must know her name," Donovan said. "She was a guest at this hotel. I'll get it."

"Sarah couldn't get it. I wonder who she talked to about the drowning?"

Donovan quirked an eyebrow. "You think she was killed because she was asking about that woman's death?"

"A more obvious explanation is that she died because she knew something about Dennis's murder. Sarah worked closely with him. She was distraught over his murder."

"And her death might have just been an accident," Donovan said.

But she didn't believe that. Not for a minute.

CHAPTER 23

RIGA STROLLED INTO THE bungalow's living area, her silk pajamas swishing about her ankles, and worked at unlatching the clasp of her charm bracelet one-handed. The windows were a black mirror at night, reflecting the cheerful cushions, the low table, the wrinkled tarot cards stacked on it. Riga did a double take. Hadn't she thrown those away?

Three of the cards had fallen to the floor and lay face down on the sisal carpet. She knelt and turned the first card over. The two of pentacles: a fool on a beach juggling two large coins. A ship labored in the high waves behind him. It was usually a card of finding balance in the midst of turmoil, but Riga knew who the fool on the beach was.

She turned over the next card. A man hung upside down by his heels, coins falling from his pockets. In Renaissance times it was the card of the traitor. Today, it could mean a time of stillness, or sacrifice. She thought of the ghostly figure hanging from the tower at the snow goddess's heiau, and a chill rippled up her spine.

Riga flipped the third card. A king and queen plummeted, headfirst, from a lightning-struck tower.

She blew out her breath. "Well, that's not good."

Bare chested, Donovan walked into the room. "What's not good?"

She swept up the cards and dropped them on the table. "These tarot cards. I thought I threw them away. Did you salvage them?"

"Not me."

Brigitte soared through the open glass doors and landed on the carpet. She skidded, and the carpet accordioned, rumpling beneath her talons. "What has happened since I have been away?"

"Brigitte, did you pull these cards from the wastebasket?" Riga asked.

The gargoyle stiffened. "I do not dig through ze trash, like a common vulture or... or... crow."

"Sorry. As to what's been happening..." Riga told her about their interviews at the lighthouse, the B&B, of Sarah's death.

"Another death, and so soon on ze heels of ze poor Mana? This necromancer, he must be growing desperate to kill with such speed."

"Right." Riga absently pinched the skin at her throat. "I'm afraid whatever he's working up to will happen soon."

"As do I. It is logical, is it not? But this necromancer is a cunning one. First he killed Monsieur Dennis Glasgow and ze mermaid and makes one murder ze cover for ze other. Brilliant. And then ze poor Mana, to die so terribly, so obviously by magic – so obvious, that no one will believe it. And now ze hotelier's assistant – her death appears to be an accident, which means it *must* be murder."

Riga raised her brows. The gargoyle's logic was straight out of a mystery novel. Donovan coughed.

"Did you learn any more about the local magic?" Riga asked.

"Not magic, no. But I found some gnomes at ze Waialeale Crater. They were very agitated, preparing for something."

Riga shuddered. How many different types of faeries were on this island? "Preparing for what?"

"Finally, I have found ze answer. I, Brigitte, have learned ze truth."

"Which is?" Riga asked.

"It is rare, but when ze earth element becomes agitated enough, it releases a... scent humans cannot smell. I do not know ze word. But this scent is powerful, it affects human behavior. Like sex."

Donovan frowned. "A pheromone?"

"Perhaps." Brigitte shrugged, her stony feathers fluttering. "But this scent makes people aggressive, violent. It has happened in other times, other places."

"That would explain all the fights," Donovan said. "But why attack mermaids? Even I know they're water elementals, not earth."

"That," Brigitte said, "I do not know."

"I wonder..." Riga tapped the edge of a tarot card against her lips. "What did our boat captain tell us? That Kauai is a place where all the elements are battling each other, shaping the island? An attack on one might cause an imbalance, set off a chain reaction with the other elements. Perhaps the mermaids were the simplest victim."

"But how does the death of a few mermaids create an imbalance on this scale?" the gargoyle asked.

"If my people were under attack," Donovan said, "I'd build my forces up to defend."

"Water is rising and the other elements, including earth, are reacting," Riga said. "They're seeking equilibrium."

Brigitte tossed her head. "If this is his game, I am not impressed. So far, all we have seen are fist fights. What is ze point?"

"Two people were killed in San Francisco," Riga said.

"People are always getting killed in San Francisco," the gargoyle replied. "It is a blip on ze statistical radar."

"She's right." Donovan slipped into a button up shirt. "The earthquake frightened people, but there were no serious injuries. If this necromancer is looking for mass deaths, he's going to have to go bigger."

"Well, he's not going to get it by killing the occasional mermaid," Riga said. "Brigitte, there's a colony of... I don't know what to call them. Travelers, I guess, who live out on the Na Pali coast. Townsend suggested they might have some inside information. Can you spend some time out there, see if you can hear anything and if there's any magic?"

The gargoyle's eyes narrowed. "You want me to join a hippy colony?"

"No. I want you to listen and observe."

"You know how I feel about patchouli. And headbands."

"I'm not asking you to go undercover. Just some surveillance."

"Fine." Brigitte huffed. "Because ze fate of ze world is at stake, I will go. I will suffer. You enjoy yourselves and drink beverages with tiny umbrellas."

"Brigitte." Donovan placed a solemn hand over his heart. "You know I would never drink anything with an umbrella."

Brigitte cast a sneer in Riga's direction. "*She* might."

"I only ask because it's nearly impossible for us bi-peds to get out there," Riga said. "It's a two-day hike, and the trail is dangerous right now."

"Whatever." Brigitte hunched her shoulders, then sprang and soared out the window.

Whatever? Riga watched the dark form pass before the moon. "It's like living with a teenager."

CHAPTER 24

SUNLIGHT SLANTED OFF THE wooden floor of the breakfast room. It was filled with chattering diners. Riga nudged Donovan and jerked her chin toward Deidre.

Dennis's widow sat alone in a booth beneath a watercolor of a Hawaiian sunset. She picked listlessly at a fruit salad, her head bowed. Wisps of straw-colored hair dangled from her loose bun.

Deidre looked up as they approached. "I'd say good morning, but it doesn't really feel like one today."

"We were very sorry to hear about Sarah," Riga said. "And sorrier to be giving you condolences twice in one week. What happened?"

Deidre motioned toward the empty bench across from her. They slid into it.

"I don't know, and I was the one who found her," Deidre said. "She was head down in the fishpond. I pulled her out and tried CPR. But it was too late." She raked her fingers across her scalp. "She shouldn't be dead."

"Another woman died here three years ago under similar circumstances," Riga said.

Deidre's green eyes widened. "Hannah?" She sucked her cheeks in, reddening.

"You knew her then?" Riga asked slowly. "Sarah wasn't able to give us her name." And she hadn't been able to find anything on the internet about it last night.

Deidre put her hands up, palms forward. "I shouldn't have said it. The family asked that we keep it private, and we've honored their wishes.

I'm sorry, I can't say anything more. And you can't believe there's a connection between a drowning three years ago and Sarah's death."

"It is strange, though," Donovan said. "I spoke to Sarah on the phone about the drowning in the morning. She died the very same way a few hours later."

"Surely that's just a coincidence," Deidre said. "I talked to her that morning about the linens in the meeting room. But I don't think she died because of tablecloths."

"When did you discover the body?" A memory fluttered through Riga's mind, just out of reach, something that jarred.

"Just before noon. I know you're trying to help, but it was an accident. A terrible, terrible accident."

"Do you really believe that?" Riga asked. "Your husband's assistant died less than a week after his murder. Do you really think it's a coincidence?"

"Yes, I do. Please, I just don't want to talk about it anymore."

A shadow crossed their table, and they looked up. Paul stood over them scowling, his dark hair mussed. "What's going on?"

Donovan leaned against the back of the booth. "We were talking with Deidre about Sarah's death."

"Why? Can't you see she doesn't want to talk about it?"

"Because there have been two deaths related to this hotel in one week," Riga said.

"My brother was shot. Sarah slipped and fell. They're not related."

"How can you be so certain?" Riga asked.

Paul flushed, his birthmark turning a deep purple. "Because it doesn't make any sense. The police don't think they're connected. Look, I get that you think you're a private investigator, but the game's over."

"She is a private investigator," Donovan growled. "And her question was perfectly reasonable. I understand – better than most – how difficult this sort of thing can be. But I also know you won't be able to live without some resolution to your brother's death."

Paul stood stiffly and breathed heavily through his nose. "Please, just leave it alone." He held out a hand to his sister-in-law. "Come on, Deidre. Let's go."

Riga and Donovan watched them leave. "I hope I haven't scotched your hotel deal," Riga said.

Donovan rubbed his jaw. "You haven't. He was controlling himself with us because he wants to sell. Badly. Strange that they refuse to see a connection between the deaths."

"They're protecting each other. Or they think they are."

Donovan threw her a sharp look. "Maybe."

"At least we're closer to the time of death – between ten thirty and noon. The fishpond is secluded, but Sarah couldn't have been in there that long without being found. So she likely died closer to twelve o'clock. We need to talk to the people in the bungalows nearby. They may have seen something."

Donovan checked his watch and slid from the booth. "Let's go before they leave to play tourist for the day."

They tackled the nearest bungalow. It was empty, no one responding to their knock. But they were in luck at the second.

A florid man in shorts, sandals, and a black polo shirt, tight around his middle, opened the door. His bushy gray eyebrows lifted. "Yes?"

"We're neighbors of yours, in bungalow six," Donovan said. "My wife is a private investigator. We wanted to ask you about yesterday."

Riga handed him her card.

"The drowning?" The man read it, looked up. "I've never met a private investigator before. What can I do for you?"

"Did you see anyone along this trail or at the fishpond between ten o'clock and noon yesterday?" Riga asked.

He looked down at his flip-flops. "Well, I don't think I was much help to the police, or I'll be much help to you. I don't exactly spend my days here staring at that trail."

"But did you see anything?" Riga persisted.

The man scratched his sunburnt ear. "I heard several people go by, but I only *saw* one. He looked a lot like me, if you get my drift," he said, patting his stomach. "Maybe a little scruffier."

"Was he a guest? I don't suppose you've seen him before," Riga said.

"Oh, I saw him before. Just about everybody did. He made a ruckus in the hotel dining room earlier this week, drunk in the middle of the day." He squinted. "Come to think of it, weren't you there too?"

Riga and Donovan glanced at each other. *Grover Garfield, the lighthouse keeper.*

"And you saw no one else?" Riga asked.

He shook his head, regretful. "Nope. Sorry."

"Thanks. I don't suppose you have a card?" Riga asked. "In case we want to get in touch with you later?"

He shambled into his bungalow and returned with a business card. "Here you go. Hope I was of some help."

"You were," Riga said.

They returned to their bungalow and sat in the deck chairs by the pool. The sun soaked into Riga's skin, leeching the tension from her limbs.

Donovan pulled a slip of paper from the breast pocket of his sheer white shirt. He handed it to her.

She unfolded it. An address. "What's this?"

"That's where Sarah lives with her mother. I mean lived."

"You're a marvel. How...? Oh. Another early morning with Ellen?"

"I thought you might want it."

"I do," she said. "Something was bothering Sarah. If she didn't tell anyone at the hotel, maybe she confided in her mother. And then there's Grover. We need to talk to him again."

"I checked a map. Sarah's home isn't far from the lighthouse." He closed his eyes.

"Convenient."

They didn't stir from their chairs.

"We really should go," Riga said, but her arms and legs felt like warm noodles.

"Yes."

"But it's very comfortable here."

"Mm."

"This is a terrible place for an investigation," she said, exasperated. "It's too beautiful. It's making us lazy."

"All right. Murder calls." He swung his feet from the chair. "We can redo our honeymoon another time, another place, and as often as we like. Let's go find Grover and Sarah's mother."

They drove down winding roads draped in green, scattering chickens in their wake. Slices of blue ocean rose and fell between the hills. And then they were curling up the narrow road to the lighthouse.

"As beautiful as it is," Donovan said, "this drive is getting monotonous."

"It's a small island," she agreed.

They parked and walked down the spit of land to the lighthouse, starkly white against the sea. Waves crashed faintly beneath them.

The lighthouse door was metal, studded with bolts, and locked. They checked the outbuilding nearby.

Its door opened at Donovan's touch, and he stuck his head inside. "Mr. Garfield?"

"Yeah? Who is it?" A disembodied voice called.

"Donovan Mosse and Riga Hayworth," Donovan said.

A pause. "Come in." Grover's voice sagged with resignation.

They walked into a small entryway. Donovan turned right and opened a door into a light-filled room. Grover sat behind a battered wooden table. Papers lay scattered across it, and a laptop computer sat open on his left.

Grover half rose, then sat down again. "To what do I owe the honor?"

"Are we catching you at a bad time?" Riga asked, not much caring if they were or weren't.

The lighthouse keeper ran a hand through his graying hair. "No. I guess not. I was just reviewing the budget for our upcoming fundraiser."

"Oh?" she asked. "What fundraiser is that?"

"The Aquatic Protection Society is holding their annual fundraiser here, at the lighthouse. We're doing it jointly this year, to raise funds for the restoration of the trail."

"The trail seemed solid to me," Donovan said.

"Yeah, because you weren't looking too closely. The land is eroding around the cliffside barrier. Sections of it are hanging free. It's a hazard."

"Did you hear about the drowning at the hotel yesterday?" Riga asked.

He nodded, and his shoulders slumped. "Yeah. Poor kid. The place really is starting to seem cursed."

"You were at the hotel when it happened, weren't you?" Riga said.

"Yeah." Grover's eyebrows gathered in. "I keep wondering... I was down by that pond. Must have left just before she slipped. If I'd stuck around a little longer, maybe..." He shook his head.

"What were you doing at the hotel?" Donovan asked.

He waved his hand toward the papers. "Meeting with the committee about this."

"Who else is on the committee?" Riga asked.

"It's a joint committee between the boards of the Aquatic Society and the lighthouse." Grover eyed her with distaste. "More detecting?"

Riga nodded and leaned her hip against the table. It lurched sideways, and she hastily straightened off it. "We met with the vice president of the Society – Carol. I guess she's the president now. Was she there?"

His bushy eyebrows rose. "No, because she's not on the committee."

"Who is?" Donovan asked.

"Me and Townsend, of course. Paul volunteered – it's not a regular board committee, you understand. We have non-board members on it too. It's just for this event." He rattled off more names. Riga pulled her notebook from her satchel and wrote them down.

"Out of curiosity," Donovan said, "what's the Aquatic Protection Society fundraising for? Anything special or general operations?"

"General ops. They do this every year. That organization is mostly volunteer, but they have office expenses – the young fellow who works there, Townsend's salary. Not that Townsend needs it, but it's only fair he gets paid."

The light in the room dimmed, a cloud passing before the sun.

"So if you were at the committee meeting," Riga said. "What were you doing alone at the fishpond?"

"You ever been on a committee? There was no end in sight to the meeting, so we took a break, and I ran for it." His eyes took on a faraway look. "I liked that fishpond. It's peaceful. Secluded."

"Did you see anyone else down at the pond?" Donovan asked.

"I didn't see anyone, no. I heard someone coming and took off – thought it might be someone from the committee come to tell me they were starting up again. It must have been Sarah though. Poor kid."

"How well did you know her?" Riga asked.

"She was Dennis's righthand man... er, woman. She came with him to all the committee meetings, to anything work related. I knew her to talk to her, but I didn't *know* her. She was pleasant but kind of kept to herself, if you know what I mean."

"Can you think of any reason why someone would want to kill her?" Riga asked.

Grover's hand jerked. "Kill her? She was murdered? It wasn't an accident?"

Riga's eyes narrowed. If it was an act, it was a good one. "That's what we're trying to figure out."

"You think she might have known something? About Dennis? Because they worked together?"

"It's a possibility," Riga said.

Grover rubbed a hand across his face, making scratching sounds of his five o'clock shadow. "I don't know. I still can't believe anyone would kill Dennis."

"Thanks for your time," Riga said. "And good luck with your fundraiser."

"I'll need it." The lighthouse keeper picked up a spreadsheet and tossed it back down in disgust. "Hey, I don't suppose you'd be interested in making a donation?"

Donovan opened his wallet and pulled out two bills. "For the cause."

Outside, Riga rubbed her arms against the chill breeze. Clouds massed on the horizon. She believed Grover. So why did she have such a bad feeling about him?

"Looks like rain," she said.

Donovan glanced up. "I'm surprised we haven't had more of it. We're in Kauai's rainy season." He stopped, however, to put the top on the Ferrari before they left the parking lot.

In thoughtful silence, they drove to Sarah's home, a purple cinderblock house with a corrugated tin roof. Chickens pecked in the front yard.

Donovan eyed the gold sports emblem that covered one wall. "Someone's a basketball fan."

He knocked on the door. A dog inside barked. There was a shuffling sound, then locks drawing back, a chain rattling.

An older woman wearing a housecoat opened the door. Her face was lined with grief. "Yes?"

"My name is Riga Hayworth. This is my husband, Donovan Mosse. We knew Sarah and are very sorry for your loss."

The woman cracked the door, sheltering behind it. "You with the hotel?"

"We're guests," Donovan said. "And I'm looking into buying it. Sarah and I met quite often over the last few days. My wife is a private detective."

The woman hissed an indrawn breath. "Come in." She turned and walked through a gloomy hall.

They settled in a tattered living room. Cheap paintings of Hawaiian sunsets lined the walls. The cushions sagged.

"Why are you really here?" she asked. "You've come a long way to bring condolences for a woman you only knew a few days."

"I'm investigating the recent deaths at the hotel," Riga said. "Dennis and now Sarah."

The woman blanched and squeezed her eyes shut. When she opened them, she took a long slow breath, exhaling through pursed lips. "You think there was something wrong with my daughter's death?"

"I don't have enough information yet," Riga said. "But we're looking into the death of a woman under similar circumstances at the hotel three years ago. And you've probably heard of the hotel owner's murder."

"Him! He deserved it if you ask me."

Riga's pulse quickened. But Dennis hadn't been the prime target. His personality wasn't pertinent to the murder. It was the first time though that someone hadn't spoken in glowing terms about him. "Why do you say that?"

"Worked her like a dog, he did. Late hours. She was always doing extra favors for him that had nothing to do with the hotel. He even had her buying gifts for his wife, sent her on all sorts of personal errands, and not during work hours. The sun rose and set by that man, and he took full advantage of it." She slumped back in her seat, wound down.

"Did she say anything to you about his death?" Donovan asked.

"What was there to say? She grieved for that man, though personally, I don't think he was worth much. I told her so." Her face crumpled. "Now I wish I hadn't. It just hurt her."

"Sarah didn't have any opinions on who might have killed Dennis?" Riga asked.

"His wife, of course. The wife always does it, don't you know? And Mrs. Glasgow just didn't understand him." She raised her eyebrows. "How many times have I heard *that* before? So you're thinking of buying the hotel? Maybe you should have this then." She rose and walked from the room into a dimly lit corridor. "The police didn't seem to think much of it," she called over her shoulder. "Far as they're concerned..." but her voice was lost in the hallway.

Riga and Donovan looked at each other. He lifted his eyebrows.

Sarah's mother returned and set a cardboard box on the coffee table in front of them. "Here. She brought these home two weeks ago. More work. She was only paid for forty hours, you know, but here she was bringing stuff home. Do you think she got a bonus for it? Not from him. Anyway, it's hotel work and I don't want it in here. You take it."

Donovan rose, scooping up the box. "Thank you. I'll return it to the hotel."

"Return it, dump it in the ocean, I don't care. Sarah's gone..." She choked on a sob and turned away. "You two can show yourselves out."

Quietly, Riga and Donovan left.

Donovan put the box in the trunk of the Ferrari. "I'm itching to see what's in that box. There's a little restaurant not far from here I'd like to try. How about we stop there for lunch and break it open?"

"Great idea. After what happened with the leiomano, I'd rather not go through this at the hotel."

The restaurant was a small, wooden building with honey-colored walls that had been slid open to reveal rolling hills and an ocean view. The waitress sat them at a central table. Their napkins fluttered away in the breeze.

Bending to pick them up, the waitress said, "I'll get you fresh ones." She handed them menus then walked to one of the doors and rolled it back into place.

Donovan set the box on the empty chair between them and opened the lid. He pulled out a manila folder and a journal beneath it. "This doesn't look like it belongs to the hotel." He handed it to Riga.

She opened it and flipped through the leather-bound book. "No, it's Sarah's journal. Her mother mustn't have known it was in the box." It was private, personal. She began reading.

Donovan opened the manila folder.

"Are you ready to order?" the waitress asked.

Riga glanced up. "The pulled pork and a glass of your house red."

"Darling," Donovan remonstrated. He looked over the menu and ordered a bottle of a hellishly expensive Zinfandel.

The waitress nodded and left.

"Two Buck Chuck has never passed your lips, has it?" Riga shook her head. But a smile played at the corners of her mouth.

"I thought you were going around the South Pacific in martinis."

"I was," she said, "but now it's time to get serious."

"This is a very serious Zin."

"A deadly Zin?"

When the waitress returned, they were back to reading. The waitress poured out the wine and dashed away.

Fifteen minutes later, the waitress put steaming barbeque in front of them. "Would you like anything else?"

Donovan grunted a negative, and she left them alone. He slapped the folder shut and put it on an empty chair, bit into the sandwich. "What did you find?"

Riga grimaced. "Sarah was in love with Dennis. So far, it doesn't look like either of them acted on it."

"Either of them? What makes you think Dennis was interested in her?"

"She seemed to think he was, but this is only a journal. It could have been all fantasy on her part," she said, trying to be fair. But sadness hung on her like a lead weight. "She says he was estranged from his wife and suspected Deidre was seeing someone as well. But she doesn't say whom. I vote for Paul as Deidre's paramour. What did you find?"

His eyes narrowed. "A second set of books."

"You're kidding." She put the sandwich down and wiped her hands. Cooking the books opened up all sorts of possibilities. And Riga had been hoping to narrow them. Had Dennis known about the fraud?

"Someone was trying to cheat me," Donovan said. "The hotel isn't doing as well as Paul and Dennis presented it. The labor disputes have taken a toll, and the hotel's been running at a loss for nearly two years. The trend is worsening."

"I'm sorry," she said.

His look turned predatory. "I'm not. I know the truth now. This property is a turnaround situation. The price just dropped."

"Are you sure you still want it?" The hotel seemed more trouble than it was worth, and the deaths had darkened her memories of the place.

"My decision has nearly been made. Nearly." He tossed the folder into the box. "For all I know, these are fakes, and they're trying to salt the mine."

She leaned back in her chair. "I had no idea the resort business was so cutthroat."

He grinned. "That's part of the allure."

CHAPTER 25

HAND IN HAND, THEY walked across the hotel lobby's tiled floor, the box of Sarah's papers under Donovan's arm.

"Donovan," a man called.

Paul hurried across the lobby, a kukui nut necklace bouncing beneath the collar of his denim hotel shirt. His face was coated in a sheen of sweat. "I'm glad I found you."

"Is something wrong?" Donovan asked.

"No," he said. "I just wanted to apologize for this morning. We've all been on edge, and I guess I feel protective about Deidre. She's been through a lot. We both have."

Donovan glanced at Riga. She nodded.

"Apology accepted," Donovan said.

"Good." He crammed his hands into the pockets of his khakis. "When can we talk about the hotel? Have you reached a decision?"

Donovan's eyes gleamed, hard and cold. "No time like the present."

"Oh. Okay. Sure. Why not now? My office?"

Donovan handed Riga the box. "You don't mind, do you? It shouldn't take long."

"Of course not." She brushed her lips across his cheek. "I'm going to go to our bungalow."

"Lead the way." Donovan strode after Paul.

She sighed and shifted the box on her hip. Between her work and Donovan's, it hadn't been much of a honeymoon. Or had it? She remembered the boat ride, the helicopter, and their time on the Big Island. And even when things had been horrible, his presence had buoyed her.

At the bungalow, she balanced the box on her knee and dug for the key card. The box fell, spilling its contents, and she cursed under her breath. She should have just put the thing on the ground.

A smattering of rain dotted the bricks as Riga bent and shoved the paper haphazardly into the file. She jammed file and journal into the box.

The rain came down harder, and she slipped inside, closing the door behind her. She dropped the box on the low coffee table in the living area and opened one of the sliding glass doors.

The sound of the rain on the pavement and the pool soothed her mind. Riga leaned against the door frame and gazed past the patio to the ocean beyond. A ship's silhouette broke the horizon, a dark blip against a pale gray sky and sea.

She found a sheaf of hotel stationary in one of the desk drawers and sat at the table, her notebook open in front of her. The executive assistant knew this hotel inside and out – enough to keep a second set of books, real or fake. Did that mean Dennis had trusted Sarah to manage fake books? Or had she taken the real books as evidence against him?

She bit the inside of her cheek, doubtful. No, this was about the seals, not the hotel. But she opened Sarah's journal, found the point she'd left off, and resumed reading.

When she'd finished studying Sarah's last entry, Riga closed the journal, sadder but no wiser. Sarah'd had no idea her life would soon end. Could she be wrong? Maybe the young woman's death *had* been an accident.

Riga's lips tightened. No. She didn't believe in coincidence.

The light faded, and she stood, stretched, turned on the overhead lamp. Riga went back to the table and returned to work.

It came down to three questions. Who could have killed Sarah? Who knew about the hotel ghost? And who knew about Mana and the leiomano? The answers pointed toward one person.

But the why of it confounded her. What did the necromancer have to gain? On the other hand, did a necromancer need a good reason for murder?

Riga put her head in her hands. She was a necromancer by birth, if not by desire. Her aunts were practitioners, and they were nuts... though in a sort-of delightful way. Would she go mad too?

She dug her hands into her hair and made an exasperated sound. Brigitte had been right. She was losing her edge. But she'd known that for a while, fumbling to find her own way, fighting this new magic inside her, fighting the blood desire...

She'd thought that by following her calling, seeking justice for the dead, she could escape madness. But her magic only seemed to work well when she used blood, and the delicious pull it had on her...

Riga shivered with longing. She wanted that dark drug. And the wanting was terrifying.

A crack of thunder startled her from her musings. She glanced at the clock. It was nearly six o'clock, and Donovan hadn't returned.

Unease lodged just below her throat, and Riga shifted in her chair. He'd said he wouldn't be long, but several hours had slipped past. She grabbed her cell phone, dialed.

Donovan's phone rang twice, three times, and then, "Hello?" a woman's voice answered.

"Hello." Riga stood. "This is Riga. I'm trying to reach Donovan."

"Hi, Riga, this is Ellen. Donovan's in a meeting right now. I'm answering his phone because he asked not to be disturbed. But if you'd like me to, I can get him."

"No." Riga touched the base of her neck and frowned. "No, that's all right. I don't want to disturb him."

"Would you like me to leave him a message?"

A gust of wind scattered the stationary on the table. Riga hurried to close the doors. "Yes. Will you please tell him I'm headed to the hotel bar?"

"Of course. Enjoy your evening, Riga."

"You too."

Slowly, Riga pocketed her phone. Then she nodded, made a decision, and picked up the room key. A drink was definitely in order.

She grabbed a jacket from the closet and strode outside. She tried to shrug into its sleeves, but the wind caught it, fought her, teasing the light fabric this way and that.

"Oh, come *on*." She ran, rain pelting her, half in and half out of her jacket, holding it over her head as a shield.

Dripping, Riga skidded into the hotel lobby. She looked around, stopped to catch her breath, and realized with a dash of shame she was hoping to see Donovan.

Shaking the water from her hands, Riga strode to the hotel bar and restaurant. The overhead fans weren't turning tonight. The sliding glass doors were shut. Small mason jars had been turned into oil lamps, and they flickered on the tables.

She turned from the dining room and walked into the sleek bar, neutral-colored with pale slate tiles. Outside the windows, the bay was a black sheet. A familiar figure sat hunched on a barstool beside two broad-shouldered men.

She stepped up beside Kimo at the bar. "Mind if I join you?"

He looked around, as if unsure whom she was talking to. "Sure. It's a free country."

The two men leaned across the bar and stared past Kimo at her. She recognized one as the guy who'd brandished a bat when he'd caught her and Donovan outside the laundry service. She winked at him and sat.

A bartender approached her. "What can I get you?"

"A glass of your best Cabernet."

"Our best Cab doesn't come by the glass."

"Then a glass of whatever Cab or Zinfandel you can pour me."

He nodded and wandered to the other end of the bar.

"You following me?" Kimo asked.

"Not tonight."

"I hear you were parked outside my laundry the other night."

She raised her eyebrows. "Your laundry? You own a laundry and a fishing boat and a restaurant? Color me impressed."

"Then you're easily impressed. I also own a chain of pizza parlors."

"The ones listed in my hotel brochure?"

He grinned. "Nepotism. It's a wonderful thing. So why were you following me?"

"I wasn't. I was following Paul."

"Aw, leave him alone."

"Can't. He's been lying to me. When people lie to me, I have to find out why. Sometimes it has nothing to do with the investigation, but I can't leave it until I know. Sometimes it's something that's embarrassing, or innocent, or private. Like being in love with your brother's wife."

Kimo sighed, stared down at his beer. "Paul never was particularly subtle."

"Did his brother know?"

"And Dennis never was particularly aware. I doubt it. Dennis was too busy empire building."

"Mm. So what about you? How'd you build your empire?"

The waiter appeared with her wine. He placed it before her.

"Piece by piece," Kimo said. "I started with the boat. People liked my catch, and I liked to cook, so I opened the restaurant. It was a success, and a friend asked me to go in with him on a pizza parlor. He had the recipes, I knew how to run the business. We did well. We opened more. And then I found out the owner of the laundry was selling. I knew how much business he did with the local hotels – it seemed like a good opportunity. I bought it, promoted one of the lower managers who seemed to know what he was doing to run the place. Made more money. Life's been good to me."

"It sounds more like you've been good to life."

"Well. Here's to life." He raised his beer, and they clinked glasses. She nodded to Kimo's two large friends. They ignored her.

"What about you?" he asked.

She sipped the wine. It was rich and peppery. "I used to own a PR company, but I got sick of it and became a metaphysical detective instead. I needed a PI license to be taken seriously – and not just by my clients. Cops like to see it, too, when you're nosing around."

"Metaphysical? Is that a good business?"

She laughed. "It's a rotten business. But I get by."

"Looks like you more than get by."

"Well, Donovan does. I'm just along for the ride. How—"

The world tilted sideways. A wave, dark and sweet, aching with desire, roared through her. She resisted, and her stomach turned. But something beckoned, and she followed it, an opiate she didn't want to kick. Blood, flowing rich and metallic.

She gasped, the pulse of her own blood humming in her veins, riding the surge of magic. *Another necromantic spell, here, on the island.* If she could follow the trail of magic now...

She stopped resisting, opened her senses. The tower rose before her. Lightning struck it, and stones crumbled, fell alongside two figures, plummeting headfirst to the rocks below.

A rough hand grabbed her arm. "Get down."

She shook her head to clear it and was back in the real world. Screams. Shouts. A bottle flew past her. It shattered behind the bar, sending other bottles tumbling to the floor.

Kimo was shaking her, his face contorted. "Get behind the bar." He shoved her, and she stumbled against a woman who had the same idea.

The woman turned and clawed at Riga. "Get away from me."

Riga blocked the blow and took a quick step back.

A fight, a brawl. Kimo's friends were in the thick of it, men and women tumbling, tables overturning, glass breaking.

She climbed onto her barstool and vaulted over the bar, landing beside a crouching waitress. Riga ducked down beside the woman.

"What happened?" the waitress shouted.

Riga grasped her head, as if to keep it from flying apart. *Another necromantic spell. Another death. Human? Mermaid? Did it matter?* A chair flew over the bar, sending more bottles crashing to the floor.

Riga shielded her face from the flying glass. The waitress shrieked. Two men, struggling, stumbled behind the counter.

"We need to get out of here." Riga duckwalked away from the men.

"And go where?" the waitress asked.

And that was the question. Was the fight only here? Or had it spread? Was Donovan safe?

Riga's chest hollowed. *Donovan.* She'd have to tell him about her reaction to the spell. It had pulled at her like a drug, and she'd responded. She'd wanted to respond.

She told herself it was because she had to follow it to the end, find the person doing this. But the blood was a narcotic to her. Now, she understood how certain necromancers became addicted. Riga's skin tightened. She pressed her hands against her twisting stomach.

One of the men stepped on the waitress's hand. She shrieked and cradled her injured hand. He staggered away.

"Riga." Donovan's head appeared over the bar. He reached toward her. "We need to get out of here."

She grasped his hand and stood. "We need to get her out too." Riga jerked her head toward the waitress.

"Her?" He leaned over the bar and his gaze landed on the crouching waitress. "Oh. Come on." He helped Riga and the waitress over the bar, edging them along it to the wall and an emergency door.

"No." The waitress grasped his wrist. "An alarm will sound."

"Even better." Donovan pushed the door open. A siren blared.

Riga hesitated, looking over her shoulder for Kimo. He and his friends battled a horde of frat boys in university t-shirts. Kimo kicked one in the crotch, and Riga winced.

"Come on," Donovan urged.

They escaped into a service corridor. A clarion wailed.

"Is the fighting just here?" Riga asked, hurrying behind him.

"As far as I know," he said. "I was still in that meeting with Paul when we got the call from security that a fight had broken out. Ellen told me you were at the bar."

"Where was security?" Riga asked.

"This isn't the sort of joint where you see a lot of brawling," he said. "They're not prepared for something like this. Paul called the cops."

"I hope they're prepared," Riga muttered.

At the end of the corridor was a door. It opened to the outside, and they ran out into the rain.

"Thanks. I'm outta here." The waitress jogged away, her arms wrapped around her waist.

Riga wiped her face. "There was another spell. And I think I know where it was cast. The lighthouse. It's the tower."

"What tower?"

"The tower in my vision. In the tarot cards. I had a vision when... Oh, just trust me!"

He put his hands on her arms. "I do. Let's go."

The door bammed open behind them. Kimo staggered out, one hand clapped to his head. Blood trickled down the left side of his face. "What's wrong with this island?"

"There's a necromancer," Riga said. "He's been killing seals and people to fuel his magic. He murdered Dennis and Mana and probably Sarah as well."

He wobbled. "A necromancer? You mean like black magic?"

"How else would Mana throw up shark teeth?" Riga said, exasperated. "The killer is at the lighthouse now. That's probably where he's killed another seal or maybe even another person. If we can catch him, we can stop him."

Kimo sputtered. "But... but..."

"You asked." Donovan grasped Riga's hand, and together they ran down the path.

CHAPTER 26

THE VALET STATION WAS abandoned. Donovan rummaged through the cabinet and found the keys to the Ferrari. They ran to the valet parking lot and jumped into the car.

Donovan revved the engine, and they screeched from the drive, their back tires skidding on the slick asphalt. Riga's head rocked back on the seat.

"Sorry," he said. "And I'm sorry about keeping you waiting, about leaving you alone."

"It's fine. You were working."

"But I knew there was danger. I got too wrapped up in the kill. I'm afraid you're not exactly seeing me at my best."

They whipped around a dark curve.

"Your best?" she asked. "You mean focused?"

"Our honeymoon was supposed to first be about us."

"And then Dennis was murdered, and magic invaded, and a simple hotel deal became something more."

"None of that was your fault," he said.

"And none of it has really changed anything. Our honeymoon is still about us. We're just not doing traditional honeymoon things. Donovan, I want to see you happy. This world – wheeling and dealing, managing properties, turning them around – it's what makes you happy."

"You make me happy."

"But necromancy doesn't."

His mouth twisted. "I don't like what the blood, the sacrifice, does to you. And it's hard to forget my first encounter with necromancy, being made dead."

"In fairness, you weren't completely dead."

He gave her a look.

"Well," she said, "you weren't."

He laughed, rich and deep. Riga smiled in response.

She rested her hand on his atop the gearshift. "I don't like what it does to me either. And I will never use blood – or any kind of sacrifice – again. I promise."

He lifted his fingers and twined them in hers. "Thank you."

Wind buffeted the Ferrari. Donovan pulled his hand free and gripped both on the wheel. "Will Brigitte be okay out in this?"

"She's flown through worse," Riga said. Though the gargoyle would be grumbling about it for days. She imagined Brigitte, saw her flying closer in her mind's eye. *Brigitte, we need you.*

"The last time a spell like this was cast," Donovan said, "you had to cast a tracking spell to find it. How did you locate the source of the magic so quickly this time?"

"I managed to mentally... catch the spell as it was being cast and follow its trail." She looked out the window. Her pale face reflected back at her. "It was intoxicating. Not like wine, like something else, something more powerful. I didn't like it." No, that wasn't quite true. She'd liked it too much.

A gray and white blur crossed in front of them. He swore and yanked the wheel to the right. The car skidded, and he corrected course. They sped onward.

"Sorry," he said. "Someone's goat got loose. What were you saying?"

"Nothing." Riga pressed a hand to her chest as if she could will the thundering there to subside. "I'd better let you concentrate on driving."

He grunted.

They turned off the highway and wended down the road to the light-house, leaving cinderblock houses and streetlamps behind. Their headlights illuminated a palm tree. It flattened, parallel to the ground, and the Ferrari skidded sideways.

"This is hurricane force now," Donovan said, slowing. The road narrowed. He leaned forward in his seat. "I don't see the lighthouse."

Riga craned her neck. The rain-coated windshield warped the darkness. She couldn't see a thing. "Neither do I, but it's got to be there."

They drove slowly into the parking lot and pulled beside a Volvo.

"You recognize it?" Donovan asked.

"No." She opened her bag and pulled out her flashlight. "The lighthouse. Its beacon is off." Riga struggled to open the car door, the wind forcing it back on her.

He grasped her arm and pointed to the horizon and a ship outlined in light. "That's an oil tanker. It's too close. The wind is driving it in to shore."

She paled. "In this storm, with the lighthouse off..." She shouted in the howl of the wind. It whipped her words away, buffeting her, and she staggered.

"Our necromancer might be trying to cause an oil spill."

"He's going to kill the seals – and everything else – en masse to fuel his spell."

"Even if that's not his goal," he said, "we need to get that light back on."

Leaning into the gale, they started down the trail. The entire trail appeared to be in motion, banana trees and other greenery rippling. Knives of icy rain bit her skin. Water streamed down her face and neck. She might as well have worn her bathing suit, for all the good her jacket was doing.

"Leave the flashlights off," he shouted. "I can see well enough without it. Let's not give this guy advance warning."

Stumbling in the dark, they made their way toward the lighthouse. Riga grounded herself, pulling energy from the in-between, creating a protective barrier around her and Donovan.

His teeth gleamed, pale in the night. "I'll be fine," he said.

"How did you know I—?"

"I just know." He pressed a hand to her lower back. "Up ahead. Do you see it?"

Something shifted in the darkness. There was a banging sound.

They hurried forward. The heavy door to the lighthouse clunked open and shut.

"Wait here." Donovan walked inside.

But she couldn't wait, couldn't let him go without her. Riga took a step and struck something solid, cold, rotting. She staggered back. "Donovan," she yelled.

He turned, brow wrinkling. "What's wrong?"

She pressed her hand against the invisible barrier and softened her gaze. Faintly, she could see it, a magical wall that glowed green as if illuminated through night vision goggles. "He's placed a magical barricade at the door. I can't get through."

Donovan walked forward, his hands extended. He jerked his hands away from the open door as if burned. "What is this?" He looked behind him, up the winding lighthouse stairs.

She ran her hands along the barrier, waves of nausea flowing through her at the touch. It wasn't like the barrier at the snow goddess temple. This was rotten, evil, powered by murder. "It's dark necromancy."

Donovan shifted his weight. "I've got to get that light on." His black hair lay plastered against his skull, his clothing stuck to the hard muscles of his body.

"It may be a trap."

"Of course it's a trap. But I need to get the light on."

She clenched her fists, the pressure of the double set of rings tightening about her finger. Fear dizzied her. She couldn't lose him. "Donovan..." Her voice was a croak.

His mouth set in a grim line. "I need to get that light on," he repeated.

God help her, this wasn't the first time she'd put him in danger. Danger he'd willingly accepted. That was the man she'd married. She gritted her teeth. "Go."

He turned and vanished up the darkened stairs.

Weak silver glowed around her feet, and she turned. The windows in the outbuilding flickered with sickly light. Goosebumps layered her goosebumps, the magic like pins dancing across her skin. The necromancer was there.

She fought the wind, forced herself out of the shelter of the lighthouse, across the slick paving stones to the outbuilding. Riga grasped the handle of the heavy wooden door. Locked. She cursed.

A dark shape crashed into the door. Riga yelped, leaping away.

The gargoyle plummeted to the ground. Unsteadily Brigitte stood, shaking her head.

"Brigitte, are you okay?"

"Of course I am not okay. There was no magic at ze hippy camp." She sneezed. "Patchouli!"

"Gesundheit."

"But dark magic is afoot, and you have called, so I braved ze storm. Where is ze magician? How shall we defeat him?"

"I'll take the magician." Riga's jaw clenched. Justice had been a long time coming to that one, but one way or another, his games would end tonight.

She pointed to the lighthouse. "Donovan's in there, trying to get the light back on. There's some sort of magical barrier at the front door. I doubt he's blocked the top windows though. Can you make it there? Try to get in another way?"

"I shall find a way." Brigitte leapt into the air and was promptly blown past the lighthouse and over the cliff.

"Brigitte!" Riga's voice was lost in the screaming wind. She closed her eyes. The gargoyle would be okay. Her hands shook. She'd be okay.

Riga turned to the door. She needed to focus on what she could deal with. And locked doors were one thing she could manage.

Riga pulled her hand fractionally away from the doorknob and called the energies, imagined the cool blue from above, the red heat from below. She inhaled, drawing them into her body, through her feet and into the crown of her head, letting them fill her.

She imagined the pins of the lock dropping into place, the knob turning. It was an old spell to unlock doors. With her new magic, it had a very different effect.

An acrid scent burned her nostrils. She opened her eyes. The knob flowed in a lava stream down the smoking door.

"Take that," she muttered.

The wind took the door, slammed it against the wall. She ran inside the narrow hallway. Coats on pegs and boots lined one wall.

A watery light leaked from the crack beneath a shut door at the end of the hall. One hand trailing along the cold, cement wall, she edged toward it.

Nothingness swallowed her. The world went black, the wall she'd been using to guide herself had disappeared. She felt nothing against her skin. Where was her skin? Where did she end, and the nothingness begin? And then something bubbled to the surface of her awareness. Despair.

She'd been too slow to figure it out, had failed. The ship had already cracked apart on the rocks, sent men tumbling, screaming into the sea. The tower cracked, the top of the lighthouse plummeting down the cliff, breaking apart, and with it, a man. She'd failed, and she couldn't breathe, had forgotten how.

She should have known sooner – that first lunch with Townsend when her magical probing had been blocked. But she'd thought it had been the kupua. Her first, but not last mistake. And there was no air. She had no lungs. And Donovan...

Donovan.

Her heart beat, aching, slamming against her ribs. And she remembered. This was a spell. Donovan was alive. He was made of magic, and Townsend couldn't touch him. A spark grew inside her.

It's only a spell. I can break this. I know how.

Riga spoke the words, embraced the nothingness. Pulling its force through her, she sent it spiraling outward.

Cold pressed into her palms and knees. She sucked in a lungful of air. The door was there again, the light beneath it fading. "Townsend," she screamed. "Where are you?"

Lurching to her feet, she ran down the darkened hallway to the door. She took a moment to let her eyes adjust to the dark, then flung it open.

The room was small, empty but for the man lying in a pool of blood, black in the weak light from the windows. Grover lay centered in a chalk pentagram, his arms outflung, legs stretched like da Vinci's Vitruvian man. She smeared one of the sigils with her foot, and knelt beside him, pressing her fingers to his neck.

He was dead.

A branch slapped a window, and Riga jumped. Her eyes made out more details. A wooden chair in the corner. An unlit candle on the floor. A door.

"Son of a…" She went to it, turned the knob. The door pushed back. She fought the wind and escaped into the outdoors.

"Townsend!" The wind tore her words from her throat.

Rain pelted her, the force of the hurricane making her squint. She closed her eyes, extended her senses. Riga sensed movement by the cliff's edge. She opened her eyes and saw a figure slip through the bushes near the metal barrier.

Riga grasped her tactical flashlight in her hands, keeping the beam off. She still had some surprises up her sleeve. Bending against the wind, she ran toward the figure.

It vanished.

She slowed to a halt beside the metal barrier. A leaf from a banana tree slapped her face, and she brushed it aside. "Where are you?"

Someone grabbed her by the hair, yanking her backwards. She twisted, yowling. Flipped the tactical flashlight on and lit up Townsend's eyes. Rain cascaded off his domed head. He winced, temporarily blinded.

She slapped him in the crotch. He let go, staggered backwards, and bent, hissing.

Riga kicked at him. He raised his elbow and connected with her shin. Pain arced through her leg. She howled, hopping backward. He drove into her, slamming her against the barrier fence. It shifted behind her, metal groaning. Her left foot swung suspended in space. She dropped the flashlight, and it rolled away.

Townsend kept her pinned to the fence, pushing her back. The shriek of metal mingled with the wind.

"Why?" she screamed. "Why are you doing this?"

"Because." He grunted. "I hate people."

She kneed him, missing his crotch. Banged her elbow into the side of his head and knocked him sideways. He staggered, low to the ground, grabbing her around the knees, taking her down. They tumbled, rolling toward the cliff. She flung a leg around his neck and flipped him.

Townsend shrieked, his lower body sliding over the cliff's edge, slipping, scrabbling. He grabbed her leg.

She kicked out with her free leg, but he was slowly dragging her beneath the low barrier rail. Riga grabbed for its metal bar. Her hands fumbled for purchase.

"It's too late," he roared. "It doesn't matter what you do. The lighthouse is going, and so is that ship."

"That's what you think." She kicked him in the face.

He hung on. The cliff crumbled beneath them. Their bodies jerked downward.

One of her hands loosened on the metal rail. She kicked again. "What have you done to the lighthouse?"

"Your husband will find out."

Her legs and hips hung over the cliff. Riga's heart exploded. Townsend thrashed, scrabbling for a toehold, weighing her down.

Her right hand slipped from the bar. She struggled to grab it, but Townsend pulled her lower, toward the rocks. She was stretched too far. Still she reached, her fingertips brushing the wet metal.

A hand grasped hers, and her breath stalled.

She looked up into Kimo's black eyes.

"Hold on," he shouted.

"It's Townsend," Riga yelled. "He killed them all."

Suddenly, she was lighter, Townsend was screaming. She was being dragged upward and across the jagged cliff, beneath the railing.

"Are you okay?" Kimo asked.

Riga nodded, gulping air. She crawled to the flashlight and shined it over the edge.

Townsend's body lay crumpled on the rocks below. She looked up. The lighthouse remained dark.

"Over here," Kimo shouted, waving to someone down the trail. Two male figures pounded toward them.

"He sabotaged the lighthouse," Riga said. "Donovan's inside, trying to fix it."

Kimo nodded. "Stay here." He turned to the two men, pointed to one. "You and I have got to get the light back on. You—" he pointed to the guy who'd once threatened her with a bat. "Stay with her."

Kimo and the other man raced to the lighthouse. They disappeared inside.

The barrier spell had been broken with Townsend's death, Riga realized, her heart leaping. She could get in too.

She struggled to her feet. "Come on."

The man gripped her shoulder and gently shoved her back. "Kimo said to stay here."

"Technically, he said to stay with me. And we need to help them get that light on." She darted from his grasp.

A hand seized the collar of her jacket. Riga wriggled free of it.

An arm went around her waist, lifting her.

"Let go." She struggled against him.

"Kimo said to stay."

She shouted with rage. Were the lights of the ship closer? It was impossible to tell.

Whatever sacrifice Townsend had made, or spell he'd cast, the elemental wind was an entity in its own right. Townsend's death hadn't ended its rampage. The tanker was drifting towards shore. Getting the lighthouse working might not be enough. But Donovan was inside, in danger.

She rocked her head back, hoping to connect with his face and hit his chest instead. Did he have to be so big? She reverse-kicked, angling for his crotch, and connected. There was a popping sound. He didn't budge.

"You're wearing a cup?" she asked, incredulous.

"There's always something new to learn." The kupua's voice came from behind them.

She twisted, startled. "Help me," she shouted.

"He wants you to stay," the kupua said. "And you can do more good here."

The man holding her didn't react. Was the voice inside her head or out of it? The menehune kupua was here, somewhere. He wanted her to do something. Something new, something she'd learned...

Reading her future in the waves? Visioning? Grokking... Grokking water, helping it change its course, encouraging it to flow in a direction it might naturally flow. And wind was not so different...

She relaxed in her captor's arms and closed her eyes, connected to the energies from the in-between. Imagined her spirit body, a duplicate Riga, stepping outside her physical body. Imagined that body whipping away in the wind, dissolving, becoming one with the element. Imagined the wind dying down, relaxing.

The hurricane battered her.

It wasn't working.

She concentrated. *Wind. I am the wind.* She flew through the air, battering against the island. There was an easier way, a happier way. All she had to do as wind was flow gently around this land.

Something struck her face. Her eyes opened, and she snarled in frustration. Dammit. She was a necromancer, not a kupua.

A necromancer...

She closed her eyes and focused on her own center. But all she could think about was Donovan. Donovan in danger, hurt. She'd waited so long to find him, and the thought of losing him, his cocky smile, the way he treated life as a game to be won rather than a problem to be solved...

And suddenly she was there, at that still point, and Donovan was with her. The tears that pricked at her eyes changed, were no longer tears of fear and potential loss. Her heart swelled.

Riga found that still point inside her, and he was there.

The world dropped away. She was everywhere and nowhere, in-between. Energy flowed through her, cool and dark, hot and light, there and not there. She let it fill her, and sent it into her energy body, into the wind. Dreamed.

Gentle winds caressing the treetops. A green island, silver in the moonlight. And Donovan. The world fell away.

She felt other energies join her, other minds. Mark. The menehune. Sal, the faery shaman in San Francisco. And other kupuas she'd never met, on other islands. Her power surged – not the sickening, drunken headiness of blood magic – the purity of the in-between.

She opened her eyes. The wind was dying. Trees rustled gently in the breeze. Above, the clouds parted, revealing a fat moon. The lighthouse remained dark.

"Weird weather," the man holding her said.

A blaze of light. An explosion boomed, and then the shockwave hit them, sending the man staggering back.

He dropped her, and she ran, her head craning upward, searching for the signs of destruction – crumbled brick, falling glass. But the lighthouse stood. A beam switched on from the top of the tower and flashed across the clouds.

She burst through the door, raced up the steps, her feet ringing hollowly on the metal. A figure loomed before her, and she crashed into him.

"Riga." Donovan pulled her close. "Kimo told me what happened. Are you okay?"

She nodded and pressed her face against his damp shirt, listened to the sound of his heartbeat, felt his chest rise and fall. He was alive.

"I heard an explosion." Relief flooded her, and she tightened her arms around him, legs trembling.

"Someone rigged an explosive in here. Kimo was on the phone to the bomb squad, but Brigitte got impatient."

"Brigitte? Was she hurt?"

"No, she took the bomb and dropped it in the ocean, well away from the lighthouse and the cliff. Don't worry. Kimo and his buddy didn't see her."

A masculine shriek echoed down the stairwell. "Menehune!"

Riga scrunched up her face. *Brigitte*. "You were saying?"

CHAPTER 27

WHISTLING, DONOVAN TOSSED A shirt into his suitcase, splayed out on the hotel bed.

Riga carried her toiletry kit into the bedroom and shoved it in her bag. "Happy to escape?"

"Just looking forward to being in our own home, getting back to the casino. There's another big poker tournament coming up. I'm ready to roll up my sleeves and get back to routine."

She laughed. "Since when did you like routine? Has our honeymoon killed your sense of adventure?"

He grasped her wrist and pulled her to him, nuzzling her ear. "Never. And for the record? Best. Vacation. Ever."

"I suppose any day that doesn't end with one of us in jail is a success."

He released her and returned to his packing. "If Kimo and his friends hadn't followed us to the lighthouse and seen Townsend attack you, we might not have been so lucky. Kimo told me that Mana and Townsend had been drinking and killed a seal three years ago."

"I wondered if they knew each other. Kimo told us that Townsend used to spend time at his restaurant. It made sense that he would know Mana as well."

Donovan studied a folded shirt. "They'd both felt so guilty that Townsend got involved with the Protection Society, and Mana confessed his sins to Kimo. When the seal killings started up again, Mana must have been suspicious."

"But on Townsend's side, I doubt guilt or alcohol played any role in his actions. He was a killer. He took over the Aquatic Protection Society for his own reasons. That was how he knew where the seals would be – convenient calls from helpful citizens. He and Jay were the only ones who knew about the most recent seal by the Spouting Hole – until he killed it, that is."

Brigitte zoomed through the open window and landed on the footboard. "So. Are we done here?"

"Just about," Donovan said. "But I'm afraid you'll have to find your own ride back to the mainland."

"Hmph. And this is ze thanks I get for my bravery. If I had not arrived in time, ze lighthouse would have been destroyed by ze bomb."

"Thank you, Brigitte," Riga said.

"Well." The gargoyle inclined her head. "You are welcome, I suppose. But I wonder what ze necromancer's final spell was to be? It would have been something powerful after ze deaths from ze ocean, natural disasters, rioting…"

"I don't want to know," Riga said firmly. She still didn't trust necromancy – didn't trust herself. And her niece had been right. In some things, ignorance truly was bliss. "What did you decide on the hotel?" she asked Donovan.

"After my accountants got through with the real set of books, I decided not to make an offer."

"Probably for the best," Riga said. "I'm not sure I'd feel comfortable coming back here."

"Why? We caught the necromancer."

"It's not the necromancer. It's the menehunes." They'd helped her, leaving hints, teaching, protecting Donovan. But she'd never really trust the fae.

"I wonder if we'll ever know the real story behind Dennis's murder?" Donovan said. "Was he just in the wrong place, wrong time? Or was he a target?"

"I got a call this morning from Carol, the Society's new president," Riga said. "She said there are some questions about the funds – whether Townsend misused them. Maybe Dennis found out. Or maybe he was just unlucky."

"The really unlucky one was Sarah," Donovan said.

"Yes." Riga looked at her sandaled feet. She'd failed that young woman. But there was another she might still be able to save. "And I have a ghost to release. Would you like to come?"

Brigitte shook her head.

Donovan looked at the open closet, and the rows of shirts and shoes still on hangers inside. "You go. You know her better."

Riga nodded and walked out the back door onto the poolside patio, down the steps past the banyan tree, to the rocky outcropping on the beach.

She called the in-between and summoned the ghost of Townsend's wife. The temperature dropped. Riga shivered.

Hannah stood before her. She wore her bathing suit, but she was dry, and a sarong was tied around her hips. A hibiscus blossom decorated her hair.

"Your husband is dead," Riga said. "He fell from the cliffs by the lighthouse last night. We know the truth."

The ghost sighed. "I know. I felt his hold on me release." She looked toward the bay. "He forced me to spy on you."

Riga nodded. The chills they'd felt in the bungalow. The ghost had done a good job hiding from them – likely helped by Townsend's magic. "And you told him about our meeting with Mana, and about the leiomano."

"I'm sorry," Hannah whispered. "I caused so much pain."

"You didn't. Townsend was responsible. He was a powerful necromancer. You couldn't have helped yourself."

"I still don't understand why he drowned me on our honeymoon."

"For your money, I think," Riga said. She thought of the small dolphin memorial with Hannah's name on it, and her fists clenched. Before it had seemed pathetic. Now it was an insult. "Your bequest fueled the Aquatic Protection Society, which Townsend came to manage. And your family had quite a bit of money, didn't they? It was how they managed to keep your name from the papers after you died here."

Hannah's ghost nodded.

But Sarah had found Hannah's name. That morning when they'd spoken with Townsend at the lighthouse, she had called him, asking for permission to reveal Hannah to Donovan. And then when Sarah had called Donovan immediately afterward to tell him the helicopter ride was set, Townsend had panicked. He'd killed her that day at the hotel, the same way he'd killed his wife.

"I thought we were so happy," Hannah said. "But he really wasn't a very good man, was he?" The air around the ghost brightened. She turned and vanished.

Riga returned to the bungalow. The glass patio doors stood open, and the bungalow was silent, still.

"Donovan?"

She wandered through the living area, and into the bedroom. On her pillow, something gleamed in shades of violet. Slowly, she walked to it, and picked up the pearl necklace. It shimmered, catching the light, and she drew the pearls through her fingers. Even to her untutored eye, she could see that these were light years above the green-tinted pearls she'd bought by the Spouting Hole.

"I picked it up a week ago," Donovan said.

She turned, startled.

He leaned against the doorframe. "I've been waiting for the right time to give it to you."

"It's stunning."

He came behind her and took the pearls from her hand, latched them around her neck. "Nowhere near as stunning as you."

"Donovan, you didn't have to—"

"I wanted to." He kissed the side of her neck. "Our honeymoon is just the beginning."

A part of her thought that sounded ominous, but she leaned against him, and decided to just enjoy the pressure of his arms circling her waist, his breath against her neck.

It was a beginning.

THE END?

Note from Kirsten

Of *course* Donovan would rent a red Ferrari in Hawaii. And you know it's true love if Riga didn't snatch the keys away. She would have loved driving it too.

When I visited Kauai several years ago (fantasies of red Ferraris in my head), the island was in the grip of a rash of seal murders. As far as I know, they're still unsolved. The killings, and the Hawaiian legend of the menhunes, formed the foundation for *The Elemental Detective*.

Not long after that trip, I was introduced to a woman who studied Hawaiian shamanism. The Hawaiian variant of shamanism functions through the spirits and the elements – earth, air, fire, water and spirit. A Hawaiian shaman, or Kahuna, learns to work with and respect the elements instead of trying to master them. For Kahunas may work to redirect lava flows, rather than trying to stop the flow of lava itself. It's a different kind of magic, working with nature rather than trying to use it to make change in the world, or to control it.

But not forcing things can be tough for Riga, especially when her loved ones are in danger. And in her next adventure, *The Hoodoo Detective*, Riga and her family face multiple threats. What starts out as another episode of her reality TV show, set in outrageous New Orleans, quickly devolves into murder. And when murder finds Riga and Brigitte, magic can't be far behind...

Can't wait to read more? Click here to buy *The Hoodoo Detective*, Book 5 in the Riga Hayworth series, today!

THE HOODOO DETECTIVE

HOODOO, HAUNTS, AND HOT Flashes.

Metaphysical Detective Riga Hayworth just wants to wrap up her supernatural TV series exploring the magic of New Orleans and go home. But when she stumbles across a corpse, the middle-aged metaphysical detective ends up a police consultant on a series of occult murders. Murders that become all too personal.

When a vampire and Riga's two necromancer-hunting aunts appear on the scene, Riga fears there's more to this case than meets the eye. And when Riga's magic changes in unpredictable ways, she's certain of it. But can she manage her powers before a killer takes someone she loves?

Delving into the Gothic cemeteries, streets and mansions of New Orleans, *The Hoodoo Detective* is book five in the Riga Hayworth series of fun, fast-paced paranormal women's fiction. If you're looking for a page-turner with a complicated, 40-something heroine, buy *The Hoodoo Detective* to start your next magical adventure today!

Turn the page to read the first chapter of *The Hoodoo Detective!*

CHAPTER 1: THE HOODOO DETECTIVE

"WHAT WE NEED IS more conflict." Sam frowned, his sandy hair stirring in the breeze from a nearby fan.

Riga Hayworth caught a waiter's eye. She pointed to her empty cocktail glass and raised a digit.

Nodding, the waiter bustled off, abandoning her to the crew of the reality TV show. Waitstaff and tourists swirled around their courtyard table in a New Orleans mix of soupy heat and raw excitement.

Both heat and excitement irritated Riga. She missed her husband, Donovan. The *Haunted New Orleans* episode so far had been a bust. And she didn't really need the money from the reality show, *Supernatural Encounters*. Her husband had plenty for them both.

And that left her awkwardly trying to demonstrate some relevance, keeping her hand in as an income earner. And why did she feel the need to prove herself in their marriage? At the thought of her husband, her annoyance vanished, replaced by longing. What was Donovan doing now?

"We need tension," her field producer went on. "It doesn't have to be a fight per se. Tension can mean two people who want different things." He was dressed for an L.L. Bean safari, but judging from his darkening freckles and ruddy face, he wasn't any cooler than the rest of them.

Summer in New Orleans. Why?

Riga glanced across the table at her slim, tousle-haired niece, Pen. One bare foot was propped on the edge of her chair, straining the knee of her cargo pants. Today's t-shirt read: KEEP CALM AND GET OFF MY LAWN, an image of a shotgun bracketing top and bottom.

At least Pen was on the *Supernatural Encounters* camera team, giving them a chance for some quality time. The opportunity to do magical research was an added bonus. One of their interviewees, a local hoodoo queen, had joined them for lunch.

Riga angled her head back and meditated on a puffy white cloud. If Donovan had been able to get away from his casino in Macau, New Orleans would have been different. Fun.

She pulled her auburn hair off the back of her neck, enjoying the play of the fan on her damp skin. Discreetly, she unstuck her white silk tank from her back and leaned forward in the wrought iron chair.

"Story is conflict," Sam rattled on.

Pen fiddled with a video camera. Her chair was slightly back from the table, angled toward her boyfriend and fellow camera tech John Wolfe. Her other foot rested, hidden, in Wolfe's lap. Pen thought no one didn't knew it was being massaged.

Angus, their sound man, turned a deeper shade of pink. He looked away from the couple.

"I mean, you're gorgeous," Sam continued. "A Rita Hayworth clone whose name is actually Riga Hayworth. The heart-shaped face, the hair. Your eyes are more of a browny-purple, which is stunning, but the point is…"

Ignoring the producer, Riga narrowed her gaze at Wolfe, still massaging her niece's bare foot. With his long sideburns and wavy, dark hair, his looks fit his name. The cameraman was a good seven years older than Pen, and though Riga liked him, the relationship made her uneasy.

Catching her eye, his face paled. He laid his broad hands on the table.

Pen wasn't old enough to drink yet. Riga was unsure what her role of chaperone entailed but had decided to err on the side of militancy.

"You're ignoring me," the field producer said. "Again."

Riga looked up, studying the spot between his pale blue eyes. "I'm not ignoring you," she lied. "Just waiting for you to elaborate."

"As am I, *chère*." Beside her, Hannah the Hoodoo Queen propped her head in her hands and fluttered her lashes. Tall, with the sculpted cheekbones of a supermodel and the muscular frame of a pro tennis player, Hannah's dark skin shimmered in the heat. Dreadlocks streamed from beneath her gold-colored turban.

Sam waved his manicured hands in the air. "Conflict. Stories are built on conflict. Our pilot show had it in spades—"

Riga's mouth turned down. "In the pilot we crossed paths with a serial killer. Do you really want that again?"

"No, no. Of course not," he said. "Just... conflict."

"We've got some great footage of Riga rolling her eyes and smirking." Pen shook her loose, chestnut-colored hair, smothering a smirk of her own.

"It's a start," Sam said. "But we need more."

"How much more?" Riga asked.

"We need conflict between people."

"It's too hot to argue," Riga said. "Whose bright idea was it to come to New Orleans in June?"

He sighed, glancing at Hannah. "Can't you two at least disagree a little? Magical practitioner to magical practitioner?"

"Why would I disagree with Hannah on anything that has to do with hoodoo?" Riga asked. "She's the specialist, not me."

"I like this woman," Hannah said.

He braced one elbow on the glass table. "Work with me here."

"So you're asking us to fake an argument," Riga said. "For reality TV."

"It's television," Sam said. "You should know by now there's no such thing as reality TV."

Hannah rose. "Sorry, Mr. Producer. I don't do catfights. And now if y'all would excuse me, I've got to meet a client in desperate need of a love potion."

"Bye," Riga said.

Hannah winked and sauntered through the restaurant. She wound past the fountain in the center of the courtyard. Pausing beside a table sheltered by ferns, the hoodoo queen nodded and disappeared through the garage-like entryway.

Sam folded his lanky arms across his chest. "Riga... We spent the night in one of America's most haunted houses, and you didn't react."

"It's not that haunted."

Wolfe's hands were under the table again. Pen smiled.

Riga relaxed, slipped through the in-between. Wolfe's drink toppled, spilling ice and mint leaves and booze into his lap. He leapt up, sputtering, dabbing at his jeans with a cloth napkin.

Pen's feet retracted onto her chair. Peeling a wet leaf from her foot, she glared at her aunt.

Riga gave her a what-are-you-gonna-do-about-it grin. After a year of struggling, her magic had had a sudden breakthrough.

Unfortunately, other parts of her magic were still wildly awry. But the possibilities both excited and terrified her.

Enemies in the magical world were like gunfighters, looking to make names for themselves by knocking off tough opponents. The more adept her magic, the easier it was to defend herself, the more people came after her.

She fidgeted, itching to return to her hotel room to study the thin file on the Old Man, the file she'd told Donovan she'd leave at home.

Wolfe tossed the soaked napkin on the table. An awkwardly positioned stain spread over the front of his jeans. "I'll be right back." He headed for the bathrooms, passing the bar.

A youngish man in a Hawaiian shirt and baggy shorts half-fell off his barstool, but managed to keep his tall, tropical drink upright. The drinking got started in New Orleans earlier than any other city Riga had visited.

"Riga, this is important," Sam said. "You need to react more. People need to see your emotion to connect with you – whether that emotion is positive or negative. For example, what are you feeling right now?"

"Annoyed."

"Great. And what do you do when you're annoyed?"

Riga's lips thinned. "As a mature adult, I express my annoyance in the appropriate time and manner. If you expect me to pitch a fit like some reality TV star—"

"You *are* a reality TV star. Or you *could* be if we get this series off the ground. Look, we've got three more days. Just... give me more reaction, okay?"

"Got it. More emotion. No problem."

Glass splintered, and they turned toward the sound. Hawaiian shirt guy had navigated off the barstool and knocked a waitress to the ground. Clumsily, he brushed an orange from her knee.

Her tray rolled along the moss-filled brickwork. A toddler in a high-chair pointed at it, laughing with delight. Clutching a fistful of napkins, the bartender hurried to the fallen waitress.

Riga's brow furrowed. *Stupid drunks.* That was *her* drink seeping into the patio tiles.

Waving a hand in apology at the waitress, Hawaiian Shirt staggered to the fountain. He crashed into a chair and stumbled into their table.

Angus stood quickly and laid a chubby hand on the drunk's chest. In spite of Hawaiian Shirt's six-inch advantage, the stranger stumbled back.

"Hey friend," Angus said, his broad, freckled face serious. "The bar's that way."

"I'm not your friend. I'm a hit man. A hoodoo hit man."

"Well, Mr. Hit Man, you need to move along." Angus oriented him in the other direction.

The man nodded and turned, brushing past Riga. His lips pressed to her ear, his breath hot and sweet on her neck. "And you're worth a cool quarter mil." He leaned into her, the gun hidden beneath his shirt digging into her shoulder. Something dropped to her lap.

Pen's face twisted with disgust.

"That's enough, buddy." Yanking him away from the table, Angus shoved him in the opposite direction.

The hoodoo hit man lurched into the dark corridor that led to the bathrooms and the rear exit.

Riga looked down at the scrap of paper folded in her lap. Hands beneath the table, she opened it:

Neither of us is alone.

Follow me and only one of us gets hurt.

At a nearby table, a father lifted his toddler off the ground and blew into the little boy's belly. The child shrieked with laughter.

Riga swallowed. There were too many targets. The waitress, bringing her a fresh Hurricane. A well-dressed couple, engrossed in their smart phones. Pen, smiling vacuously at Wolfe and oblivious to the danger.

Riga clenched her hands, a wave of dizziness surging through her body. Abruptly, she stood.

"Now that's an emotion," Sam said. "That's what I want to see on your face. What have we got? Anger? Anxiety? Stress?"

"Indigestion." Riga followed the hit man.

Walking into the cool shadow of the wood-paneled corridor, she unclenched her fists, her heart slamming in her chest. In magic, fear and stress worked against her. Riga fought to relax, rolled her shoulders.

It didn't help. Tension sputtered through her system.

A humming fluorescent light illuminated the narrow hallway in flickering sepia tones. On her left, two bathroom doors, black and splashed with red paint. Further down, a cart stacked with dirty dishes. A sliver of light gleamed at the end of the hall. The rear door stood ajar.

So he wanted her there, outside.

Which meant he was probably in one of the restrooms. Centering herself, she pulled in energy from above and below – hot molten red from the earth, cool blue from the sky.

Riga shoved open the door to the ladies room and checked the stalls. Empty.

Riga sidled into the hallway. She walked to the men's room, her sandaled feet clicking lightly on the tile floor. Riga flung open the door.

Wolfe, braced before a urinal, whipped his head around. "Hey!"

"Anyone in here with you?"

"What are you... No!"

"You sure?"

"Of course I'm sure. Do you mind?"

"Sorry." She ducked out.

So the hit man really was waiting for her in the alley, unless he could hide on the ceiling like a bat. Glancing up, she blew out her breath. No vampires or hit men crawled across the ceiling. Not that she really believed there would be. Riga paced down the corridor, energy rippling between her fingers.

Heat drifted in from the cracked door. Licking her lips, she tried to ignore the fluttering in her stomach and pressed her fingertips to the dark wood. She extended her senses beyond it, a gentle push on the auric bubble that surrounded her, forcing the bubble outward. She felt no one before her, outside. Which meant...

Riga spun, panting, palms extended outward, fingers curled like claws.

The corridor was empty.

Sounds of normalcy – the clatter of dishes, laughter, light jazz music – flowed down the corridor from the restaurant.

She stared at the alley door. *What. The. Hell.*

Extending her senses again, Riga probed more carefully. A flicker of life sparked on the edge of her awareness. But it was too small to be the hit man. A cat? The gorge rose in her throat at a familiar pull, sickly sweet.

She pushed open the door. A wave of damp heat struck her and the scent of copper and rotting garbage. A narrow brick alley. Tumbled cardboard boxes. A garbage can, tipped on its side. A hand, lying on the pavement, wet with...

Gripping the door, Riga took another step into the alley. She stared, breathless.

The hoodoo hit man lay on the ground, blood spreading from the gash in his neck in a ghastly smile. Blood soaked his Hawaiian shirt. Blood puddled, trickled, spattered.

She stumbled back, dizzy, the warm door handle tethering her to reality, keeping her upright.

Something prickled at the edges of her consciousness, hot and cold and electric. At the end of the alley, a tall figure wavered in the heat, its head strangely bulbous. It stretched, extended, darkening, pulling light inside it.

"What's going on?" Wolfe asked.

Riga jumped, gasping. She turned and looked into a camera lens. "Dammit, Wolfe."

Riga glanced down the alley. The figure had vanished.

Wolfe smiled, one eye glued to the viewfinder. "I figured you were up to something when you busted into the men's room, so I went back for my camera."

Riga couldn't trust herself to speak. She longed to punch him, to wipe that infuriating grin from his mouth.

"What...?" He turned the camera, panning down the alley. The camera dipped, swayed. "Oh."

Digging into the pocket of her skorts for her cell phone, she called 9-1-1. Her hands trembled.

"At least the cops can't say you did it," he said. "I saw you go into the alley. I've even got it on tape."

Riga grunted. "Small favors." Forcing down the fear and shock, her mind registered the scene.

The hit man had probably been attacked from behind. But the spatter would have been hard for the killer to completely avoid, and she shuddered in spite of the furnace-like heat rising from the macadam. It cooked the garbage, the blood, the body.

There was something horribly intimate about a knife attack. It was close, personal. She'd rather face a gun.

The hit man's shirt was ruched up, exposing his weapon, a Walther PPK. He'd never gotten a chance to draw it.

Click here to get your copy of The Hoodoo Detective so you can keep reading this series today!

ACKNOWLEDGEMENTS

I'D LIKE TO THANK the many people who assisted me with research and other elements of the book. First, , who not only suggested the idea of the earth giving off pheromones but also introduced me to , a teacher of Huna. She not only allowed me to pick her brain on huna, but also recommended several excellent sources, including books on Huna by Serge Kahili King. You can read my interview with Julie . I'd also like to thank Stephanie Taylor for advising me on how the police might react if they found the same tourist couple at the site of two suspicious deaths in a week. And as usual, Mike Agoff of for assisting me with the martial arts moves in the fight scenes.

Any mistakes I've made in the book are my own. In one case it was intentional. Kauai's Kilauea lighthouse looks pretty much as I described, but it's not a working lighthouse.

I'd also like to thank my editors, Diana Orgain, Kassandra Lamb, and Stacy Green, as well as my beta reader, Robin Rodricks and my "delta" reader, my sister, Alice.

MORE KIRSTEN WEISS

THE PERFECTLY PROPER PARANORMAL Museum Mysteries

When highflying Maddie Kosloski is railroaded into managing her small-town's paranormal museum, she tells herself it's only temporary... until a corpse in the museum embroils her in murders past and present.

If you love quirky characters and cats with attitude, you'll love this laugh-out-loud cozy mystery series with a light paranormal twist. It's perfect for fans of Jana DeLeon, Laura Childs, and Juliet Blackwell. Start with book 1, *The Perfectly Proper Paranormal Museum*, and experience these charming wine-country whodunits today.

The Tea & Tarot Cozy Mysteries

Welcome to Beanblossom's Tea and Tarot, where each and every cozy mystery brews up hilarious trouble.

Abigail Beanblossom's dream of owning a tearoom is about to come true. She's got the lease, the start-up funds, and the recipes. But Abigail's out of a tearoom and into hot water when her realtor turns out to be a conman... and then turns up dead.

Take a whimsical journey with Abigail and her partner Hyperion through the seaside town of San Borromeo (patron saint of heartburn sufferers). And be sure to check out the easy tearoom recipes in the back of each book! Start the adventure with book 1, *Steeped in Murder*.

The Wits' End Cozy Mysteries

Cozy mysteries that are out of this world...

Running the best little UFO-themed B&B in the Sierras takes organization, breakfasting chops, and a talent for turning up trouble.

The truth is out there... Way out there in these hilarious whodunits. Start the series and beam up book 1, *At Wits' End*, today!

Pie Town Cozy Mysteries

When Val followed her fiancé to coastal San Nicholas, she had ambitions of starting a new life and a pie shop. One broken engagement later, at least her dream of opening a pie shop has come true.... Until one of her regulars keels over at the counter.

Welcome to Pie Town, where Val and pie-crust specialist Charlene are baking up hilarious trouble. Start this laugh-out-loud cozy mystery series with book 1, *The Quiche and the Dead.*

A Big Murder Mystery Series

Small Town. Big Murder.

The number one secret to my success as a bodyguard? Staying under the radar. But when a wildly public disaster blew up my career and reputation, it turned my perfect, solitary life upside down.

I thought my tiny hometown of Nowhere would be the ideal out-of-the-way refuge to wait out the media storm.

It wasn't.

My little brother had moved into a treehouse. The obscure mountain town had decided to attract tourists with the world's largest collection of big things... Yes, Nowhere now has the world's largest pizza cutter. And lawn flamingo. And ball of yarn...

And then I stumbled over a dead body.

All the evidence points to my brother being the bad guy. I may have been out of his life for a while—okay, five years—but I know he's no killer. Can I clear my brother before he becomes Nowhere's next Big Fatality?

A fast-paced and funny cozy mystery series, start with Big Shot.

The Doyle Witch Mysteries

In a mountain town where magic lies hidden in its foundations and forests, three witchy sisters must master their powers and shatter a curse before it destroys them and the home they love.

This thrilling witch mystery series is perfect for fans of Annabel Chase, Adele Abbot, and Amanda Lee. If you love stories rich with packed with magic, mystery, and murder, you'll love the Witches of Doyle. Follow the magic with the Doyle Witch trilogy, starting with book 1, *Bound*.

The Riga Hayworth Paranormal Mysteries

Her gargoyle's got an attitude.

Her magic's on the blink.

Alchemy might be the cure… if Riga can survive long enough to puzzle out its mysteries.

All Riga wants is to solve her own personal mystery—how to rebuild her magical life. But her new talent for unearthing murder keeps getting in the way…

If you're looking for a magical page-turner with a complicated, 40-something heroine, read the paranormal mystery series that fans of Patricia Briggs and Ilona Andrews call AMAZING! Start your next adventure with book 1, *The Alchemical Detective*.

Sensibility Grey Steampunk Suspense

California Territory, 1848.

Steam-powered technology is still in its infancy.

Gold has been discovered, emptying the village of San Francisco of its male population.

And newly arrived immigrant, Englishwoman Sensibility Grey, is alone.

The territory may hold more dangers than Sensibility can manage. Pursued by government agents and a secret society, Sensibility must decipher her father's clockwork secrets, before time runs out.

If you love over-the-top characters, twisty mysteries, and complicated heroines, you'll love the Sensibility Grey series of steampunk suspense. Start this steampunk adventure with book 1, *Steam and Sensibility*.

CONNECT WITH KIRSTEN

You can download my free app here:
https://kirstenweissbooks.beezer.com
Or sign up for my newsletter and get a special digital prize pack for joining, including an exclusive Tea & Tarot novella, *Fortune Favors the Grave.*
https://kirstenweiss.com
Or maybe you'd like to chat with other whimsical mystery fans? Come join Kirsten's reader page on Facebook:
https://www.facebook.com/kirsten.weiss
Or... sign up for my read and review team on Booksprout:
https://booksprout.co/author/8142/kirsten-weiss

About the Author

I WRITE LAUGH-OUT-LOUD, PAGE-TURNING mysteries for people who want to escape with real, complex, and flawed but likable characters. If there's magic in the story, it must work consistently within the world's rules and be based in history or the reality of current magical practices.

I'm best known for my cozy mystery and witch mystery novels, though I've written some steampunk mystery as well. So if you like funny, action-packed mysteries with complicated heroines, just turn the page...

Learn more, grab my **free app**, or sign up for my **newsletter** for exclusive stories and book updates. I also have a read-and-review tea via **Booksprout** and is looking for honest and thoughtful reviews! If you're interested, download the **Booksprout app**, follow me on Booksprout, and opt-in for email notifications.

BB bookbub.com/profile/kirsten-weiss

g goodreads.com/author/show/5346143.Kirsten_Weiss

f facebook.com/kirsten.weiss

O instagram.com/kirstenweissauthor/

Introducing the UnTarot App: Step into the Enchantment of Kirsten Weiss's Mystery School Series!

Embark on a journey that intertwines fiction and reality as you dive into the captivating world of Kirsten Weiss's upcoming Mystery School series. With the UnTarot app, you can wield the very cards the characters from the books utilize, tapping into a wellspring of ancient wisdom and boundless magic.

Imagine harnessing the power of the UnTarot cards to unlock hidden insights and unravel the threads of fate. With the UnTarot app, you gain access to a treasure trove of captivating readings and interpretations. As you explore this mystical experience, you'll be drawn into a world where the boundaries between fiction and reality blur.

- **Authentic Connection:** Immerse yourself in the enchanting ambiance of the Mystery School series. The UnTarot app faithfully captures the essence of the books, allowing you to connect with the characters and their adventures on a whole new level.

- **Ancient Wisdom, Modern Convenience:** The UnTarot app marries centuries-old divination techniques with cutting-edge technology, creating an accessible experience for both seasoned practitioners and curious novices.

- **Free Exploration**: Yes, you read that right! The UnTarot app is entirely FREE, ensuring that everyone can join in the magical journey of self-discovery, insight, and revelation.

Ready to embark on a journey that defies the boundaries of time and space? The UnTarot app beckons you to step into the wondrous world of Kirsten Weiss's Mystery School series. Download the UnTarot app and let the magic unfold before your very eyes!

Download the UnTarot app for FREE today and embrace the enchantment that awaits!

Manufactured by Amazon.ca
Acheson, AB

33135554R00144